STAY OUT OF SPACE!

By
DWIGHT V. SWAIN

I0541524

ARMCHAIR FICTION
PO Box 4369, Medford, Oregon 97504

FROM THE DARK, DARK DEPTHS OF THE VOID...

John Goss had been trying to get accepted for the new deep space expedition for quite some time. It was his dream—hell, it was the dream of the whole human race to someday visit the stars. However, all previously scheduled missions had been postponed—the Huu giving any and all sorts of reasons.

For John Goss, though, this expedition was to be different, he was certain of that. But the Huu had different ideas. They secretly wanted to prevent space travel—period. To the Huu, Goss' kind spelled potential disaster, because they knew that going into space would provide their mortal enemies, the Shan, with a break in the Earth's force field. The Shan had been waiting a long time for that, and if they were successful, they planned to wipe out every living creature on the planet.

FOR A SECOND COMPLETE NOVEL, TURN TO PAGE 83

ABOUT DWIGHT V. SWAIN...

...Dwight Vreeland Swain was born November 17, 1915 to John Edgar Swain, a railroad telegrapher, and Florence Marietta Vreeland. Growing up in Rochester, MI, he showed early promise as a writer, selling non-fiction to a Sunday school paper while in high school. He got his BA in journalism at the University of Michigan in 1937, then started working as a newspaperman and editor. He had a wide variety of other jobs, including door-to-door sales, working as an ordinary seaman, acting as a press agent for a mind reader, and interviewing murderers for true crime books. Over the next twenty years, he sold over a million words of pulp fiction—mostly space opera short novels. Often these novels were assignments to write a tale for an already completed illustration. Dwight Swain's best known work was probably his novel, "The Transposed Man," which appeared in an early Ace Double. Outside of writing, his hobbies included the harmonica, the violin, swimming, travel, reading, psychology, archaeology, and economics. Dwight Swain passed away on February 24, 1992 in Norman, Ok.

CHAPTER ONE
Captured

THE GREY-HAIRED woman spoke into a transitron, cool and decisive: "All units, this is Dey Z'ulle speaking. Goss is coming now. He'll be here in a minute. Stand by present positions and prepare to give us cover as needed. Confirm, please."

A clipped feminine voice from the transitron: "Unit One, Dey Z'ulle. Order confirmed."

"Unit Two—confirmed."

"Unit Three—"

"Unit Four—"

"Check." With swift precision, the woman called Dey Z'ulle thrust back a lock of iron-grey hair and adjusted her rayscope's eyepiece. "Watch it, now! He's stepping into the hall...turning this way...climbing the ramp...Tuber, get ready!"

She gestured as she spoke. Instantly, the two girls who stood behind her in the narrow alley stepped forward. The darker of the pair brought up a Karak tube; rested it on the pudgy blonde's shoulder. Cross-hatch sights framed the duraloid door of the building across the street.

Eyes still glued to the rayscope, the older woman moved aside a fraction. "Get ready!" she repeated.

"Ready," the girl with the tube echoed. Her stocky blonde helper made only a small, vaguely affirmative sound.

Silence, then; silence, and the slightest hunching of shoulders.

Across the street, the duraloid door slid back. A man stepped out onto the walk and turned right, moving easily and with no discernable sign of tension.

Now Dey Z'ulle spoke again, and for the first time her voice bore the echo of a nerve-honed edge: "Hold it, now— hold it! We need to catch him flat against the building, where he can't run." Her hand came up. "Steady—on target—"

Five seconds, perhaps, while the man walked briskly onward. Four seconds...three...two...one...

"Fire!" clipped the woman.

The dark girl depressed a button at the Karak tube's base. Like magic, a cone of faint blue haze enveloped the man. He halted in mid-stride, literally, as if all at once turned to stone. Then, rocking off balance, muscles still rigid, he crashed to the pavement.

"Now!" Dey Z'ulle's voice rasped in the transitron, hoarse and urgent. "Hurry! Hurry!"

Two women darted from an entryway before her words could even die. An open seal-sack dangling loose between them, they raced to the fallen man and flung the shroud-like sheet down on him; rolled him in it.

The plastic sealed to itself with small sucking sounds. In seconds, the victim lay more tightly cocooned than any mummy.

Dey Z'ulle expelled a quick, gusty breath. Then, cool and in command once more, she stepped forth from the alley and joined the women from other units now gathering about the prostrate, unconscious man called Goss. "Good work, all of you. You'll be commended by The Council.

"Right now, though, what we need is action. Get this man to Sarah Corley's laboratory—before it's too late!"

IT WAS DARK here—dark, and with a strange feeling best described as nothingness...no heat, no cold, no drafts, no sounds, no tastes, no smells, no pressures.

Then, suddenly, silvery radiance rushed in and drove away the murk. Machinery whispered. Faint sounds rose of respiration, shifting bodies. The air took on the measured chill of artificial cooling.

Footsteps, approaching. Close at hand, a voice—a woman's voice, perhaps—? said, "Back, please, all of you. Let me see him." And then: "So. This is the famous John Goss."

Involuntarily, Goss stiffened. Or rather, his brain sent out the proper message.

Only something seemed to be wrong with his autonomic nervous system. Or, maybe, with his muscles.

In any case, his body lay still and chill as ice, paying no heed to his mind's commands.

It would have been frightening, had he been able to react with proper tension. But as things stood, not even fear seemed able to take form—a unique tribute to the old James-Lange theory of emotion, Goss decided. His intellect still functioned, but everything else seemed at a halt.

Another voice: "Save your sarcasm, Doctor Corley. Your feelings on this matter are common knowledge."

"They are—" Yes, surely this was a woman speaking; a relatively young woman, at that, poised and intelligent and with a wit-edged tongue. "Then you know I wasn't being sarcastic, Dey Z'ulle. John Goss is famous. You've made him so, with this whole nonsensical business. For my part, I—"

"I'm not interested, doctor. Your personal prejudices don't concern me; only your professional findings. My responsibility is to The Council." An older voice, this one; and again, that of a woman. Cool and competent, she spoke with that slight edge of authority, which comes only to those who hold command.

The younger woman: "I wish it were that simple; I really do. But as an examiner, a psycho-geneticist—"

"You're wasting time, Doctor Corley...time The Council may feel could have been better spent."

The slightest of hesitations. Goss sensed a mounting tension. Clothing rustled nervously, as if silent onlookers were drawing back.

Then, precise and clipped, the younger voice said, "Very well, Dey Z'ulle. As you say, it's you The Council will call to account."

A shoe scraped barely audible. A hand brushed Goss' face. Deft fingers turned back his eyelid.

Again, it was the strangest of sensations. For while light flooded in, such was the paralysis that gripped Goss that he could not even bring his eye to focus. At one point, far distant, he glimpsed shining lines of plated piping. All else remained foggy, indistinct. The figure towering above him though a golden halo seemed, to surround the head, he couldn't even tell whether the face belonged to man or woman.

The fingers let go. The lid fell shut again.

Goss swore—intellectually. Frozen this way, he couldn't so much as muster anger.

Now a pressure came to the inside of his left wrist, firm and continuing.

But like an echo, the crisp voice of the woman called Dey Z'ulle interrupted: "He isn't applying for insurance, doctor. And the pulse rate hardly seems pertinent to our mission."

The fingers on Goss wrist stiffened. "Perhaps you'd like to conduct the examination yourself?"

"I'm afraid The Council would hardly feel me qualified, doctor. Not as a psychogeneticist. But under the circumstances, I think my suggestions at least rate respectful consideration." A sudden sharpening of tone. "Begin with the fluoroscope, please."

For a long moment, nothing happened. Then, as if in response to a gesture, angry or resigned, air changes and faint rustlings told of movement. Goss felt himself lifted. Strong hands maneuvered him bodily...tilted him, turned him, walked with him, slid him down at last onto a smooth, hard surface. Shadow blocked off the silvery radiance. A switch clicked, sharp and clear over a backdrop of shufflings and whispers.

Dey Z'ulle speaking: "Well, doctor?"

Sarah Corley: "See for yourself. Or can't you count to thirteen?"

"Thirteen!"

"That's right, thirteen, precisely as you predicted. A normal series of seven pairs of true ribs, costal cartilage connected directly with the sternum. But below that, six sets of false ribs instead of the usual five—a thirteenth pair, an extra set at the bottom. Three pairs of floating ribs instead of two."

Goss could hear the quick intake of Dey Z'ulle's breath. "Then I'm right! The Council—"

She broke off sharply. Command replaced elation in her voice. "Put him under the cortical filter."

"The cortical filter—!"

"You heard me!" The older woman spoke with driving tension now, harsh and domineering. "We've got to turn this creature's brain inside out, discover what he and his kind are plotting. That's why we chose your laboratory for this examination. Your filter unit stands head and shoulders above the others."

CHAPTER TWO
Old Blood

A PAUSE. A faint drumming, as of fingers on a table. Then, voice surprisingly calm, Sarah Corley said, "Dey Z'ulle, you outrank me. Questioning your judgment amounts to insubordination. But no matter what it costs me, I won't let you do this. My filter unit wasn't designed for other than experimental use on humans. Even if you could make a deep probe with it—pull this man's thoughts out, strip his mind bare—you'd leave him a gibbering, subhuman wreck."

"You don't have a choice in the matter, doctor," Dey Z'ulle retorted flatly. "It's The Council's responsibility to defend all of us against the Shan. If that requires the sacrifice of this creature, it's a negligible cost, believe me." Again, a direct order: "Take him to the filter!"

Hands grasped Goss, lifting.

Sarah Corley spoke rapidly:

"How can he tell you anything when he's in Karak shock? His vocal cords are paralyzed. He can't move a muscle."

The hands that held Goss hesitated. Dey Z'ulle groped: "What—?"

It was most interesting, Goss decided. His time had run out; even his minutes were numbered. Yet thanks to the Karak tube, he couldn't muster a single tremor. It was as if he was some sort of overlord god more than human, surveying his own plight with almost academic detachment.

"If you're going to use the filter on him in spite of me, then at least do it properly," pressed Sarah Corley. "Bring him out of shock first. Check his coordination, his comprehension."

"We don't dare!" Dey Z'ulle suddenly sounded worried. "These creatures' daring is incredible; they'll try anything. All the old records prove that. If we bring him out of shock, he's liable to destroy us."

"If you don't, you'll get no answers," Sarah Corley retorted coolly. "Of course, you can explain it all in your report to The Council: 'Subject was captured and transported to the secret laboratory without event. But the dey in charge was afraid to bring him out of Karak shock, so no information was forthcoming.'"

"That's enough, Doctor Corley!" The older woman's voice shook with fury. "This creature's very existence proves the presence of an alien menace in our midst—menace we'd thought long extinct. Given the slightest chance, he and his kind would destroy us, betray us to the Shan. The very circumstances of his discovery the time and money and scheming that went into his efforts to get into space—they prove how dangerous these beings are, how far their plotting's gone. Yet you stand here mocking me, even with the living evidence before you!"

"Perhaps we differ as to what constitutes proof and evidence." A cool gloss of self-possession overlaid Sarah Corley's words. "The fact is, this man has an extra set of ribs. At worst, he's representative of a tiny, unassimilated remnant of a primitive race. More likely, he's a sport or an atavist or a chance deviation from the norm. Until I'm convinced otherwise, I see no reason to treat him like a wild animal running amok."

"I'm curious, doctor." Now Dey Z'ulle, too, spoke calmly, as if she had regained her momentarily strained poise. "Before this, I thought of you merely as resenting my rank, my authority as dey. But now…What was that term you used? Atavist?"

"What—?" Now it was Sarah Corley who sounded startled.

"It means throwback, doesn't it, doctor? A reversion to a more primitive type?" Dey Z'ulle's tone grew even more thoughtful. "Take a mixed race like ours—Huu blood, basically, but with a strong infusion of the old Earth strain. With that sort of history, Earth tendencies might occasionally crop up among us. As in your own case, for instance."

"You realize, of course, you're talking nonsense," Sarah Corley interjected icily.

"I doubt that The Council will think so." The older woman's voice now rang with open triumph. "As a matter of fact, I'd say your only chance lies in setting an extremely high standard of cooperation."

"I see." For the first time, something close to a tremor invaded Sarah Corley's speech.

"Well, what about it? Shall I report you as an atavist; recommend that we run you through the filter?"

A long pause. Then: "What is it you want me to do?"

"Conduct a proper psychogenetic examination, obviously." Dey Z'ulle spoke with crisp precision. "First, put proper safeguards on the prisoner. Then, bring him out of shock, if that's really necessary, and check his brain with the cortical filter."

"Very well," The younger woman suddenly sounded weary. "Post guards on the exits. Then, move Goss to the infradation table."

Orders. Mumblings. Movement. Bleakly, Goss wondered what it would feel like when they turned on the filter.

If they succeeded in turning it on...

A succoring thought, that last. A tribute to his heritage. Had Goss had control of his muscles, he'd have smiled grimly.

Only then, abruptly, there were needles in his body—a million billion pricking, sticking, flaring, flaming needles. His brain exploded in a mad kaleidoscope of color.

THEN, AS QUICKLY as they'd come, the colors and the needles vanished. Goss opened his eyes.

A strikingly beautiful blonde girl of perhaps thirty was speaking across him with Sarah Corley's voice: "so it's simple, really. Thirty seconds of infradation reverses the flow-pattern established by the Karak tube."

"And that gives back control of the muscles?" Dey Z'ulle, obviously...a spare, brisk woman with iron-grey hair and a face and manner too cold for comfort.

"Yes." Doctor Sarah Corley turned to two other women, white-coated lab assistants. "Help him up, please."

The pair took positions, one on either side of Goss, and gripped his arms.

Repressing a first impulse to rise unaided, he lay limp; forced the women to heave up his full weight.

With an effort, they got him on his feet. Half walking, half dragging, he let them maneuver him over to a huge, cone-like apparatus suspended from the ceiling, with a counterweight to move it up and down.

Sarah Corley spoke to another lab assistant: "Put a chair under the filter. He's too weak to stand."

The white-coat hurried to obey. Still sagging in his captors' grasp, Goss let his head loll loose while he surveyed the scene through lash-masked eyes and weighed his chances.

The wall to the right had two doors. Through one, slightly ajar, Goss glimpsed a corridor.

Unfortunately a woman bearing a snub-nosed weapon of unfamiliar design stood by each of the twin exits.

The second wall, the one directly in front of Goss, had no doors. Neither did the wall behind him.

To his left, there were windows, a whole row of them—and three more guards.

Goss cursed under his breath.

Then, abruptly, Sarah Corley stepped closer; gestured.

The attendants who held Goss' arms lowered him into the chair. The third pulled down the cortical filter. Box-like, it walled Goss in, its lower edge cutting into his shoulders.

The attendants fumbled with a chin-strap.

Goss sucked in a quick breath. Scooting forward limply on the chair-seat, he slid from it to the floor.

The maneuver not only got his head out of the filter; it pulled his captors off balance. They teetered precariously, unable to support his weight.

Goss chuckled, deep in his throat. With a single convulsive movement, he jerked forward.

Choked cries. The two lab attendants toppled.

Goss surged up. Lunging, he drove for the counterweight of the filter and heaved it high into the air.

The filter, released, crashed to the floor with a jangle of shattering glass and clanging metal.

Now the guards at doors and windows were leaping forward, shouting. Their snub-nosed weapons blazed streaks of pale green light.

Ducking, Goss dived for Sarah Corley.

The lovely blonde psychogeneticist still stood frozen, close by the fallen filter. Before she could even open her mouth to scream, Goss had an arm about her waist. Locking her before him like a shield, he charged for the nearest doorway.

CHAPTER THREE
Sky Terror

AN ESCAPE under fire is never to be undertaken lightly. But some stand out as worse than others.

For John Goss, the laboratory scramble ranked close to the top of his personal list. Weak to begin with, and dropped down in an unfamiliar setting, he hardly knew which way to turn. Streaks of green light lanced at him from all directions. Sarah Corley writhed like an eel, more adversary than hostage, so that what had started as a mad dash for freedom now seemed likely to deteriorate into a wrestling match.

Then, to make matters worse, something hit him from behind—a numbing blow to the shoulder. He lurched round, reeling.

Dey Z'ulle stood poised hardly more than an arm's length away, a length of pipe already drawn back club-like for a second onslaught.

It was no time for chivalry. Ducking under the grey-haired woman's swing, Goss kicked for her shin-bone.

Dey Z'ulle's eyes went wide with panic. She tried to twist away. But the movement only brought her round so that Goss' foot connected with the back of her knee. Her leg hinged. She pitched sidewise; sprawled on the floor.

Simultaneously, Sarah Corley tore free of Goss' grasp and, in her turn, grasped him, digging long-nailed fingers into his hair and scalp with convulsive violence.

Goss tried to wrench away; failed.

A guard hurled herself at his legs. A second clutched him about the waist.

Desperately, Goss stomped down on one's foot. The other he knocked clear with his elbow.

But even as he did so, out of the corner of his eye he glimpsed Dey Z'ulle, still on the floor where she had fallen.

Now, though, she had a pistol-like weapon in her hand. She was leveling it at him.

Sarah Corley, still clinging to him, picked that moment to wrench his head around to where he was anchored off balance.

It came to Goss, in a sort of numb paralysis, that this time he couldn't dodge, and Dey Z'ulle couldn't miss.

And that would spell the end of John Goss.

That instant dragged long as eternity. Goss forgot to breathe, waiting for a blast to cut him down.

Then, without warning and for no apparent reason, Sarah Corley let go of Goss' hair. She stumbled past him, knocking him aside even as she fell.

Her shoulder hit one of the girl guards. The guard crashed into Dey Z'ulle. Dey Z'ulle fired wild.

To Goss' mind, chance didn't set up double plays that good. But he wasn't about to stop to ask questions. Swinging Sarah Corley up bodily, once more he lunged for the door.

This time, by some miracle, he made it. Stumbling out into the corridor, he stiff-armed another girl guard and lurched on, seeking an exit.

A single glance told him the odds were hopeless. More armed women barred the way at both ends of the hall.

Grimly, Goss changed course, stumbling through a doorway on the side of the corridor opposite the laboratory.

The room beyond was equipped as an office, but unoccupied. Hastily, Goss slammed the door behind him, bracing it against his pursuers with boot and hip while he threw the bolt.

Sarah Corley picked that moment to claw at his eyes. Wearily, Goss fended her off with one upflung arm, then punched her in the stomach.

The girl's breath went out of her with a sound that was half cough, half indignation. Clutching at her middle, she skittered backward to the wall behind her and slid down it to a sitting position.

Goss watched her slump with a certain dour satisfaction. He was getting tired of women, he decided; and even a lovely blonde eventually should make up her mind as to where she stands. A man had too much to do at times like these without wasting energy trying to guess whether his hostage intended to save his life, or blind him.

Now Sarah sobbed for breath, but Goss paid her no heed. Ramming the nearest desk against the door—a door already quaking under the assault of his pursuers—he leaped to a window.

He recognized no familiar landmarks. Outside, and perhaps seven feet below the sill, lay what appeared to be a small, tightly-fenced supply yard, with piles of lumber, mounds of sand and gravel, oil and chemical drums, rusting equipment.

Goss pivoted. In three strides he was beside Sarah Corley.

SHE SCRAMBLED up before he reached her. The soft blonde hair hung disheveled now, golden halo no longer. Her lovely face was stiff with fright.

Goss said sharply, "Stop that! I'm not going to hurt you."

The girl's eyes widened. "What—?"

Goss jerked a thumb at the window. "We're getting out. You're safe enough, unless you give me trouble."

Catching the woman's slim wrist, then, he jerked her to the casement.

The hammering on the door stopped in the same instant. Dey Z'ulle's voice echoed: "Goss! John Goss!"

Goss didn't answer.

"Give up, Goss! We can burn through this door in two seconds!"

Pulling his captive down to a sitting position on the window sill, Goss lifted her legs and shoved them outside.

"We'll burn through, Goss! We'll cut our way in!"

"Go ahead," Goss yelled over his shoulder. "Only when you slice that door, just remember it's Sarah Corley you're chopping in two, not me!"

He nudged Sarah. Fearfully, she slid on out the window, clinging to Goss' arm for support. Bracing himself, he lowered her as far as he could, till she was only a foot or so above the ground. Then, releasing her wrist, he let her fall.

She landed awkwardly, pitching to hands and knees. By the time she got up, Goss stood beside her.

But a crash above told of the office door giving way. Shrill cries of triumph rose. Feet pounded towards the window.

Whirling, snatching at Sarah Corley, Goss raced for the shelter of the nearest stack of lumber.

They made it just ahead of a fiery green streak that set boards smoking behind them. Crouching, Goss pointed to a long, low parapet of sacked cement. "Quick! Over there!" He shoved the woman forward.

Ignoring the sacks, she darted left instead, out into the open. She screamed as she ran: "Help! He's here, behind that lumber—"

Goss stopped short. Doubling back on his own tracks, he sprinted the length of the woodpile, then dived behind a mound of sand, worming his way along flat to the ground in a desperate effort to find more cover. His belly was a tight knot of fury—fury not so much at Sarah Corley—who, after all, had only followed her own penchant for the unpredictable as at himself, for being such a fool as to give her the opportunity.

But there was no time now for rage, even. The supply yard seemed suddenly alive with prowling girl guards, each armed and with weapon at the ready. It was all Goss could do to duck from straggly shrub to wrecked earthmover; from tarpaulined stationary engine to gravel hummock.

Then, at last, he reached the edge of the yard, the fence.

A fence, which he now discovered, rose straight from reinforced concrete footings, without breach or burrow...a fence so high and tight and well-constructed as to appear proof against anything short of a cutting torch or Iphax detonator.

As if that were not enough, someone fired at Goss before he could even approach the barrier. Cursing, ducking like a scared rabbit, he threw himself back out of sight.

Only that was a game that couldn't last long, and he knew it. In minutes, the searchers would be upon him.

Desperately, he looked this way and that for some hiding-place, some refuge.

The closest he could come to such, it seemed, was a shallow sump pit in the lee of a stack of oil drums. And even as he reached it, slid into it, a new cry rose, and he knew that once again his whereabouts had been discovered.

Grimly, he clawed rocks from the ankle-deep grease and slime in which he stood...piled them on the edge of the pit in vain token of his defiance.

A woman stepped into view around a gravel-heap. Savagely, Goss hurled a stone at her.

The woman's jaw dropped. Falling over her own feet in her haste, she stumbled back out of sight and range.

It wasn't respite, and Goss knew it. Rather, call it the beginning of the end.

Only then, abruptly, a different cry rose from his pursuers: A frightened cry, far off to one side.

Another voice joined in; another.

Then, close at hand: "Look! Discs! Fear-discs!"

And from another throat, in tones of utter, shrieking panic: "Tal Neeni help us all, the Shan are coming!"

Simultaneously, a flicker of movement caught Goss' eye. He whirled, staring.

High overhead, and far off, a spiral of strange, shining, coin-like discs were whipping down out of the sky.

Goss stood forgotten. His pursuers of a moment before now themselves were screaming, fleeing.

Overhead, more of the discs swept into view with every passing second. Full half the sky seemed spotted with them.

CLOSER THEY CAME, and closer, spinning earthward. Dust spurted as one struck the ground far off. A second sliced through the roof of a building.

The third landed less than twenty feet from the sump pit.

For Goss, it was a baffling moment. Instinctively, and from the women's panicked cries, he knew the discs had some dangerous function. Yet from the evidence of his own senses, he knew also that he himself was not affected.

Frowning, he tried to analyze his reactions. The only change in sensation he could pinpoint was a slight feeling of psychic pressure—queer, soundless buzzing in his brain that seemed to make him tense and edgy.

Beyond that, nothing.

Still frowning, Goss climbed from the pit and surveyed the disc more closely. About three feet across, the thing was formed of some shining metal unfamiliar to him. He couldn't tell whether it was cast or machined, one piece or several.

One thing was certain, though: The closer he came to the disc, the more intense grew the feeling of psychic pressure in his brain.

The knowledge roused new wariness in Goss. He backed away.

It was then he heard the sound, the moaning. Turning, he searched for its source...at last glimpsed a woman's foot protruding from behind the stack of oil drums by the sump pit.

For an instant, Goss hesitated. Then, picking up a rock, he crept stealthily towards the other.

He need have had no fears. His quarry lay prostrate, face down, her whole body convulsed with spasmodically violent tremors. The sounds that rose from her throat were incoherent. An upset can hid her head and shoulders.

Goss ran to her. Shoving back the oil drum, he turned her over.

Dun-colored hair spilled about her face. Eyes white-rimmed with terror stared up, wide and unseeing.

Goss shook the woman; slapped her.

She only trembled harder, her whole body aquiver in pulsing, rhythmic patterns.

Eyes narrowed, Goss surged to his feet and ran through the yard till he found another prostrate woman.

Pulsations rippled through her with the self-same ebb and flow as in the other.

Goss checked still more crumpled forms, more moaning women. All showed the identical tremor-pattern.

Smiling thinly, Goss strode towards the yard gate. He felt a certain smug satisfaction at seeing his adversaries so neatly hoisted on their own petards.

Only then he thought of Sarah Corley, lying somewhere too. His smile died.

But she'd fought him, as well as saved him, and that took the edge off. Resolutely, he pried back the gate latch, left the yard, and hurried on around the building.

It was the first time he'd seen the place from the outside. Yet seeing, he still knew no more about it than before. It looked just like any other small, two-story commercial building...a local clinic, perhaps, or the regional headquarters of some fraternal order. There wasn't even a nameplate over the entrance.

Goss gave it small attention. More important, in his eyes, were on the carrier and three pelcars lined up in front.

Running to the first car, Goss jerked open the door.

A man was already in it—a man whose whole body twitched and jerked as he slumped over the wheel.

Goss shivered and stepped back; looked up.

Overhead, the strange discs had vanished as quickly as they'd come. But meanwhile, men as well as women lay here shaking...

Again Goss shivered. Moving on to the second pelcar, he climbed in and depressed the lift-pedal. The gravs took hold. Rising to the standard eighteen-inch adjustment, the car swung out into the street and hovered.

Goss pushed forward the repeller. The car picked up speed.

But as it did so, a body came into view, off to one side—a woman's body, with a tousled mop of blonde hair.

GOSS BRAKED by sheer reflex. The pelcar jolted to such a sudden halt, both vertical and horizontal, that he was thrown hard against the dial. Ignoring the pain in his chest, he lurched out and hurried to the woman.

But her hair was yellow, not golden. She wasn't Sarah Corley.

For the fraction of a second Goss hesitated. Then, with a curse, he wheeled and ran back towards the supply yard behind the laboratory building. Up one aisle and down the next he searched...peered back of lumber piles and around sand-heaps.

Why had she had to save him back there in the laboratory, damn it? That is, *if* she'd really saved him. Because he couldn't even be sure of that, really. Maybe it all had been an accident. Maybe she'd slipped. Maybe, at heart, she hated him and his kind as much as Dey Z'ulle—

He found her in a crumpled, shaking knot, close by a rack of old pipe. It was hard to believe she was the same woman who'd stood before him in the laboratory, so cool and poised and lovely. Now her smooth oval face was alternately stiff and flaccid, jerking in time with the tremor-rhythm. Spittle drooled from one corner of her mouth.

Tight-lipped, Goss bent to lift her.

But at the first touch, the first pressure, she shrieked in wild, wordless anguish. A new convulsion shook her.

Sweat carne to Goss' forehead. Breathing hard, he tried again.

Again, the shrill scream of a soul in torment.

Goss stumbled to his feet, hesitated one more moment, and then turned and headed at the double for the disc that had fallen by the sump pit.

The thing still lay as before—glinting, glistening. Gingerly, Goss bent and touched it.

It seared like white-hot iron. Sucking his fingers, Goss dragged up a length of scrap lumber, shoved it beneath the disc's edge, and exerted leverage.

The craft—if that was the right name for it—moved easily. It couldn't have weighed much more than an equal bulk of magnesium. Poking and prying, Goss skidded it across the packed dirt of the yard and into the sump pit.

Water hissed. Oil smoked. Goss began scraping sand from the nearest pile and dumping it into the pit on top of the disc. In two minutes, the thing was buried; in four, the pit itself well-nigh filled.

Off to one side, someone gave vent to a loud groan. Goss turned sharply.

It was the woman by the lumber pile. Sitting up, she leaned back against the stacked planks, gripping her head in her hands.

Goss swore under his breath. So much for his fond hopes that he might bring Sarah Corley some relief from the fear-disc's influence without endangering himself too seriously. He'd be lucky if she even recovered consciousness before he had to run for his life once more.

Pivoting, he jumped the sump pit and trotted towards the spot where Sarah lay.

He didn't even see the woman by the woodpile rising, nor the streak of green fire that brought him down.

CHAPTER FOUR
Death Rides An Asteroid

NOW THE ASTEROID came into focus on the screen—a smallish asteroid, probably not more than thirty feet in circumference. It moved against the backdrop of The Belt: hundreds of other worlds-in-miniature, all spinning slowly along their appointed orbits through the boundless black void of outer space.

Then, as the asteroid revolved, a figure came into view—the terror-taut figure of a straining, struggling man whose wrists and ankles were chain-shackled to the rock. A plaston oxygen helmet encased his head, space boots his feet. The garments between had been torn to rags.

The asteroid continued to revolve. A second shackled figure appeared.

This one was beyond terror—long beyond. Where once another spaceman had fought fetters, now only bare bones remained.

The asteroid kept on turning. Slowly, first living man and then skeleton disappeared from view.

Close beside Goss, Sarah Corley spoke over the hum of the projector: "Now you see why you can't go into space, why no one can. Earth is an island, one tiny, helpless world adrift in a hostile sea. The Shan are out there, every moment—watching, waiting, dreaming of the day when they'll breach our force field—"

Like an echo, two ships of strange design hurtled up from one corner of the screen. Spurting flame-trails, they climbed faster and faster, passing close to the doom-asteroid and the man and skeleton who now, once again, had moved into the foreground.

Sarah Corley shuddered; pressed closer to Goss.

He made it a point not to respond in kind. Instead, holding his voice carefully casual, he remarked, "I wonder about that business, just a little."

"You wonder—?" The woman stiffened ever so slightly. "What is there to wonder about?"

"Quite a few things. For instance, how were these films made, if it's so dangerous to go into space?"

A switch clicked. The picture vanished from the screen. "Unmanned remote-control carriers, of course." For an instant Sarah's voice seemed the barest trifle tart. "Seventeen years ago, after the first three expeditions sent into space disappeared so mysteriously, the International Interplanetary Exploration Board secretly ordered complete film coverage on the fourth run. These pictures are what came back. Naturally, the Board couldn't release them; they'd have caused a public panic."

"Naturally," Goss agreed. He smiled wryly in the semi-darkness. "Especially with such fine detail. It's quite a feat, holding a carrier that close on target by remote control."

"Umm…"

"The Shan, too," Goss went on thoughtfully. "Their psychology interests me. Why do they chain prisoners to asteroids?"

A vague, noncommittal sound, Sarah moved away a fraction.

"There must be a secret, of course; a treatment." Goss spoke with determined sobriety. "Otherwise, there's no way I can think of that anyone could keep a skeleton intact that way. And probably there's a special Shan astrogation section assigned to keeping track of the asteroid till the Earth expedition comes along."

Beside him, abruptly, his companion sat up very straight. "What you really mean, of course, is that you don't believe any of this I've told you," she observed in a brittle voice.

"That's right," Goss nodded. "I don't. Sure, there's something going on, all right; something big. But all this nonsense about force fields and Shan bogey-men prisoners— chained to asteroids—no, thanks; save that for the magazines that specialize in bug-eyed monsters."

"I see." The woman rose quickly. "Very well, then; I'm sorry I've wasted your time. But at least you can leave here safely now; there's no one on guard."

She turned to go.

Goss came forward in his seat; reached out fast and caught her wrist. "Not yet, doctor!"

It brought the woman up short. She teetered. "What—?"

"I said, not yet." Goss rose now, also and stood beside her, still gripping her wrist. "Just because I can't swallow what you've said so far doesn't mean I don't have questions."

"That's unfortunate, Mr. Goss. Because I don't have any answers for you."

"You will." Goss smiled thinly. "Let's start with fundamentals: What's your role here? Where do you stand in all this?"

"I've told you that already, I'm an Exploration Board psychogeneticist."

"And this chamber of horrors is a Board laboratory?" Goss snorted. "Don't make me laugh!"

THE SLIGHTEST of tremors ran through the girl. Not speaking, she looked down at Goss' hand, tight on her wrist.

Goss said, "We'll try it again. Are you really a Board psychogeneticist?"

"Yes."

"But this isn't a Board laboratory?"

"No."

"Then why was I brought here today? Who are you people? What are you up to?"

No answer.

"The Board doesn't have anything to do with all this, does it? It couldn't have. It's planning new expeditions into space; you're trying to stop them."

Golden hair rippled. The woman's lovely face lifted. "I'm not answering any more questions, Mr. Goss. So you may as well let go of my wrist."

"On the contrary." Iron suddenly replaced the velvet in Goss' voice. "You're going to talk, and now, if only because you don't want your friend Dey Z'ulle to know you saved my neck—smuggling me in here, letting her think I'd escaped."

"So now it's blackmail!"

"Precisely."

"You really think I'm that easily bent?"

"Who knows? But the Board certainly will be interested in what you're doing."

Contemptuous silence.

"Dey Z'ulle, too. She'll enjoy being right about your atavism, your recessive traits. Especially when I explain how you worked with me from the start, and tell about the way you pressured that woman in the yard into forgetting that she'd knocked me over with her fire-gun—"

"You wouldn't!" For the first time, a note of panic rang in Sarah Corley's voice.

"Wouldn't I?" Goss pressed close; tightened his grip. "Tell me about Dey Z'ulle."

His companion's full lips drew to a thin, straight line. She didn't speak.

Goss prodded: "Look at me, Sarah."

No response.

"Are you afraid to? Is that it?"

Still no answer.

Very slowly, Goss twisted the girl's wrist.

For a long moment, nothing happened. Then, quite suddenly, her nostrils flared. Her lips parted. "Wait! Please—" And then, as Goss relaxed his pressure: "She's—it's—dey's a rank, a title. Her name—it's a Huu name."

"A *what*—?"

"A Huu name. A name of—my people."

"Your people."

"The Huu. We came here from another planet, thousands of years ago. We were fleeing the Shan. That's why we still have to have the force field: to protect us from them—" The girl broke off; bit her lip. "You, whether you believe it or not, the Shan *are* out there in space, waiting for a chance to take Earth and wipe out the Huu."

Goss hesitated, hardly knowing whether to frown or lift an eyebrow. "And how did I become involved in all this?" he asked finally.

His companion stared. "Don't you see? You wanted to go into space. You applied for a place in the new expedition."

"You mean everyone who signs on draws this treatment?" Goss baited. "Sorry, doctor; that's just not good enough."

Mouth tightening, Sarah Corley rose to the lure: "Perhaps I know more about you than you think, Mr. Goss."

"You do?"

"Not every applicant refuses to accept rejection. You're the only one I've heard of who's come back three separate times, each time with a new name and credentials."

"Oh?" Goss held his face expressionless.

"Dey Z'ulle has a theory on it, Mr. Goss. It might even prove correct." The girl's eyes sparkled. "She thinks you're a survivor of the old Earth strain—one of the primitives, the race of Adam that's chronicled in your Bible legends."

"Which accounts for the fluoroscope, the rib-count?"

"Of course, the old race had an extra pair of ribs, a thirteenth set. Only then we Huu came to Earth—the Eyes of the Bible, the female element in the present race, just as the primitives were the male. When the two species inter-bred, various characteristics of each changed. One set of the Earthling's ribs disappeared completely. That's why the story says Eve was created from Adam's rib."

"And why should a pair of ribs be so important?"

"They're not; they're just identification. It's the strain that counts—menal traits, attitudes, attributes of the old species."

Goss frowned. "It really matters?"

"Security always matters." A shrug; a sigh. "We Huu understand; the Shan wrote it for us in blood."

"And the—primitives—?"

"They were crude and savage. To them, excitement was always worth the candle. They'd gamble their lives for a new adventure."

Goss nodded slowly.

"It wasn't too important, at first," the woman went on. She sounded ever so weary. "Only then Sikkema invented his magnetic flow drive, and space travel became practical; not like the early days, when men still were playing with rockets.

"But to leave Earth, a ship has to breach the force field. And once it's warped, the Shan can come in."

"So through the years, your secret Huu Council has played a game with the rest of the human race." Goss spoke almost as if to himself. "You've let men set up Interplanetary Exploration Boards, and make plans, and build ships. Only we never had a chance; not really. Because you Huu saw to it there were always difficulties, always accidents and problems; always some reason why men couldn't get out into space."

And Sarah: "We didn't have a choice. We knew what the Shan would do. We had to keep Earth secure, walled in."

Goss chuckled softly.

The woman looked up. "What—?"

"I was thinking about what you said. It's too bad, isn't it?"

"Too bad—?"

"That you've failed."

Sarah stared. "I wasn't aware that we had."

"You mean you thought I'd quit?" Again Goss chuckled. "A man who'll try three times will try four, doctor. And this trip I'm going to make it."

No comment.

Goss said, "You're wondering if I'm crazy, aren't you? You can't imagine how I could even think I'd have a chance to make it." And then, with sudden violence: "All right, I'll tell you: Three times I've applied for this new expedition; and three times they've turned me down.

"But stupid primitives like me don't care about Shan bogeymen or odds or danger. All I know is that there's a ship over in the Exploration Board reservation right this minute, ramped and ready. It's a showpiece, an exhibition item— something to confuse the yokels, convince them the Board's really trying, even when it isn't.

"I've studied that ship—studied it till I know every weld and rivet in it. I've checked the plans. I've memorized the manuals. I've scraped barroom acquaintances with half the men who've helped to build it.

"You know what that means, Doctor Sarah Corley? It means all I need now is a pass to get me past the reservation fence, some sort of permit so I can enter the ramping area.

"Just a pass, Sarah. And a Board psychogeneticist can give me that.

"You see, now? Congratulations are in order! After all this time, and in spite of all the tricks you Huu can think up, tonight I blast for outer space!"

CHAPTER FIVE
Voyage to Nowhere

A GUARD STOOD by the ramping-area gate. Boldly, Goss marched Sarah towards him, gripping her elbow iron-tight under a mask of manners.

"Well, what do you want?" scowled the corpsman, in classic disregard of all specified procedures.

"Board psychogeneticist coming in," Goss retorted. "She's got orders to run a special emergency check on the ship's neurodynamic test equipment." He fumbled out the girl's pass. "Here. Here's her permit."

The guard lounged over to the pass window and reached through.

Simultaneously, Sarah Corley cried, "No! He's a—"

Goss leaped for the guard's extended hand before she could complete the sentence. Catching the man's wrist, he heaved back with all his might.

The other came violently forward, yanked completely off his feet by the suddenness of the assault. His head hit the pass window's metal frame with a meaty *thunk*. He went limp.

Spinning, Goss leaped after Sarah Corley, now fleeing. In half-a-dozen steps, he had her by the shoulder.

She halted, unresisting. Grimly, Goss led her back to the now-unguarded gate.

The guard still lay in a heap beside the window. He had the look of a man who'd be a long time rousing.

Not pausing, Goss hurried Sarah across the ramp in the direction of the spaceship that thrust up in slim, dim silhouette against the star-studded night sky.

Closer it loomed, and closer, till at last they entered its very shadow, where the loading-ladder touched the ground.

Another guard here. Goss handed him the pass with one hand, and smashed a blow to his belly with the other.

The man bent double. Goss kneed him under the chin and left him where he fell.

Sarah Corley started up the ladder.

Goss caught her arm. "No."

"No——?" She stared at him incredulously. "You mean I'm not going with you?"

Goss couldn't help but laugh; her expression was that ludicrous. "That's right. You can go back now and spend the rest of your life being a good Huu; keeping Earth secure."

Still she stared at him, unblinking. "But—but why——?"

"Why?" For some reason, the question sobered Goss. He considered it for an instant. "Because you're you, I guess. Because you can't help what you are."

"Oh."

"The business of being a woman; the way you—most women—feel about security—I can see it, even if I think you overplay it. So maybe if you try hard enough, you can see the other side too."

"The—other side——?"

"My side, the side of the people you call primitives." Goss laughed harshly. In spite of him, his voice deepened; took on resonance. "Security never built a culture, doctor. But plenty have died because the people reached the place where they were scared to take a chance. When you build a wall around yourself, you're not just shutting enemies out; you're locking yourself in. Pretty soon, you get so you're afraid to strive, afraid to be wrong. And after that——"

Off in the direction of the gate, a siren screamed.

Again Goss laughed. "You see? Too much philosophy, too much talk. Action's what I need."

He started up the ladder.

Sarah darted close; snatched at his ankles. "John, wait! You mustn't go! You mustn't!"

"I must, you mean," Goss corrected gently. "You see, I can't help being what I am, either." And then, as the siren rose again, speeding closer: "Just one question, Sarah: When you saved me at the laboratory this afternoon—why did you do it?"

"Why—?" The girl fumbled. "You know why. You stopped to bury the fear-disc. So, then—"

"Not that time," Goss interrupted. "The other, earlier. Back when I was trying to break free, and you fell and spoiled Dey Z'ulle's aim."

Even in the darkness, he would have sworn that Sarah's cheeks flushed. Her words came low:

"I...felt responsible, I guess."

"Responsible? But why?"

"Because I was the one who discovered you'd applied three times, under different names. It showed up on the psychogenetic indices and I—I notified Dey Z'ulle."

"Spoiling her aim makes up for it," Goss said quietly. "I just wanted to say thanks."

Then he was climbing, scrambling full-tilt up the ladder, cursing himself for having delayed so long. Yet he knew in his heart the things the two of them had said were worth the hazard; it was that kind of a moment.

HE ALMOST thought he heard the girl cry, "Good luck!" through the siren's scream as he swung through the hatchway.

But that was impossible, of course. No Huu could utter such words to anyone who threatened the security of her kind.

Inside, now—inside, and levering the great hatch shut; spinning the locking wheels.

The control board, then: levers and dials, knobs and switches. He knew them all, knew them with the intimacy of one who has memorized the wiring diagrams and cross-checked every single circuit. Like an automaton in action, he raced from one panel to another…ran control tests, zeroed instruments.

Then, suddenly, there was a feeling of lightness, incredible lightness, and he knew that Sikkema's marvelous magnetic flow drive had taken hold, and that he and this ship were free of Earth and hurtling out across the void into reaches no man had ever seen.

Flipping on the artificial gravity switch, he crossed quickly to the visiscreen and, through it, watched the planet of his birth recede.

It was a feeling to conjure with. He, of all his kind, had at last slashed off the home-world's chains and set his sights on new frontiers.

They'd be proud of him, all of them—the old men, his counselors, giving of their wisdom and their courage; the young boys, admiring with eyes aglow; his friends, trying with him, only at last to fall short of the pinnacle, the dream.

So, now, he was here for all of them. His was the hand to strike this blow for the old Earth strain, his the destiny to fulfill the blood heritage of Adam and adventure. His was the spirit of daring that ever rode his kind—rode them and goaded them and drove them, one and all.

What was it his father had said, those long years gone—? "Live till you die, John; and live with daring. It's a poor man who accepts blind fate without a fight and covers his eyes against his dream."

And again: "What if you do fail, John? Life's in the game, the striving. You'll never know how far you might have gone unless you try. Don't worry about odds. They'll flip for a man who can spit in destiny's eye and laugh in death's black face."

Goss laughed aloud. He'd never felt better, never more alive.

Once again, he checked his instruments, his controls.

All in order; everything in hand.

Back to the visiscreen, now. Back to take one last look at Earth.

Earth wasn't there.

But something else was. A big something else, vague and shimmery, like a tremendous canopy hanging suspended in the sky.

Tight-lipped, Goss spun the controls.

Nothing seemed to happen. The ship held to its same disastrous course, lancing straight for the weird shape that loomed ahead.

Whirling, Goss whipped round the mobile screen.

It picked up Earth easily enough, but in the wrong place— far off to one side, beyond all possibility of navigational error or parabolic drift.

And still the ship refused to answer to its controls.

It dawned on Goss, then.

Savagely, he cursed the Huu and all their works. What good did it do to memorize manuals, trace through wiring charts, when someone else could secretly sabotage the mechanism behind the builders' and designers' backs?

The ship was moving into the canopy's shadow now, drawn as if by invisible lines of magnetic force. Like a matchstick in a maelstrom, it swung round, faster and faster, racing towards the whirlpool's vortex.

Then, suddenly, in a rush, with a silent sound like the blast of bottled thunder, the craft swept into and through the focal point.

Instantly, all pressure, all tension, seemed to fade away. Eddy-swirled no longer, the ship drifted aimlessly, as in a strange intraspatial sea.

Stiff-fingered, Goss spun his dials; checked his screens.

AND THERE, incredibly, lay all the galaxies, all the heavens—the whole vast realm of outer space. It was as if the canopy, the maelstrom, hadn't been there; did not exist.

Goss gaped, still not quite believing.

Then, while he stared, a sphere moved into focus on the mobile screen...a sphere somehow familiar in its size and shape.

Goss flicked to a stronger lens...studied the sphere in extreme close-up.

It was an asteroid, apparently; a smallish asteroid, probably not more than thirty feet in circumference, revolving slowly as it drifted through the sky.

As it turned, heavy gyves came into view...great forged metallic shackles designed to fit tight about human wrists and ankles. But the fetters hung empty now, without a victim, swinging free from the spikes that anchored them to the asteroid's living rock.

The boulder kept on turning.

More shackles, now...shackles locked to a skeleton's dangling bones.

Obviously, this was the asteroid of Sarah Corley's film. Baffled, scowling, Goss flicked back to the mobile screen's other lens.

The broader field revealed that things had been happening while he stared. Other asteroids had joined the first—a whole covey of them, assorted as to shape and size. While Goss watched, one drifted slowly closer to the tiny world that bore the shackles; bobbed against the skeleton with what appeared to be crushing force.

But nothing happened. Not a single fragile bone snapped. The delicate rib-cage dangled as before, unharmed. As leisurely as they had come together, the two asteroids moved apart once more.

Bleakly, Goss pondered, trying to dredge up answers to the jumbled questions that tumbled through his brain.

The next instant, the whole ship shuddered, rocking violently under a hammer-blow of impact. Goss sprawled on the control-room's floor.

Another blow—less violent, this time. Scrambling to his feet, Goss swung round the mobile screen.

The Great Nebula in Andromeda loomed, so bright and clear and close as to make Goss jerk back by reflex from the screen.

It was incredible, impossible. Hastily, once again he swung the viewer.

Other clusters, other nebulae, flashed by. In seconds, he found himself shifting from Omega Centauri to The Crab...from a close-up view of Venus' dust-clouds to the Leonid meteor swarm in scintillant display.

Then, again, the ship bumped into something.

Abruptly, Goss laughed.

It was a sour laugh, though; a laugh both bitter and heavy with chagrin.

Because at last he'd figured out the answer to his questions, all of them. At last he'd pinpointed the key, the angle.

The only possible angle.

How could anyone, any ship, bridge the gulf between Venus and Omega Centauri in less than half-a-dozen seconds? What conceivable procedure could range through whole galaxies as if they were mere rods apart?

Coupe all that with the bumps, the impact. Throw in the asteroids and the skeleton that didn't smash. Consider the Huu—their slyness, their trickery, their schemings.

Together, they told him precisely where he was—

Where else but in a vast planetarium—a gigantic model of the universe, all the heavens, created with an infinitude of realistic detail and then somehow suspended in the sky!

CHAPTER SIX
The Force Field

GOSS NEVER could be sure quite when he fell asleep.

The awakening was a different matter. It came with a bludgeon-blow of light, shot square into his eyes. A woman's voice lashed harshly, "Up, you! On your feet! Move!"

Groping, blinking, Goss lurched to his knees—and then discovered that he no longer lay in his stolen spaceship's control room.

Nor in the ship itself, for that matter. Instead, now, he faced walls of a weird green metal, put together in proportions surely alien. The styling of the place was different, too, and based on an unfamiliar motif. Patterns, furnishings, decorations—everything seemed slimmer, more graceful.

But his captors—two women of the type he'd come to think of as 'girl guards'—gave him no time for contemplation. Jerking him erect, they shoved him through the nearest doorway and down a long, narrow corridor beyond.

Another doorway, then; another room. A table, king-size and a spare, unpleasantly familiar figure with cold face and iron-grey hair cut short.

Dey Z'ulle.

Goss said, "The fear-discs must have raised an uncommon lot of hell. Can't you figure them out?"

For the wildest of guesses, the longest shot among off-beat conversational gambits, the effort proved singularly effective. Dey Z'ulle came half out of her seat, as if stabbed with a needle. "You know about them? The mechanism? The control system?"

"Would I tell if I did?"

The woman sank slowly back into her chair. "You do know, then."

"I do?"

"Of course. Otherwise, you wouldn't dare mock me."

Goss held his face expressionless.

It seemed to infuriate the woman. Her knuckles grew white, pressing against the table. "Stop smirking! Don't think I won't break you if I have to!" She pushed back a lock of iron-grey hair with fingers that shook ever so slightly. "In the eyes of The Council, as well as by my own estimate, this was the most dangerous Shan assault on Earth in generations. It was only a test, of course, and on a limited scale. But it paralyzed the area. You were the only person in range not completely incapacitated."

"So?"

"Don't play stupid!" Dey Z'ulle's nostrils flared with the effort of bridling her anger. "Obviously, we need to find out how the discs work. We take it for granted there's some sort of wave-principle involved—vibratory impulses, tuned to stimulate the human hypothalamus in such a way as to evoke paralyzing terror. But the details, the practical aspects—"

Abruptly, she broke off. Her voice took on a new, even harsher quality—a cold relentlessness, grim and unbending. "The danger's too pressing to waste time on talk. You can cooperate voluntarily, or you can make me force you. Take your choice."

Goss felt a tiny knot of tension growing in him. "Just because the discs didn't freeze me doesn't mean I know anything about them."

It was as if he hadn't spoken. Eyes flicking to the guard, Dey Z'ulle clipped, "Get Doctor Corley."

Silently, the woman stepped to a nearby door and pushed it open; gestured.

Heels clicked. Sarah Corley entered. Her face was pale and drawn, the blonde hair not quite so smooth and neatly-groomed as usual. She kept her eyes straight ahead, avoiding Goss.'

Dey Z'ulle said, "Connect the filter."

"It's ready."

The knot of tension in Goss tightened. He broke in quickly, angrily: "What's the matter with you? Work on the discs, not me. That's the way to get your answers."

Dey Z'ulle's glance washed him in cold contempt. Wordless, she rose; flicked a switch.

The top of the big table at which she had been sitting blazed light. Startled, Goss stepped closer.

Now he saw that what he'd assumed to be a table was, rather, a large, flat box with a transparent top. Inside lay one of the fear-discs, dully gleaming.

Still wordless, Dey Z'ulle moved a lever set in the case's side wall.

A jointed metal arm swung up inside the box. An elongated cylinder with double-serrate snout was mounted on the end.

Goss stared. "Is that a Rhondyke cutter?"

A CURT NOD. Deftly, now, the woman manipulated the tool's control knob. Like an extension of her own hand, skilled and precise, the metal arm within the case pressed close to the disc. The cutter's twin rows of teeth spun, in opposite directions. Purple light speared from the snout, the beam razor-edged as it traced lined patterns on the disc's surface.

"This cutter," Dey Z'ulle observed tightly, "will slice through any substance known to the human race in seconds."

"But it won't touch this?"

"Would you like to microcheck for scratches?"

"Have you tried impact, too? Corrosion?"

Dey Z'ulle's face twitched as if Goss has pricked a nerve. She turned on him; lashed out: "Stop it! I'm sick of your stalling!"

Goss rocked back. "What—?"

"I said, quit stalling! Or shall we use the filter on you?"

Narrow-eyed, Goss studied the woman for a long, taut moment. "All right," he said finally. "Let's talk about the discs."

A tremor of excitement crossed Dey Z'ulle's face. Her eyes grew hot and eager. "The mechanism, first—" She was already groping for a diagram scaler.

Goss cut her off with a slashing gesture. "You buried them, didn't you—like I did?"

All color fled the other's cheeks.

Her breathing seemed to hang suspended.

"The old Huu pattern: Security first, last and always. Play it safe." Goss chuckled softly. "I demonstrated that the discs won't work through dirt, so you insulated dump rigs or graders and poured on sand by the ton.

"Only then...when it came time to run tests, you found the discs had all disappeared. Right?"

Dey Z'ulle pressed her palms down flat on top of the disc-case, as if to keep them from trembling. In a ragged voice, she spoke to the guards: "Take—him. We'll try the filter."

"Before your precious council finds out how badly you've fouled up?" Goss laughed aloud this time. "It's too late, believe me. Even your bosses can't help but guess that burying those discs was an invitation to corrosion; that some soil element combined with their metal to destroy them. So who ordered them buried—?" He shrugged, spread his hands. "You see? There it is, no matter how you play it— that big black smear across your record!"

For a moment he thought that Dey Z'ulle would surely strike him.

Only then that tempest passed, and her shoulders slumped, and of a sudden she was just a fearful, aging woman, with face well-nigh as grey as her hair.

She said, "You're right, of course. It was—an error of judgment. But before I realized it, all the discs were gone, except for this one that had wedged in the roof of a house where we couldn't get to it as quickly as the others."

If he hadn't seen the core of ruthlessness that lay within her, Goss could almost have felt sorry for the woman.

She spoke again, now, low-voiced and tense: "You're right about my record, too: I don't want it smeared. But there's more to this than that."

Another pause, even longer than that previous.

Then, almost in a whisper: "The force field."

Goss frowned, ever so slightly. "It exists, then? It *really* exists?"

A sigh. "Yes, it exists. It's been Earth's shield against the Shan till now—the only barrier they couldn't breach." Dey Z'ulle turned, years hanging heavy on her. "Here. Let me show you."

She crossed the room to the one door not yet opened in Goss' presence. After a moment's hesitation, he followed her.

Even this portal itself was strange...a great, vault-like thing, double the normal size and set on a center spindle instead of hinges. The chill glitter of antiquity was in its greenish metal.

Dey Z'ulle said, "You understand, all this is very old—this whole ship. The true, pure Huu, our ancestors, came here in it, a thousand light-years across the void from their own planet. Their science lies behind all present cultures, just as their wall of energy, the force field, still protects us."

She touched one side of the massive door, the barest pressure. Smoothly, easily, it pivoted.

Beyond lay wonder—wonder such as John Goss had never dreamed of. Awestruck, he stared.

For this was a place incredible, a place of dazzling brilliance. Everywhere, light blazed, radiating out as from some huge jewel's facets

GOSS THREW up an arm to shield his eyes. Beside him, Dey Z'ulle said, "This room is designed to simulate a gigantic asymmetric crystal. It serves as a focal point for energy transmuted from the radiation of cosmic dust. The principle's related to that you get in the piezo-electric effect utilized in the primitive quartz clocks Earth astronomers sometimes use."

Goss drew back a step, out of the chamber; turned away from the pulsing, blazing display of light. "Would I understand the details if you explained them to me?"

"Probably not. I'm not sure I grasp it all myself." For the first time Goss could remember, his companion gave vent to what might have been a small laugh. "The important thing is that a chain of these crystal chambers is hung in space all around Earth. There's one in the sky-scoop that trapped your spaceship: another on the dark side of the moon; two more riding artificial orbits based on conic projections from the poles. Together, these and all the others, they lock planes of energy to each other, so not even the Shan can blast a path through."

She closed the great door as she finished; leaned against it, balancing on the vertical spindle in its middle and staring bleakly at the floor.

Goss looked from her to Sarah Corley and the guards. "And the discs—?" he prodded finally.

"I don't know. A new principle, maybe. Or maybe a chink in our armor—some spot the force field warps round; some rift or dead area." A pause. "That's why it's so vital you help us, John Goss, no matter what your race." And then, when Goss still said nothing:

"Tell me: Have you ever seen a Shan ship?"

Goss shook his head.

"Here, then; let me show you." Of a sudden it seemed that the woman could not help Goss enough. Leading him to what appeared to be a scanner-plate in one corner, she manipulated a series of slides.

The thing was like a visiscreen. Swiftly, it swept out from Earth, far below, to search the void beyond.

Then, abruptly, it stopped in mid-shift. A moment's blurring, and all at once the ship was on the screen.

Without quite knowing why, Goss found himself shivering. The craft was that peculiar, that alien. Amorphous, amoeboid, it seemed at first without form. Even its coloring was muddy and hard to pin down.

Dey Z'ulle said, "Watch, now!" and pressed a button.

A sudden spear of light lanced out of nowhere, straight at the dark ship.

But faster even than the bolt, the amorphous mass shifted. The light-spear hurtled past.

Dey Z'ulle turned off the scanner. "You see? We can't touch them. That's why we lost; why the Huu had to flee here. But so long as we had the force field, we could wait them out. Now, though—"

She stopped, cold-eyed. "Well, Mr. Goss, you've seen it now. Everything. So…"

Goss waited, not speaking.

"The discs, Mr. Goss; the discs! What about them?"

"What do you want me to say? That I know something I don't?"

A silence came upon the room, so heavy it echoed like thunder. Dey Z'ulle's eyes locked with Goss' unblinking.

Then, quite suddenly, she pivoted. "Doctor Corley!"

"Yes?"

"I told you we'd gain nothing this way; that the only things these fools can understand is death and violence! Time, we need it so desperately; and then to waste it on a creature like this!"

Goss clipped, "If time's so important, get to work on that fear-disc!"

"You'd like that, wouldn't you?" Dey Z'ulle blazed. "Your kind would love to see me squander more precious hours!"

To the guards: "Take him!"

Goss stepped back quickly. "No, you don't!"

"Take him, I said!"

The two women moved closer.

Goss said, "Quit asking for trouble. The first person to touch me won't walk for a while."

Dey Z'ulle: "Weapons, both of you! Paralyze him if he moves again!"

From beneath their jackets, the two guards brought out the snub-nosed fire-guns; swung them round. Grimly, Goss fell back yet another step, behind the case in which the fear-disc lay.

Dey Z'ulle: "I'm going to have them paralyze you, Mr. Goss, for a little while. But before they do it, I want to give you something to remember for the hours that lie ahead."

Triumph rang in the woman's voice now. Her eyes gleamed in fanatic fury.

"You see, you're going to help us, Mr. Goss! On our terms, this time. The Council's already given me permission. They recognize now that you and your kind are natural allies of the Shan; that so long as one member of the old race remains alive, Earth can't be safe.

"That's why we brought you here from the spaceship. That's why I've given you every chance to prove you're on our side.

"But you wouldn't accept our friendship; you wouldn't cooperate. All you could think of was your barbaric compulsion to adventure; your cursed, insatiate drive to break free of Earth and out into space.

"It proves my point: You can't be trusted—not you, personally, nor any of your kind. You'd gamble Earth and all our great Huu-rooted culture on stupid, savage impulse.

"So, now, Doctor Corley's going to make a new tracing of your psychogenetic patterns…a special kind of tracing, one we can use to screen whole populations for your racial drives and traits.

"Then, when that tracing's finished, and for the benefit and security of all, we're going to check every man and woman and child on Earth against it.

"Any who fit it will die within that hour.

"Congratulations, Mr. Goss! With you, your race comes to an end!"

CHAPTER SEVEN
Breakthrough

NUMB DISBELIEF spread through Goss, stealthy and deadening. So great was his shock that for a moment even perception lost its focus. The women looked strange, the room distorted. The pounding of his heart and of his pulses hammered in his brain like giant timpani.

"Wait, now—" he fumbled, loose-lipped. "Killing me—that's one thing. But the others—my race, my people; the mixed bloods who happen to have some of the same traits—you'll find plenty who stand as more Huu than human—"

Childish words. The speech patterns of a low-grade moron.

Only that was the way with such moments. They bore too much impact, came too unexpectedly. It gave a man's brain no room to function.

Dey Z'ulle gave no sign of having heard him. She spoke to the guards: "Now! Paralyze him!"

The command seemed to cut Goss free; to slash through the bonds of numbness. Of a sudden he was in a fighting crouch-feet spread apart; head down and forward; elbows in; hands up.

"Try it!" he snarled savagely. "Try it and die!"

For the fraction of a second the women hesitated, flicking uneasy glances one to the other.

Dey Z'ulle: "Fire, damn you, fire!"

Spasmodically, the weapons centered on Goss.

No more time for words, now. No more time for anything but desperate action.

Goss flung himself down and forward bodily, into the shelter of the case that held the fear-disc.

Above him, green fire laced the spot where he'd stood. Dey Z'ulle shrieked, "Get around there, in behind him!"

The ankles of one of the guards raced past the stand. Lunging, Goss caught a foot. The woman crashed headlong to the floor.

But before he could seize her weapon, there was a rush of other feet. Women swarmed over him—dozens of women, it seemed from where he lay. Their hands clawed at him—clutching and pushing, pinning him down. He couldn't even find room to swing a fist.

Desperately, he rolled to one side, hard against the uprights of the stand that held the fear-disc.

But still the women pursued him. Nails clawed at his face. Arms wrapped around his legs. And still there seemed no end to their numbers, their reinforcements.

Ten seconds more, and he knew they'd have him.

His head hit the stand, then.

The stand. The fear-disc.

Inspiration.

The hands were pulling him away now, out from under the case. Bodies fell atop him, deadening his struggles.

Only he couldn't give up. Not now, not when at last he had the answer.

With a violent lurch, he tore his arms free from his assailants. Clutching one leg of the stand, he groped blindly along the case that held the fear-disc, searching for the lever that controlled the Rhondyke cutter.

Buttons, knobs, switches—

The lever.

Goss seized it in a death grip, moved it this way and that, as far as he could in all directions.

Fingers gouged his wrist. Someone dropped on his chest like a sack of cement and began hammering methodically at his face.

Still Goss clung to the lever. The gouging fingers exerted yet more pressure. Pain shot up Goss' arm as his opponent twisted. He knew, instinctively, that something was going to have to give. Grimly, he braced himself for the snapping of the bone.

The next instant, someone shrieked.

It was the moment in the laboratory supply yard all over again. One moment, Goss lay helpless, sore beset. The next, his assailants were falling from him like flies, crumpling to the floor in helpless paroxysms of terror.

Unsteadily, breathing hard, he pulled himself free of their weight and lurched to his feet.

The room was a shambles, a mass of wrecked equipment. And everywhere lay women—choking, gasping, shivering, shaking.

Goss managed a wry smile. Then, swaying with fatigue, he turned to the case that held the fear-disc.

It was as before, save for one thing: The Rhondyke cutter had slashed a great, gaping hole in the transparent top.

Again, Goss became aware of the sense of psychic pressure building up within his own skull. Involuntarily, he shuddered.

Only then, for no good reason he could ascertain, the pulsing seemed to fade. It was as if the rhythmic waves from the disc were ebbing, dying.

But that was absurd on the face of it, for—

He threw a quick glance at the case; stiffened involuntarily.

The disc's casing had crumbled. Now the whole thing was disintegrating, disappearing, before his very eyes!

A SPASMODIC tremor ran through one of the prostrate women close by. She went limp, no longer convulsive in her tension. Another sobbed for breath and tried to pull herself to a sitting position.

Goss swore aloud. With desperate haste, he dragged the nearest of his erstwhile opponents to the corridor door and dumped her out. Then another...another...

But there were close to a dozen of the guards crowded into the room's cramped confines. Before the fourth was out, one was on her feet; a second struggling to rise.

Dey Z'ulle's voice came feebly: "Catch him! Hold him! Don't let him get away!"

Goss charged for the door.

But now someone had him by the ankle. He sprawled at full length on the cluttered floor. Before he could recover, the door rang shut like the knell of doom.

Dey Z'ulle, in triumph: "Doctor Corley, prepare to make the tracings!"

Savagely, Goss cursed her; cursed the fear-disc, too, and the blind fate that had made it choose this moment to lose its power and disappear.

In front of him, another woman clambered to her feet.

Beyond her, on the floor, lay one of the ugly, snub-nosed fire-guns.

Goss lunged for it. When the guard clutching his ankle tried to hold him back, he kicked her in the throat. A second and a third scrambled away before his fists' fierce impact.

And then, at last, his hands were closing on the weapon.

One assailant went down under a butt-stroke. When a second would have argued the point, Goss squeezed the fire-gun's trigger.

The woman's face seemed to freeze in the middle of a grimace. She fell like a tree crashing in a windstorm.

The others stood statue-rigid, panic written in every line.

But Dey Z'ulle only laughed, fierce and contemptuous. "So where do you go now, you fool?" she jibed. "Do you think you can get away, with that hall door locked and my people on the far side?"

Still breathing hard, Goss fell back a step till he was pressed against the wall. He didn't answer.

"Mr. Goss, you're trapped here!" Again Dey Z'ulle's bitter laughter pealed forth, vindictive and triumphant. "You're here, and you can't escape, and before we're through we'll have your patterns!"

"Maybe." Goss worked to iron the unevenness from his breathing. And then, suddenly biting off his words: "Or maybe you'll die first!"

But if he'd hoped to gain anything from the threat, it was wasted effort. Dey Z'ulle no longer seemed the same person he'd known earlier. The chill self-control, the tight-lipped competence and unbending manner—they'd vanished utterly, replaced by a sort of reckless desperation. It was as if the woman had some precognition of disaster, and so had given herself over, unchecked, to wild impulses born of rage and hate long in repression.

Now, again, she sneered at him and mocked him. "What would that matter? Do you think I've kept all this secret? The Council's other members, on Earth, would carry out our plan, even if you should somehow destroy this whole ship!"

"They would?"

"They would!"

"I wonder..." Goss smiled, ever so slowly. Then, suddenly straightening, he gestured with the fire-gun. His words crackled: "Get over there! Crowd to that side of the room!"

The women exchanged quick, questioning glances. Tight-lipped, Goss triggered a streak of fire, high, to speed them on their way.

They fell over each other in their hurry to reach the wall he'd designated.

The move left another wall bare...the wall that held the great double-door leading to the crystal chamber.

With swift strides, Goss crossed to it; then paused and checked his weapon.

There was a dial on the gun's side, and an arrow that pointed to the stamped word PARALYSIS.

Coolly, Goss turned the dial till the arrow pointed to another word, a word at the opposite end of the intensity scale: DEMOLITION.

ALL AT ONCE, Dey Z'ulle was no longer laughing. "What are you doing?"

"Killing you, if you move another inch," Goss retorted, leveling his weapon.

The woman fell back to a spot beside Sarah Corley.

Dey Z'ulle and Sarah…study in contrasts, as opposite as day and night.

But both of them were on the same side here. Both stood for the Huu, symbol of the female component of Earth's population. They weren't content to be part of a single race, a homogeneous species. They had to draw apart, to form themselves into a tight little secret conclave of ancestor-worshippers, condemning those traits that made for progress, made for striving. Security meant too much to them. It had become an ultimate, a god to hallow. They bowed to it blindly, so hypnotized by its enticements that they stood eager to instigate the murder of all who didn't share their point of view.

The murder of all his kind, his people.

Only so long as he lived, so long as he had an arm with which to strike, that would never, never be.

He said tightly, "You've talked a lot about the Shan, and what they'll do to the human race. I don't know. I haven't seen them at that close range; haven't had to fight them.

"But I do know what *you'll* do, because you've made your point all over me with bruises. You want to wipe out a way

54

of feeling and of thinking; slice away every brain-cell that holds a spark of daring. You intend to kill everyone who's seen the stars and dreamed a dream.

"That's why I'm not here just as me, John Goss. Right now, I represent all the rest of the human race—every single man, woman and child, except for your scared, security-swilling little handful.

"That means I'm not on your side, nor the Shan side either. As far as I'm concerned, the only thing that counts, is that the general population should get its chance to find out some answers for itself and do the things it wants to do—whether that means sticking tight to Earth, or sailing off across the void exploring.

"Win, lose or draw, the water's going to find its own level without any secret Huu dams in the way to stop it!"

He moved aside a fraction as he finished; poked at the great door's edge with his right elbow.

As smoothly as before, as easily, the door swung open. Again, light blazed dazzlingly from the inner chamber.

Goss said, "Friends, here goes your force field!"

He whirled; triggered the fire-gun.

Thunder exploded inside the crystal chamber—an avalanche of sound and violence. The whole ship rocked under its impact.

Then, suddenly, there was no more light; no more sparkling jewel-like facets. Dust filled the air. Feminine voices rose, babbling and screaming.

The blast had driven Goss halfway across the room and left him stunned and sprawling. He lay there, limp, through long, chaotic seconds.

Then a cry cut through his shock-hazed brain. Dragging himself up, he looked around wildly, searching for its source.

The voice rang out again: Dey Z'ulle's voice, shrill with rising horror. She stood in one corner beside the scanner screen, hunched over the slides in frantic tension.

There was something in her stance and tone that stood out even amid this echoing world of tumult. Unsteadily, Goss came up behind her and stared over her shoulder.

The reason for her terror was there, spread on the screen plain enough for anyone to see.

Already, the weird Shan ship was hurtling towards Earth.

CHAPTER EIGHT
Escape

FEAR IS an infectious thing. It leaps from heart to heart and brain to brain, and those touched merge and meld, joined in and by a mighty wave of welling panic.

So it was in that green-walled room aboard the ancient Huu ship. One moment, Dey Z'ulle stood alone before the scanner screen. The next, her cry had drawn her comrades to her. A glance at the screen, and tunnel vision took over. Like magic, they had eyes only for the dark, amorphous mass of the Shan invader. Terror twisted them in its grip. The individuality of each was lost, swept into the surging millrace of shared emotion. They became one: Fear, Incarnate, alive and breathing.

To Goss, it seemed like an ideal time to make a quick return to Earth. Quite casually, he let the horror-stricken guards press past him, while he looked around for Sarah Corley.

She stood at the edge of the group crowding closest to the scanner. Stepping up behind her, Goss touched her arm.

At first she didn't even notice. Then, when he pulled her back bodily, she whirled—eyes dread-distended, lips already peeling back to scream.

Like lightning, Goss simultaneously jerked her close and clamped a hand over her mouth.

The women knotted at the scanner didn't even notice.

Goss spoke into the girl's ear: "Is there an intercom system on this old hooker?"

His prisoner didn't answer. But her eyes involuntary flicker called his attention to a narrow grill set in the wall beside the corridor door.

Goss said, "In thirty seconds or a minute, that Shan ship's going to be close enough to do us damage. As an artificial satellite, this outfit's a sitting duck. Our only chance is to get it down to Earth before the opposition sets up target practice. But I can't do anything about it as long as I'm locked up here."

A little of the terror in the grey eyes faded. Goss could almost see intellect battling to stem the flood tides of emotion.

He tried again: "Don't you understand? If the Shan catch us here, they'll blast us all to atoms. But if we can get down fast enough, reach Earth, we'll have a chance to fight them off."

The flood tides definitely were ebbing now. The tight unity of blind fear was broken.

So, if intelligence would only bend a little in the right direction...

"You're human, Sarah. Not like Dey Z'ulle, these others. It's time you recognized it and gave your race a break."

Without another word, then, he dropped his hand from the girl's mouth and shoved her at the grillwork. He didn't even bother to grip her wrist or stay in grabbing distance. It was one of those things. Either it would work, or it wouldn't. And second chances seemed, to say the least, unlikely.

For the fraction of a second the grey eyes stayed tight on him, as if measuring. Then, swiftly, the girl pressed one of a row of buttons and spoke into the grill: "Guard? This is Doctor Sarah Corley. You can open the door now. We've got Goss; he's all through giving trouble. But Dey Z'ulle's hurt, so hurry!"

"Yes, doctor!"

Goss snatched up his fallen fire-gun in one swift flow of motion.

A quick, clicking sound. The door swung open.

Face strangely pale, not even looking at Goss, Sarah Corley stepped out into the corridor.

The move gave Goss ideal cover. Heart hammering, he crowded through the exit close behind her.

There were four women in the hall. Before they could realize what was happening, Goss had them covered. Hastily forcing them into the room he'd just departed, he slammed and bolted the door behind them in the same moment Dey Z'ulle's voice rose in furious discovery.

On again, now, Sarah leading the way in abysmal silence. On endlessly—through corridors; down ramps and ladders.

Then, at last, they came to another door, set at the end of a long, tube-like passage, and Sarah said, "This is the control room. That's what you want, isn't it?"

"Yes."

"There'll be people here. Get ready."

She pushed a lever. The door swung open.

Two women, this time—technicians, apparently, lounging in a narrow chamber virtually walled with what appeared to be instrument panels and control mechanisms of unfamiliar type.

Goss said, "We're leaving now. For Earth."

THE WOMEN LOOKED round, blank-faced; then scrambled up in a panic of indignant haste.

Goss gestured with the fire-gun. "Hurry up! Get this thing moving!"

An uneasy exchange of glances. Then, stubbornly, one of the women said, "This ship's been in orbit a good five thousand years, they say. We can't throw it out without special orders from The Council."

"To hell with your council! This is an emergency!"

"To hell with you, you mean!" The first uneasiness. of the woman doing the talking seemed to have faded. Now she appeared to take considerable satisfaction in speaking up to Goss. "Our orders are to hold this ship in orbit, under any and all conditions and without regard to individual instructions to the contrary by whomsoever given." A leer. "That's it. She stays in orbit."

Cold-eyed, Goss leveled the fire-gun. "This talks louder than words or orders either."

"Does it? We wouldn't know." The woman leered again. "Fire away, if you want to. Maybe it'll even teach you how to read these."

Her gesture took in the chamber's walls; the panels with their banks of unfamiliar instruments, strange symbols; the devices which might, for all Goss knew, just as well be decorations as controls, and vice versa.

He swore under his breath. Apparently his adversary caught it. Blithely, she dropped back into her seat again and made a business of resuming her conversation with the other woman.

Stalemate.

Grimly, Goss started towards the techs.

The next instant, he was slamming violently into a corner. The room careened to a crazy angle, still rocking, clangorous with a deafening din of metal crashing against metal.

The women had been thrown wide too. With Sarah, they lay against a far wall—jaws agape, eyes shock-glazed.

Bracing himself against sprung wall-plates, Goss hauled himself erect. But before he could so much as open his mouth to speak, the women were up too, spinning dials and clawing levers.

Another lurch, another shock of impact, more violent even than the first.

But with it, a sudden swift sense of acceleration. Tensely, the tech who'd talked to Goss announced, "We're moving out of orbit."

A third shock, severe beyond either of the others.

Desperately, Goss clung to a stanchion, wondering how much more such punishment the great Huu ship could take.

As if in answer, one of the control banks tore loose from its fittings, hurtled in a line drive straight across the narrow room, and smashed into and through an instrument-studded panel.

A wail from the tech: "We're out of control! We can't steer!"

Goss headed for Sarah Corley.

Wordless, she stumbled along the wall to meet him caught his hand, and pushed on, leading him towards the door through which they'd entered.

More passages, more ramps and ladders, while new thunder-claps of impact burst about them. A dozen times they fell. Full half their progress seemed to be on hands and knees, or sliding.

Then, abruptly, they came out into a loft-like area where slim, silvery two-place carriers stood lined up, row on row.

Simultaneously, a voice cried out behind them. There was a snapping sound, as if some missile had struck metal close at hand.

Sarah broke into a run, Goss following close behind her.

Ahead, a long chute that looked like a launching-tube yawned, one of the carriers already drawn up and locked tightly in position.

Goss jerked back the tiny ship's hood. Clambering over the cowling, he lifted Sarah bodily and set her down in the pilot's seat beside him.

She pressed a button. Instantly, the hood overhead slid shut.

Another button. The carrier swept down the launching-tube faster and faster. Blackness closed in on them. A high, shrill whine developed, growing louder every second.

Then, suddenly, the whine cut off, as if sliced with a razor. Star-spangled heavens leaped into view to drive away the black.

Most important of all, Earth loomed ahead, a ball of faintly glowing green, heartwarmingly familiar in contrast to the endless void that stretched about it on all sides.

THEN A SHADOW seemed to fall across the carrier. Goss twisted sharply in his seat.

The dark, amorphous mass of the Shan ship hovered above them, a cloud of menace against the sky.

Now, too, the Huu ship came into perspective—a great green globe, an Earth in miniature.

While he watched, more carriers darted from the launching-tube, silver specks racing away before the Shan advance.

Some made it. But for many, the huge, shape-changing craft was moving far too fast. It swept them up, enfolded them in its dark cloud. Like stars blotted out, they blinked and disappeared.

Now bolts of what might have been lightning lanced forth from the dark cloud-craft of the Shan. Straight at the green Huu ship they struck—bolt after bolt, blast after blast.

At first, they seemed to have no effect.

Then, suddenly, a jagged crack appeared along the surface of the huge metal globe. Faster it spread, and faster— branching, dividing, reaching out in a spidery pattern that touched every monstrous metal plate.

The next moment, the globe broke up, first into segments and then fragments. In seconds, it was like a handful of greenish crumbs, flung broadside across the sky.

In spite of himself, Goss shuddered.

But that was futile, and he knew it. For now, the important issue was to get back to Earth.

He said, "Sarah…"

She didn't answer.

"Sarah! Are you all right? Can you hear me?"

A glance, quick and scornful, biting as the raw wind that sweeps across the arctic sea.

But no words. Not one.

It stayed that way, minute after minute, while the tiny carrier hurtled on through space at ever-faster speeds, and Earth grew and grew till it filled the ship's entire vision slot.

Then at last they were circling, landing…dropping down on a small, square ramp thick-fringed with trees.

Sarah led the way to one of a dozen or more parked pelcars.

Unhappily, Goss got in with her.

In an hour, they were in the city, pulling up beside the building where he'd stayed…the selfsame building from which he'd stepped out into peril and chaos hardly more than a day ago.

The pelcar dropped down onto its blocks. Tight-voiced, Sarah Corley said, "Get out."

It was an order not a request. For a second Goss hesitated, staring at the girl. But he couldn't find the right words so, shrugging, he slid to the pavement and started away.

"Wait."

Sarah again. Tight-lipped, Goss turned.

The girl said, "I think there's something you should know, Mr. Goss. I'm not really stupid. Back there on the ship, when you asked me to help you, I knew all you wanted was to get away.

"I wanted you to, too. That's why I told the guards to unlock the door. I betrayed my people for you; doomed Earth, broke my oath, threw away my honor.

"Now I never want to see you again."

Gravs grinding, the pelcar raced away.

CHAPTER NINE
Last Gamble

THE AMPLIFIERS were blaring again now: "Attention, all! Another Shan message has been intercepted! Apparently invasion preparations are under way. Landings may be expected at any time. Meanwhile, take shelter, but do not panic. Further disc attacks are coming! The first wave is expected to arrive within three minutes—"

Goss hurried faster. The weight of the heavy suitcase had grown to well-nigh more than his weary arms could handle; and to be out in the open during a disc raid was the last thing he wanted. It called too much attention to the case, and to his own unique immunity to the waves of fear that radiated from the discs. Sooner or later, some sharp-eyed Security man would note and link such items, and then—

Goss cringed at the thought.

Yet time was so precious he dared not postpone action by even a single moment.

But what if Sarah Corley was gone? What if he couldn't find her?

Grimly, Goss shifted the bulky case to his other hand; pushed the thought out of his mind.

Just managing to maintain your sanity on Earth, this past twenty-four hours, had been an achievement. Time after time, the world had wakened to the screams of sirens. And time after time, likewise, thousands upon thousands of shining disc-shaped craft had swept down from the distant Shan ship.

Terror came with them…the same, rhythmic, panic-pulse Goss had witnessed back in the first experimental raid.

Now, though, the discs struck everywhere, not just in limited areas. While islands and coastal districts took the least punishment, relatively speaking, there was no dearth of the flat, coin-like craft anywhere. It seemed unlikely that any land-bound human had succeeded in totally avoiding contact with the fear-waves, even for this short a time.

Nothing seemed to damage the discs, either. Diamond drills, explosive shells, corrosive washes, electrical charges, radiation. Earth had tried them all, but not one disc had broken.

Yet within a few hours, incredibly, all disintegrated, disappeared!

Even more startling had been the messages.

Whether they were really messages or not, and whether or not the cryptanalysts and linguists actually had succeeded in making sense of them, there seemed no question but that Earth's electronic listening devices had picked up a variety of strange wave-patterns radiating from the Shan ship. "Interpretive decryptments" had been made, allegedly to the effect that a Shan invasion was imminent.

And if it really was—Goss shuddered and drew his aching, sweating fingers tighter about the suitcase handle; lengthened his weary stride.

An intersection. Goss checked the sign.

It was the street on which the directory said Sarah Corley had her apartment. Pivoting, Goss strode right, checking house numbers.

Only that turned out to be unnecessary, because suddenly a slender blonde girl darted down the steps from a building entrance just ahead, golden hair dancing.

Sarah Corley. Goss broke into a stumbling run.

Sarah's eyes came round at the sound of his feet. At the sight of him, her face stiffened. Whirling, she raced headlong in the opposite direction.

Goss swore. Gingerly, he lowered the suitcase to the sidewalk, then sprinted after the girl.

He was panting before he finally caught her.

For a moment, she fought like a wildcat, kicking and scratching.

Then, when Goss' superior strength at last cut short her struggles and dragged her back to the suitcase, she turned frigid—standing stock still, unmoving save for the quick rise and fall of her breasts, grey eyes hot with anger in a cold and hostile face.

Goss said, "Go ahead, hate me. But I had to find you. It's our only chance against the Shan."

"Against the Shan?" The girl's laugh was bitter as tea steeped hours too long. "I must have misunderstood you, Mr. Goss. The Shan wouldn't even be here if it weren't for you."

"Correction. The first discs landed while I was still in your supply yard. The Shan aren't doing anything they hadn't already done before I knocked your force field down."

"I don't care to discuss it."

"Then let's not." Goss swung her round. "Come on."

"Come on? Where?" Of a sudden a panicky note crept into Sarah's voice despite its surface shell of ice.

"To that carrier you brought us back to Earth in. You've got to play pilot again."

"No!"

"Do you think I want to ask you?" Goss had trouble keeping his own voice steady as he picked up the heavy suitcase. "I'd do it myself, if I knew how the thing works."

'I said no! I won't do it!"

"You will!"

"No!" With a sudden twist, Sarah jerked free and ducked past Goss.

"Stop!" He snatched at her as she passed; caught sleeve instead arm; felt the garment rip even as his fingers tightened.

But the fabric's tug had pulled the girl off balance. It slowed her a second. Letting go the suitcase, Goss grabbed her wrist.

"Hey, what gives?" A man speaking, come out of nowhere. A big man, burly and belligerent.

A SINKING FEELING began to take form in Goss' midriff. "It's nothing, mister."

"Oh, no? Well, maybe I don't see it that way."

"All right, all right, so you don't."

"Another thing: What's in that bag?"

The sinking feeling grew into full-fledged knot of tension. "Nothing, nothing important. Just some stuff of mine. I'm moving, trying to find some place where there aren't so many of these damn discs."

"Let's take a look in the bag."

"Now, wait a minute, mister—"

"You wait. I'm Security. Open up."

Tight-lipped, Goss stared down at the gold badge the man displayed.

It was all his nightmares come to life. Shifting his weight a fraction, he debated his chance. A good, solid right to the man's bulging belly, perhaps—

"Hurry it up, you!"

Goss breathed in carefully, trying not to telegraph his punch.

But before he could strike, a flicker of shadow passed across his face. The next instant, a crash echoed close at hand.

Simultaneously, Sarah Corley and the belligerent man both crumpled to the pavement, their bodies convulsing with rhythmic tremors.

Startled, unbelieving, Goss looked up.

Overhead, Shan fear-discs speckled the sky like swarming insects—discs by the hundreds, by the thousands—

Goss lifted Sarah and slung her across his shoulder, heedless of her anguished screams. Running to the nearest abandoned pelcar, he loaded her in.

Back for the suitcase, then. Loading it in beside the girl, he took the pelcar's controls and headed the vehicle at full speed for the secluded field where the sleek Huu carrier lay.

He still wasn't quite sure what he'd do when he got there. Once the Security man recovered consciousness, the alarm in all likelihood would go out; not even the stupidest official could fail to spot the coincidence of heavy case and disc-immunity.

Then the hunt would start—not a blind hunt, this time, but one with a description of one John Goss to guide it.

Even worse, Sarah unconscious was also Sarah useless, so far as piloting was concerned. And while a variety of equipment already had come into use to provide insulative protection against the fear-discs' waves, none of it was light or compact enough for use aboard the tiny skycraft.

In the end, that problem proved fortuitously simple of solution. A disc lay less than a dozen yards from the carrier. When Goss shoveled it under, Sarah promptly regained her self-control.

Goss squatted down beside her. "Lie quiet a minute. You're going to need your strength."

No answer.

"The place I've got to reach," Goss pressed on, "is that planetarium affair your people used to film those horror shots of the man chained to the asteroid. Once you land me there, you can go your way. You won't be bothered with me any more."

Still no response.

"Would you rather I talked about responsibility? You Huu share it, you know. If it hadn't been for the way you kept men out of space, Earth might have managed to develop some weapons against the Shan."

Silence.

Goss' tension turned to sudden anger. "You can't be this big a fool! Don't you realize what all this means—this fear-disc business? The Shan are softening us up—preparing to occupy Earth, make us a colony! That's why they haven't blasted us like they did your Huu ship. They want our world intact, undamaged."

Sarah Corley's lips drew together slightly.

"You don't believe me?"

"Should I?" The woman threw him a cool, contemptuous glance. "You give me no credit for having a mind at all, do you, John Goss? You take it for granted I can't see past your pseudo-logic."

"*Pseudo*-logic—!"

"What else would you call it? If what you say is true, why haven't the Shan already landed? Why should they hold off this way, bombarding us with discs and more discs?"

"Do you think they check their plans with me, every hour on the hour? How should I know?"

"If you don't, I can't understand why you're so anxious for me to fly you out to that old Huu space platform."

Goss slumped down, all at once overcome with a weariness that seemed to reach clear to the marrow of his bones. He didn't even try to answer.

Sarah again: "Do you know what the word 'erratic' means? Freakish? Inconsistent? You're all of them, and more! Twenty-four hours ago, I told you I never wanted to see you again, and you didn't even shrug your shoulders. But today, here you are back again, staggering across my doorstep with a suitcase—"

A sudden pause. "That suitcase. What's in it?"

GOSS STARED at the ground briefly. Then, quite calmly, he answered, "An Iphax detonator."

"An Iphax detonator—!"

"Yes."

Sarah Corley's eyes distended. Her expression held a sort of frantic horror. "No. It can't be. No one could get one."

"You'd be surprised what you can get," Goss observed dryly, "if you can walk around wherever you feel like while everyone else is having disc convulsions."

"But what will they do to you—?"

"Shoot me on the spot, probably. Security doesn't care much for characters who steal top-priority weapons."

"But why, John? Why?" Of a sudden Sarah Corley was on her knees beside him. "You must have known what you were doing. Or didn't you realize—?"

"I realized, all right." Bleakly, Goss stared off into the distance. "Only sometimes a man runs into things he has to do, no matter how crazy they look to other people."

A low moan from Sarah. She buried her face in her hands.

Then, after a moment, she rose, swift and graceful.

Goss looked up, questioning.

"Come on." She gestured to the tiny carrier. "I don't pretend to understand you, John. But if what you want is to go out to the platform with that case, I'll see that you get there."

"Thanks."

There was silence, then…what seemed to Goss like endless silence. Clumsy with fatigue, he loaded the suitcase into the flyer and climbed aboard himself. Beside him, Sarah pressed buttons. In seconds, they were speeding upward, into the bright vault of the sky.

Then, ahead, at last, he glimpsed the strange, shimmery shape of the huge enclosure that was the Huu space platform, with its monstrous planetarium and artificial asteroids.

The place where he would rendezvous with destiny.

Of a sudden, his eyes burned, and his mouth was cotton-dry. The muscles in his middle drew tighter and tighter.

Skillfully, Sarah maneuvered the carrier through some sort of lock; let it hover, unmoving, in the strange sky-microcosm beyond.

Narrow-eyed, Goss searched out the asteroid with the skeleton, the shackles. When the carrier came close enough beside it, he slid back the cowling, hooked the shackles to the flyer so the two craft couldn't drift apart, and set about his appointed task.

Close up this way, the asteroid looked less forbidding. Skeleton, shackles, and planetoid alike were shaped of painted plastic. And since the plastic cut easily, it was no trick at all to hack a hole through the outer shell and wedge the Iphax detonator inside the hollow sphere.

By the time he'd finished, the contact points were attached to the wrist shackles, and the hole in the asteroid repaired so that only the closest of close-range scrutinies revealed that surgery had been performed.

Now, once again, he turned to Sarah Corley. "Is there a way we can get this thing out of here—let it float free in the void?"

"I think so. The locks should carry it through if we work it close enough." The girl shot him a half-worried, half-questioning glance. "What's it you're trying to do?"

Goss smiled, ever so thinly. "I thought you'd guess. The Shan are impregnable to outside attack, so far as we know. But an Iphax detonator going off inside their ship—"

"Inside—!"

"Why not? The Shan picked up as many Huu carriers as they could catch when the big ship blew. If they see a thing like this asteroid floating through the void close by, it may arouse their curiosity enough so they'll want to scoop it up so they can look it over.

"Then, once it's in, I'll fire the detonator, and that's the end of the Shan, because the Iphax is a catalytic unit. It sets up a chain reaction, renders all elements fissionable and explodes them, so long as there's anything left at all to feed the blast. That's why Earth put them under Security jurisdiction. Trigger one on any world, and there's a good chance the whole planet would be destroyed."

A shiver ran through Sarah. "But how can you fire it? A remote unit—?"

"Not remote. Proximity." Goss managed a dry chuckle. "You see, I'm the bait; the hook to catch Shan interest. I'll ride the asteroid right in, just like in your films. And then..."

Breaking off in the middle of the sentence, he clambered up onto the carrier's cowling; snapped the first of the shackles into place around his ankle.

Sarah Corley still hadn't spoken. She sat as if paralyzed—face stiff, eyes wide with incredulity, disbelief.

GOSS SNAPPED the shackle around his other ankle.

The sound; the movement, seemed to break the woman's spell. She cried out—a hoarse, choked, gasping cry, not quite coherent.

"Easy, girl."

"John, no! No!" She came up in her seat; threw herself towards him. Hysteria was in her voice.

Awkward, off balance, Goss still managed to catch her by the shoulders and push her back down. "This is one of those things, Sarah. You can't do anything about it."

The girl's babble didn't even make sense now. She struggled till it was all Goss could do to hold her.

"Stop it, damn it! Do you think I want to do this?" In desperation, he shoved her back again and slapped her hard across the face.

The hysterical keening died. Still staring at him, she brought one hand to her cheek, touching the scarlet marks left by his fingers.

Goss said tightly, "Heroics aren't my specialty. But you just might be right—all those things you said about me dooming Earth by breaking down the force field and letting in the Shan. So I figure the least I can do is try to repair the damage."

Turning, he snapped the shackle onto his left wrist.

But now, like lightning, the girl flung herself bodily upon him, leaning far out of the carrier to catch him in a convulsive grip, arms tight about his waist.

It was more than Goss could take. Savagely, he drove his free right fist to the point of the other's jaw.

Sarah went limp; and for a moment it seemed to Goss that poised as she was she must surely fall.

Only then, somehow, he managed to get hold of her and to maneuver her clumsily back into the carrier's seat. For one last moment, he stared down at her, trying without avail to control the tightness that kept closing off his throat.

But time was too short for that sort of thing. Already, the Shan attack might be getting under way. Grimly, Goss slid on his oxygen helmet, then unhooked the last shackle from the carrier cowling and shoved off, swinging the bulky *ersatz* asteroid awkwardly into the platform locks.

It was the end of something, and he knew it. But thanks to his own efforts, Huu control of his home world was ended, and in a few hours more, with luck, the Shan threat too would be forever dead.

It was almost enough to take the sting out of dying.

The asteroid began to move now, bouncing and bumping into the locks.

Tight-lipped, Goss turned, straining for one final look at the carrier, and Sarah.

Only now, incredibly, two carriers hovered side by side where one had lain before.

Two carriers; and in one sat a spare, aging woman with iron-grey hair cut short and a cold, too-competent face.

She turned at the same moment as did Goss. "A fine idea, Mr. Goss," she called across the widening space between them. "I approve heartily. And since Earth and I both apparently are going to survive, you can count on it I'll live to see the Huu back in full control!"

Her hand came up in a mocking salute as she finished. She was still laughing when the edge of the space-lock cut her off from Goss' view.

CHAPTER TEN
The Shan

BEGIN WITH a dark, amorphous mass that somehow moves itself with lightning speed across the vastness of the void.

Then, introduce a flap of sorts—a kind of sky-scoop that opens, in the mass to suck in prey.

For Goss, even planning it; expecting it—the experience was born and bred of terror. One moment, he was drifting through the star-spangled, everlasting night of outer space, shackled to an artificial asteroid in a role no man had ever played before.

The next, the great Shan ship was hurtling towards him. The scoop opened. Man and asteroid alike swirled in to utter blackness.

Desperate, hanging onto reality by the barest thread, Goss clenched his teeth.

More blackness—echoing eternities of blackness, so black as to make a man cry out aloud for the sheer solace of hearing a human voice.

Then, abruptly, the darkness faded...gave way to a haze of pale violet light.

Grimly, Goss waited, biding his time.

Still the asteroid moved on, deeper and deeper if to the Shan ship's bowels. The light grew brighter—a dazzling light, now, almost overpowering in its intensity.

Another moment, and the asteroid bumped against a low, shelf-like ledge. Beyond lay banks of tall, thin, vertical tubes, each spilling out eddies of the violet light. Other tubes, horizontal, bored straight into the walls like tunnels, though their diameter was too small—less than a foot—for Goss to imagine intelligent creatures moving through them.

In any case, he could see no opening anywhere large enough to allow for human use.

Which made this the end of the line where the asteroid was concerned…the terminal point for one John Goss.

Because he'd come for one purpose, and one only: To fire the Iphax detonator inside the Shan ship's hull.

The quicker, the better. Now, before something happened; before he lost his nerve.

Sarah Corley—? He didn't even dare think about her.

As for Dey Z'ulle…

Frustration, helpless fury, roiled in Goss. Cursing, he shoved the detonator contact shut.

Nothing happened.

A numbness came to Goss—a terrible aching, quaking anguish that was more than he'd thought it possible to bear. Jerkily, he fumbled loose the catches on the wrist shackles; tried again to fire the detonator, and yet again.

Still nothing.

It dawned on Goss that he was shaking, sobbing.

Was this what he'd thrown his life away for? Had he played out his game in the face of all the odds, only to find here at the end that the prize was clay beneath the gilt?

Yet that would be the way of it, of course. Of course. The Shan wouldn't take in foes without some control device, some mechanism or suppressant to protect them against just such schemes as this.

Or perhaps the flaw was at the other end, in the detonator. After all, what did he really know about it? Maybe the things he'd read were wrong.

For that matter, consider Security's angle: Would the men in charge have dared to leave even one such device in working order, anywhere on Earth?

So this was how it ended. All his plans, all his dreams—a psychiatrist could have told him beforehand they were the product of a disordered mind.

He wondered how long it would be before his oxygen gave out.

In the same instant, he heard the drone behind him...barely perceptible, at first, but growing louder.

Lurching, swearing at the shackles that still held his ankles, Goss craned, searching the great arched passageway that led to the scoop and out into the void.

And there, incredibly, was a tiny, two-place Huu carrier sweeping in.

Sarah Corley sat at the controls. At least, Goss thought she did, though he couldn't be sure for a moment, because his eyes kept hazing till he couldn't see.

Then, so fast he could hardly believe it, she was there beside him...clambering out of the carrier onto the violet-lighted ledge...fumbling, trying to help him with the catches of the ankle shackles—

A sound, then...a new sound, one such as Goss had never heard before.

Instinctively, he looked up, searching for the source.

IN THE SAME MOMENT, something slid from the nearest of the horizontal tubes, the tubes that bored like tunnels straight into the glowing violet walls.

It was a worm, Goss thought at first—a gigantic, loathsome, dead-white worm, full seven feet long and moving swiftly towards them across the shelf-like ledge.

Then, looking closer, he saw that the thing had legs of sorts—at least two pairs per segment, like a millipede.

There again, though, the analogy was deceptive, for certainly this creature was like no millipede ever seen on Earth.

Desperately, Goss kicked his left leg-iron, and tore his nails bloody on the right.

But the catch still stuck, somehow. It wouldn't give. It wouldn't turn him free.

Savagely, he shoved Sarah Corley backward, away from the advancing worm.

The next instant, the thing was upon him.

Hanging precariously to the wrist shackles, Goss kicked violently at the creature, aiming for what appeared to be primitive eyespots set high in its head.

Like lightning, the thing dodged. A pincer-like foot—or was it a hand?—whipped up something that looked like a pencil and speared a thin beam of black light at Goss.

The ray caught him high in the shoulder; and such was the pain of it that involuntarily he screamed aloud.

Then another scream slashed through his. By sheer reflex, he swung round.

Sarah stood with her back to the ledge's edge. Three of the worm-things were advancing on her.

But Goss' own adversary was writhing closer, too. Again, black light lanced out. Again, Goss screamed.

This time, though, he kicked as he screamed. His heavy boot struck the worm-thing. The creature recoiled, moving with a jerkiness that told of unvoiced hurt.

The retreat gave Goss precious seconds. Frantically, he tugged and tore at the ankle shackle.

Then, when he had all but given up hope, it pulled free. Goss spilled forward bodily onto the ledge.

In an instant, the worm-thing was upon him, rushing at his head.

Spasmodically, Goss twisted sidewise and drove both feet at the loathsome, segmented body.

The blow struck home with solid impact. The worm skidded sidewise, off the ledge's edge, there to hang

suspended in space, not falling because of the lack of grav-
itational pull, yet unable to progress because of the lack of
anything to cling to.

Scrambling up, Goss raced towards Sarah.

She stood with her back to one of the glowing vertical
tubes, now, away from the ledge's edge—a mistake, certainly,
for it gave her no area of refuge from the worm-things.
Already, they were crowding in closer and closer, each time
more daringly, as if searching out the girl to find if she were
in any wise dangerous.

In a rush, Goss was upon them—kicking and stomping,
dodging and charging.

But it was hopeless, hopeless. While his boots might hurt
the worms, they didn't seem to kill or cripple.

And there were three worms—no; seven now—to one of
him. Against such odds, he couldn't last more than a couple
of minutes.

But at least, he could try.

Fiercely, he lunged at the largest of the worms. Hooking a
boot beneath it, he flipped it partly over and drove in,
smashing at the ugly thing's smooth underside.

The creature's segments drew together in a convulsive,
self-protective movement. Its feet, its legs, dug into Goss'
knees, gouging and slashing. Again, pain raced through him.
He felt blood spurt.

So now there was crimson on the dead-white of the worm;
the violet-lighted ledge. And still Goss fought, leaping high
into the air and driving his heels down in his efforts to smash
through his foes' smooth, hard integument.

Another worm lashed back at him. More blood spurted.

Then, suddenly, one worm was writhing from Goss' path
and shriveling. A second followed. A third.

The others seemed to freeze. An instant later, they were turning on their own tracks, racing for the tunnel-tubes from which they'd come.

Goss stared after them incredulously, unable to believe his eyes.

But now Sarah Corley was crying out; running to him.

Three steps she took—and on the third, the ledge gave way beneath her. Barely in time, he caught her and dragged her on across a spreading crevice.

Face fear-strained, she stared down at it. "What—?"

Goss slapped a hand down on his right knee. It came away smeared with blood. Pivoting, he strode swiftly to the nearest vertical tube and smudged the blood along it.

For an instant, nothing happened. Then, with a hissing sound, the tube dissolved before their very eyes.

"The blood—!" Sarah gasped. "That's it! The blood!"

But Goss spun her around. "Quick! The carrier!"

As one, they raced towards it...scrambled hastily aboard.

ALMOST in the same moment, turbulence churned the thin atmosphere about them. In seconds, the carrier was swept like a torrent-tossed chip back in the direction from which it had comeback through the giant arch, the passageway; back into the blackness of the scoop.

And then, with amazing swiftness, out again—out into the star-lighted black velvet of the void.

The Shan ship had already disappeared from view before they could even know for sure they'd left it.

Now, looking out at the skies about them, they knew it had been traveling even before it spewed them from its maw. These were unfamiliar worlds; strange galaxies. Nowhere, nowhere, could they find even one star that they could name.

For a long moment, they sat in silence. Finally Goss said, "At least Earth doesn't have to worry any more about the Shan."

"No." Sarah Corley sighed a little, "I still can't realize it, quite. It seems too simple."

"The salt, you mean?" Goss laughed, a trifle sourly. "We should have known, of course. Everybody should. Why else would the Shan refuse to land, except that our world held some element they couldn't tolerate? It accounts for so many things—the way they avoided the sea with their fear-discs; the way the discs disintegrated whenever they were buried or exposed to air too long; the very fact that their ship was shrouded in some sort of covering—obviously, a scheme to protect the metal, in case of accidental contact with saline atmospheres."

"But apparently they didn't know that human blood is salty too." This from Sarah. And then, with sudden laughter: "Oh, what a glorious point nine-tenths of one per cent that salt in our blood is!"

"So, no more Shan." In spite of himself, Goss said it just a trifle grimly.

"On Earth, you mean?" The laughter in Sarah's eyes and voice went dead. Then, after a moment, she added, "No more Huu, either."

Goss looked at her, not speaking.

The grey eyes brimmed. The ripe lips trembled. "John—John, I killed her. Dey Z'ulle. She tried to stop me, when I came to and found you'd gone and knew I had to follow. I didn't care what happened to me; I only knew I couldn't let you die alone. So when she pulled the fire-gun, I wrestled with her, and then—and then—"

Her shoulders shook. Ever so gently, Goss put his arm about her; held her to him.

The moment passed. Slowly, Sarah raised her face. "John—" a helpless gesture— "these worlds—they're none at all we know."

"Does that matter?"

Hesitation, for the barest fraction of a second. Then, slowly, Sarah shook her head. "No, I guess it really doesn't. Not if we can find one that's habitable before what little fuel this carrier holds gives out."

"We will," Goss said. "Count on it. We've come too far for our luck to play out now."

"It's time we started, then." Deftly, Sarah pushed three buttons...stopped short with a sound that might have been a giggle. "John..."

"Yes?"

"Shall I call you Adam?"

"Sure thing, Eve," he grinned back.

Truly, it was a lovely world they found.

THE END

MARS FOR THE MARTIANS!

Dark Kensington had been dead for twenty-five years. It was a fact; everyone knew it. Then suddenly he reappeared, youthful, brilliant, ready to take over the Phoenix, the rebel group that worked to overthrow the tyranny that gripped the settlers on Mars.

The Phoenix had been destroyed not once, not twice, but three times! But this time the resurrected Dark had new plans, plans that involved dangerous experiments in mutation and psionics.

And now the rebels realized they were in a dangerous situation fraught with double jeopardy. Not only from the government's desperate hatred of their entire movement, but also from the growing possibility that a new, terrible breed of mutated creatures would soon get out of control and bring forth terrors, the likes of which, had never been known to man.

ABOUT CHARLES L. FONTENAY...

CHARLES L. FONTENAY was born on March 17, 1917, in Sao Paolo, Brazil. His parents moved to Tennessee where he was raised from infancy. In his early years he worked as a journalist for three newspapers, including *The Nashville Tennessean*. Before the war he wrote for the Associated Press.

He became a member of James Quinn's *If* science fiction magazine stable of writers with the publication of his first story, "Disqualified", in September of 1954. He also wrote three sci-fi novels over the next decade: "Twice Upon a Time" (1958), a space-time adventure; "Rebels of the Red Planet" (1961), an intrigue set on Mars, and "The Day the Oceans Overflowed" (1964), a wild tale about oceanic disasters.

In his later years (1995-2000) he returned to writing science fiction again with the long series of "Kipton" juvenile stories featuring a young girl in various adventures on Earth and in space. Charles Fontenay passed away in Memphis, Tenn., at the age of 89, on January 27th, 2007.

REBELS OF THE
RED PLANET

By
CHARLES L. FONTENAY

ARMCHAIR FICTION
PO Box 4369, Medford, Oregon 97504

*For more information about Armchair Books and products, visit our
website at…*

www.armchairfiction.com

Or email us at…

armchairfiction@yahoo.com

CHAPTER ONE

It is a sea, though they call it sand.

They call it sand because it is still and red and dense with grains. They call it sand because the thin wind whips it, and whirls its dusty skim away to the tight horizons of Mars.

But only a sea could so brood with the memory of aeons. Only a sea, lying so silent beneath the high skies, could hint the mystery of life still behind its barren veil.

To practical, rational man, it is the Xanthe Desert. Whatever else he might unwittingly be, S. Nuwell Eli considered himself a practical, rational man, and it was across the bumpy sands of the Xanthe Desert that he guided his groundcar westward with that somewhat cautious proficiency that mistrusts its own mastery of the machine. Maya Cara Nome, his colleague in this mission to which he had addressed himself, was a silent companion.

Nuwell's liquid brown eyes, insistent upon their visual clarity, saw the red sand as the blowing surface of unliving solidity. Only clarity was admitted to Nuwell, and the only living clarity was man and beast and vegetation, spotted in the dome cities and dome farms of the lowlands. He and Maya scurried, transiting sparks of the only life, insecure and hastening in the absence of the net of roads which eventually would bind the Martian surface to human reality from the toeholds of the dome cities.

In that opposite world which was the other side of the groundcar's seat, Maya Cara Nome's opaque black eyes struggled against the surface. They struggled not from any rational motivation but from long stubbornness, from habit, as a fly kicks six-legged and constant against the surface tension of a trapping pool.

Formally, Maya was allied to Newell's clarity and solidity, and she could express this alliance with complete logic if called on. But behind the casually blowing sand she sensed a depth. The shimmering atmosphere, hostile to man, which sealed the red desert was a lens that distorted and concealed by its intervention.

The groundcar was a mechanical bug, an alienness with which timorous man had allied himself; allied with it against reality, she and Nuwell were hastened by it through reality, unseeing, toward the goal of a more comfortable unreality.

The groundcar bumped and slithered, and an orange dust-cloud boiled up from its broad tires and wafted away across the sculpted sand. The desert stretched away, silent and empty, to the distant horizon; the groundcar the only humming disturbance of its silence and emptiness. The steel-blue sky shimmered above, a lens capping the red surface.

The groundcar rolled westward, slashing toward its goal from the distant lowland of Solis Lacus. Far away, two men, machineless, plodded this same Xanthe Desert toward the same goal; but they plodded southward, approaching on a different radius.

They were naked. In a thin atmosphere without sufficient oxygen to support animal life or even the higher forms of terrestrial plant life, they wore no marsuits, no helmets, no oxygen tanks.

The man who walked in front was tall, erect, powerfully muscled. His features and short-clipped hair were coarse, but self-assured intelligence shone in his smoky eyes. He moved across the loose sand, barefoot, with easy grace.

The man that shambled behind him was as tall, but appeared shorter and even more muscular because his shoulders and head were hunched forward. His even coarser face was characterized by vacuously slack mouth and blue eyes empty of any expression except an occasional brief frown of puzzlement.

Toward a focal point: from the east, two people; from the north, two people. If in the efficient self-assurance of Adam Hennessey could be paralleled a variant harmony with the insistent surfaceness of S. Nuwell Eli, does any coincidental parallelism exist between Brute Hennessey and Maya Cara Nome?

Puzzlement was the climate of Brute's mind. This surface film of things through which he ploughed his way, the swarming currents below the surface—all were chaos. He grasped vaguely at comprehension without achieving, the effective coalescence of electric ideas always falling short before reaching consciousness.

The two men plodded, naked, through the loose sand. Above them in the Mars-blue dome of day, the weak sun turned downward, warning of its eventual departure.

A two-passengered groundcar and two men, widely apart, and yet bound for the same destination...

The destination was a lone, sprawling building in the desert. It could have been a huge warehouse, or a fortress, of black, almost windowless Martian stone. The only outstanding feature of its virtually featureless hulk was a tower which struck upward from its northern side.

As the summer afternoon progressed, Dr. G. O. T. Hennessey paced the windy summit of the tower, peered frequently into the desert north beneath a sunshading hand, and waggled his goat beard in annoyance under his transparent marshelmet.

Had the helmet speaker been on or the air less thin, one might have determined that Goat Hennessey was utilizing some choice profanity, directed at those two absent personages whose names were, respectively, Adam and Brute.

The airlock to the tower elevator opened and a small creature— a child?—emerged onto the roof. Distorted, humpbacked and barrel-chested, it scuttled on reed-thin legs to Goat's side. It wore no marsuit.

"Father!" screeched this apparition, its thin voice curiously muffled by the tenuous air. "Petway fell in the laundry vat!"

"For the love of space!" muttered Goat in exasperation. "Is there water in it?"

When the newcomer gave no sign of hearing, Goat realized his helmet speaker was off. He switched it on.

"Is there water in the vat?" he repeated.

"Yes, sir. It's full of suds and clothes."

"Well, go fish him out before he soaks up all the water. The soap will make him sick."

The messenger turned, almost tripping over its own broad feet, and went back through the airlock. Goat returned to his northward vigil.

Miles away, Nuwell slowed the groundcar as it approached the lip of that precipitous slope bordering the short canal which connects Juventae Fons with the Arorae Sinus Lowland. He consulted a rough chart, and turned the groundcar southward. A drive of about a kilometer brought them to a wide descending ledge down which they were able to drive into the canal.

Here, on the flat lowland surface, the canal sage grew thick, a gray-green expanse stretching unbroken to the distant cliff that was the other side of the canal. Occasionally above its smoothness thrust the giant barrel of a canal cactus.

Nuwell headed the groundcar straight across the canal, for the chart showed that the nearest upward ledge on the other side was conveniently almost opposite. The big wheels bent and crushed the canal sage, leaving a double trail.

The canal sage brought with it the comforting feeling of surface life once more. This feeling, for no reason that he could have determined consciously, released Nuwell's tongue.

"Maya," he said, in a voice that betrayed determination behind its mildness, "I don't see any real reason for waiting. When we've cleared up this matter at Ultra Vires and get back to Mars City, I think we should get married."

She glanced at his handsome profile and smiled affectionately.

"I'm complimented by your impatience, Nuwell," she said. "But there is a good reason for waiting, for me. When we're married, I want to be your wife, completely. I want to keep your home and mother your children. Don't you understand that?"

"That's what I want, too," he said. "That's my idea of what marriage is. But, Maya, if you insist on finishing this government assignment, that could be a long time off."

"I know, and I don't like it any better than you do, darling," said Maya. "But it's cost the Earth government a great deal of trouble and money to send me here, and you know how long it would take for them to get a replacement to Mars for me. I don't feel that I can let them down, and I don't think it would be much of a beginning to our marriage for me to be running around ferreting out rebels during the first months of it."

"That's another thing I don't like, Maya," said Nuwell. "It's dangerous, and I don't want anything to happen to you."

"It's your work, too, and it's not absolutely safe for you, either. I'll be sharing it with you when we're married, and for you it will go on for a long time. I have a specific mission here, to locate the rebel headquarters, and as soon as I've done that I'll be more than happy to become just a contented housewife and leave the rest of it to you."

Nuwell shrugged, a little disconsolately, and turned his attention to the task of negotiating the groundcar up the ascending slope.

She was a strange creature, this little Maya of his. She had been born on Mars and, orphaned by some unknown disaster, had been cared for during her first years by the mysterious, grotesque native Martians. When they took her at last to one of the dome cities, she was sent to Earth for rearing. And now she was back on Mars as an undercover agent of the Earth government, seeking to ferret out the rebels known to be engaging in widespread forbidden activities.

Often he did not understand her, but he wanted her, nevertheless.

Nuwell steered the groundcar slowly up the slope, over rubble and ruts, avoiding the largest rocks. At last they reached the top, and the groundcar arrowed out over the desert again, picking up speed.

Far to the left and ahead of them there was another dust-cloud drifting up, one that was not of the thin wind, but nearly stationary. Nuwell found the binoculars in the storage compartment and handed them to Maya.

"What's that over there?" he wondered. "Another groundcar? Take a look, Maya."

Maya trained the glasses in the direction indicated, through the groundcar's transparent dome. It was difficult to get them focused, for the groundcar swayed and jolted, but at last she was able to make brief identification.

"They're Martians, Nuwell," she said. "Can we drive over that way?"

"You've seen Martians before," he said.

"But I'd like to speak with them," she said. "I talk their language, you know."

"Yes, I do know, darling, but that's utterly foolish. They're only animals, after all, and we have to get to Ultra Vires before night, if we can."

He kept the groundcar on its course.

Maya lapsed into disgruntled silence. Nuwell stole a sidelong glance at her, his breath catching slightly at the curve of the petite, perfectly feminine form beneath the loose Martian tunic and baggy trousers. He reached over and patted her hand.

But Maya was offended. She kept her black head turned away from him, looking out of the groundcar dome across the desert.

At their destination, Goat Hennessey peered eagerly into the distance, searching.

This time, his watery blue eyes picked up two tiny figures on the horizon. He watched them as they approached, finally detailing themselves into two naked, pink creatures of manshape and only slightly more than mansize.

"They made it," he muttered. "Both of them. Good!"

He turned and entered the airlock. As soon as its air reached terrestrial density and composition, he removed his marshelmet.

Goat rode the elevator to the ground level, left it and hurried down a corridor, reaching the outside airlock in time to admit the two figures.

Adam entered first, easily confident, carrying his head like a king. Brute shambled behind him.

"Everything go all right?" asked Goat, his voice quavering in his anxiety.

"Fine, father," said Adam, smiling to reveal savage, even teeth."

"Nothing unusual happen?"

"Nothing at all, sir."

"You forget, Adam?" mouthed Brute eagerly. "You forget you fall?"

Adam spun on him ferociously, raising a heavy hand in threat. Brute did not cringe.

"I forget nothing!" snarled Adam. "You crazy Brute, I say it is nothing!"

"But, Adam—"

"I say it is nothing!" howled Adam and sprang for him.

"Stop it!" snapped Goat, like the crack of a whip, and they froze in the moment of their grappling. Sheepishly, they parted and stood side by side before him.

"I'll listen to details after supper," said Goat. "The children are hungry, and so am I."

CHAPTER TWO

Adam and Brute followed Goat Hennessey down the corridor, towering over him like Saint Bernards on the heels of a terrier. They turned into the dining room, a big square room centered with a rude table and chairs, one wall pierced by a fireplace in which a big cauldron steamed over smoldering coals.

The dining room swarmed with a dozen small creatures, human in their pink flesh, more or less human in their twisted bodies. As soon as Goat entered with Adam and Brute in tow, the assemblage set up a high-pitched howling and twittering of anticipation and began beating utensils on the dishes, table and walls.

"Quiet!" squawked Goat over the tremendous clatter, and the noise subsided. They stood where they were, bright eyes fixed on him.

These were "the children." Some of them were humpbacked, like Evan, the one who had carried the message to the tower. Some, like Evan, were grotesquely barrel-chested, with or without the hump. Some were as thin as skeletons, with huge heads; some were hulking miniatures of Brute. One steatopygean girl was so bulky in legs and hindquarters that she could waddle only a few inches with each step, yet her head and upper torso were skinny and fragile.

Goat sat down at the head of the table, and immediately there was a tumbling rush for places. Most of the children sat, chattering, while two of the larger girls moved around the table, taking bowls to the cauldron, filling them with a brownish stew and returning them.

They ate in silence. When supper was ended, the children scattered, some to play, others to chores. Goat beckoned to Adam and Brute to follow him. He led them down the corridor and into his study.

Goat turned on the light, revealing a book-lined, paper-stacked room focused on a huge desk. He removed his marsuit to stand in baggy pants and loose tunic. Adam and Brute stood near, shifting uncomfortably, for the study was normally forbidden ground.

Goat stood by a thick double window, looking out over the desert to the west. The small sun disappeared beneath the horizon even as he looked, leaving the fast-darkening sky a dull, faint red. Almost as though released by the sunset, pale Phobos popped above the horizon and began to climb its eastward way. The desert already was dark, but a stirring above it bespoke a distant sandstorm.

Goat turned from the window and faced the pair.

"Well," he snapped harshly, "what happened?"

Adam smiled confidently.

"We did as you said, father," he answered. "We walked to the edge of the canal, and we walked back. We had no water and we had no air. We did not feel tired. We did not feel sick."

"Fine! Fine!" murmured Goat.

"Father…" said Brute.

Goat turned his eyes to Brute, and savage irritation swept over him. With that word, at that moment, Brute gave him a feeling of guilty foreboding.

"Don't call me 'father!'" snapped Goat angrily.

"But you say call you father," protested Brute, the puzzled frown wrinkling his brow. "What I call you if I not call you father?"

"Don't call me anything. Say 'sir.' What did you want to say?"

"Father, sir," began Brute again, "Adam forget. Adam fall."

With a muted roar, Adam swept his powerful arm in a backhanded arc that caught Brute full on the side of his head. The blow would have felled an ox, but Brute was not shaken. Apparently unhurt, he stood patiently, his blue eyes on Goat with something of pleading in them.

"Adam, let him alone!" commanded Goat sharply. "Brute, what do you mean, Adam fell?"

"We come back. We not far from canal. Adam fall. Adam sick. Adam turn blue."

"It is lies, father!" exclaimed Adam, glaring at Brute. "It is not true."

"Let him finish," instructed Goat. "I'll decide whether it's true. What did you do, Brute?"

"I find cactus, father," answered Brute. "I make hole in cactus. I put Adam inside. I put hole back. Adam stay in cactus. Then Adam break cactus and come out again. We come back."

Goat cogitated. If Adam had shown, symptoms of oxygen starvation… The big canal cacti were hollow, and in their interiors they maintained reserves of oxygen for their own use. More than once, such a cactus had saved a Martian traveler's life when his oxygen supply ran short.

He turned to Adam.

"Well, Adam?" he asked.

"I tell you, father, it is lies! I do not fall. Brute does not put me in the cactus."

"And why should he lie?" asked Goat blandly.

This stumped Adam for a minute. Then he brightened.

"Brute wants to be bigger and stronger than Adam," he said. "Brute knows Adam is bigger and stronger than Brute, Brute does not like this. He tells you lies so you will think Brute is bigger and stronger than Adam."

"I know you are bigger brother, Adam," objected Brute, almost plaintively. "I not try to be bigger. Why you say you do not fall?"

"I do not fall!" howled Adam. "I do not fall, you stupid Brute!"

Goat held up a stern hand, enforcing silence.

"I can't certainly settle this disagreement, but I'd be inclined to accept what Brute says," said Goat thoughtfully. "You're smart enough to lie, Adam. Brute isn't. The only thing I can do is to run the experiment over. You shall go out again tomorrow, and this time I'll go with you."

"You'll see, father," said Adam confidently. "Adam will not fall."

"Perhaps not. But I must be sure. As much as I prefer your more human characteristics, Adam, it's entirely possible that Brute has some survival qualities that you lack."

"Is true, father," said Brute eagerly. "Some things kill Adam, they not kill Brute."

"You lie!" cried Adam again, turning on him. "Why do you lie, Brute?"

"No lie," insisted Brute. "You know, is true."

"Lie! Lie!" shouted Adam. "Adam is bigger and stronger! What do you say can kill Adam that does not kill Brute?"

"This," replied Brute calmly.

With an unhurried lunge, he picked up a heavy knife from Goat's desk. In a single easy movement, he turned and slashed Adam's throat neatly.

Choking and gurgling, Adam sank to his knees, bright blood spouting from his neck, while Goat stood frozen in horror. Adam fell prone, he kicked and threshed convulsively like a beheaded chicken, then twitched and lay still in a spreading pool of blood.

Brute calmly wiped the knife on his naked thigh and laid it back on the desk.

"Adam dead," he said without emotion. "Brute not lie."

Dismayed fury erupted through Goat's veins and a red haze swept over his eyes.

"You idiot!" he squawked. "So that won't kill you?"

Goaded beyond endurance, Goat seized the knife and swung it as hard as he could against Brute's neck. It thunked like an ax biting into a tree trunk, biting halfway through the flesh. Brute recoiled at the impact, tearing the handle from Goat's feeble hands and leaving the knife blade stuck in his throat.

Brute staggered momentarily. Then he reached up and jerked the knife away. Blood spurted through his severed throat. Brute clapped a hand to the wound, tightly.

For a moment, blood oozed through his fingers. Then, pale but steady, Brute dropped his hand.

The wound had closed! Its edges already were sealed, leaving a raw, red scar that no longer bled.

"Brute not lie," said Brute, the words forced out with some difficulty. "It not kill Brute."

Stunned by astonishment and disbelief, Goat stared at him, his mouth moving soundlessly.

"Go away," he whispered hoarsely at last. "Go out of here, monster!"

Obediently, Brute shambled out of the study. As he passed through the door, Goat regained his voice and called after him:

"Tell the children to come and take away Adam's body."

Kilometers away, Maya Cara Nome and S. Nuwell Eli rode a groundcar that moved swiftly across the interminable waves of the red sand. It swayed through hollows and jounced over multiple ridges, Nuwell steering it with some difficulty. In the steely sky, the small sun moved downward, its brightness unimpaired by the occasional thin clouds which moved before it.

The sun touched the western horizon, seemed to hesitate, dropped with breathtaking suddenness, and the stars immediately began to appear in the deepening twilight sky.

They stopped and had a compact meal, heated in the groundcar's short-wave cooker. Then Nuwell switched on the headlights and they went on again.

Soon afterward, a faint spot of light appeared in the desert far ahead of them. As they approached it, it became a yellow-lighted window in a huge black mass rearing up against the night sky. They had reached Ultra Vires.

Nuwell announced their arrival over the groundcar radio and swung the groundcar up beside the building's main entrance. He sealed the groundcar's door to the building air-lock so they would not have to don marsuits.

After a few moments, the airlock opened. They passed through it and were greeted by a skinny, shriveled little man with watery blue eyes and a goatee.

"I was expecting you, but not tonight," said this person, rather sourly. "Well, come on in and I'll have the children fix you something to eat if you haven't eaten."

"I'm S. Nuwell Eli," said Nuwell, holding out a hand which the other ignored. "This is the terrestrial agent, Miss Maya Cara Nome. You are Dr. Hennessey, I assume."

"That's right," said Goat. "Do you want supper?"

"No, thank you, we ate on the way," said Nuwell. "I'd like to get started with the inspection as soon as possible."

"Inspection or investigation?" suggested Goat, sniffling. "Well, no matter. I have nothing to hide."

He led them down a dim, dusty corridor, stretching deep into the dark bowels of the building, and turned aside into a paper-stacked room which evidently was his study. He went straight to a big desk, sat down, swiveled his chair around and waved them to seats. Nuwell shuffled a little uncomfortably, then sank into a chair, but Maya remained standing by the door, her small traveling bag in her hand, indignation rising in her.

"Before you settle down to charts and questions, Dr. Hennessey, do you mind showing us to our rooms so we may wash away some of the travel dust?" she asked icily, black eyes snapping.

At this, Goat jumped to his feet, sincere contrition in his face wiping out all traces of his irritated gruffness.

"I'm very sorry!" he exclaimed. "I hope you will forgive my manners, but I've lived and worked here alone in the desert so long that I had forgotten the niceties of civilization."

This apology cleared the air. Goat showed them their overnight quarters, adjoining rooms which were not luxurious but were reasonably comfortable, and after a time the three of them congregated once more in Goat's study, all of them in better humor.

"Let us have some wine first," suggested Goat. "This is very good red wine, imported from Earth."

He went to the door and shouted into the corridor.

"Petway!"

Goat returned to his chair. A few moments later, a twittering noise sounded in the corridor, then a horrible little apparition appeared in the door. It was a child-sized creature, naked, grotesquely barrel-chested and teetering on thin, twisted legs. Its hairless head was skull-like, with gaping mouth and huge, round eyes.

Maya gasped, profoundly shocked. The little creature looked more like a miniature Martian native than a human, but the Martians themselves were not so distorted. She saw her own shock reflected in Nuwell's face.

"Petway, get us three glasses of wine," commanded Goat calmly.

Petway vanished and Goat turned briskly back to his guests.

"Now," he said, "I shall outline the progress of my experiments to you and answer any questions you may have."

CHAPTER THREE

Maya's education was extensive, but it did not include the genetic sciences. She was able to follow Goat's explanations and his references to the charts he hung, one after another, on the wall of his study, but she was able to follow them only in a general sense. The technical details escaped her.

Nuwell seemed to have a better grasp of the subject. He nodded his dark, curly head frequently, and occasionally asked a question or two.

"Surgery is performed with a concentrated electron stream on the cells of the early embryo," said Goat. "I call it surgery, but actually it is an alteration of the structure of certain specific genes which govern the characteristics I am attempting to change. Such changes would, of course, then be transmitted on down to any progeny.

"The earlier the embryo is caught, the easier and surer the surgery, because when it has divided into too many cells the very task of dealing with each one separately makes the time requirement prohibitive, besides multiplying the chance for error. The Martians have a method of altering the physical structure and genetic composition of a full-grown adult, but this is far beyond the stage I've reached."

"The Martians?" repeated Nuwell in astonishment. "You mean the Martian natives? They're nothing but degenerated animals!"

"You're wrong," replied Goat. "I know that's the general opinion, but I had considerable contact with them a good many years ago. Perhaps most of them are little more than strange animals. No one really knows. They live simple, animal-like lives, holed up in desert caves, and they're rarely communicative in any way. But I know from my own experience that some of them, at least, are still familiar with that ancient science that they must have possessed when Earth was in an earlier stage of life than the human."

"This...child...that brought us the wine is one of the products of your experiments?" asked Nuwell.

"Yes. Petway's pretty representative of the children, I'm afraid. I've been trying to determine what went wrong. It could be an inaccuracy in dealing with the genetic structure itself, or a failure to follow exactly the same pattern of change in moving from one cell to another in the embryo. If I could only catch one at the single cell stage!

"None of the children has turned out as well as my first two experiments, Brute and Adam. Both of them were born about twenty-five years ago—terrestrial years, that is—and developed into normal, even superior physical specimens. Unfortunately, their mental development was retarded. Adam was the brighter of the two, and Brute killed him tonight, shortly before your arrival."

Maya shivered.

"Somehow, it seems horrible to me, experimenting with human lives this way," she said.

"It's being done for a good cause, Maya," said Nuwell. "Dr. Hennessey's objective is to help man live better on Mars. After all, there is nothing nobler than the individual's sacrifice of himself for his fellows, whether it's voluntary or involuntary."

"But what about the mothers of these children?" asked Maya.

"The big problem is to reach them as soon as possible after conception," said Goat, misinterpreting her question. "We do this by magnetic detectors, which report instantly the conjunction of the positive and negative. The surgery is performed, as quickly as possible, utilizing the suspended animation technique which is being developed toward interstellar travel."

"I wasn't asking about the technical aspects," said Maya. "What I want to know is, what sort of mothers will permit you to experiment this way on their unborn children, especially seeing the results you've already obtained?"

Goat started to answer, but Nuwell forestalled him.

"There are some things that are none of your business, darling," he said. "The terrestrial government sent you here on a specific assignment, and I don't think you should inquire into matters which are classified as secret by the local government, which don't have anything to do with that assignment. Now, Dr. Hennessey, just what sort of survival qualities have you been able to develop in these experiments?"

"There's no witchcraft involved," retorted Goat, with a sardonic grimace.

"I haven't accused you," said Nuwell quickly.

"No, but I keep up with events, even out here, well enough to know that you're the Mars City government's chief nemesis where there's any suspicion of extrasensory perception. I doubt that you chose to make this trip yourself without reason, Mr. Eli."

"It's merely a routine inspection," murmured Nuwell.

Goat indicated one of his charts, showing a diagram of genes and chromosomes in different colors.

"This is my original chart," he said. "I copied it from one belonging to the Martians many years ago, and my genetic alteration of Brute and Adam were based on it. But I must have miscopied it, or else the Martians didn't have the objective I thought they did in it, because I could find no alteration of genes affecting lung capacity or oxygen utilization. My own subsequent charts, on which later experiments were based, are alterations of this."

"But just what is your objective, and how well have you succeeded?" persisted Nuwell.

"Ability to survive under Martian conditions."

"I know. This is stated in all previous inspection reports. I want something more specific."

"Why, ability to survive in an almost oxygen-free atmosphere, of course. As well as can be determined, the Martians do this by deriving oxygen from surface solids and storing it in their humps under compression, very much like an oxygen tank.

"I've succeeded to some degree with my children. All of them can go an hour or two without breathing. What I don't understand is that no capacities like that were included in the genetic changes on Adam and Brute, and yet they've gradually developed an ability to do much better. Both of them were out on the desert the entire day today without oxygen."

Nuwell was silent for a moment, tapping the tips of his fingers together, apparently in deep thought. Then he said:

"Maya, I think we've reached the point where you had better retire to your room and let us to talk privately. You can question Dr. Hennessey in the morning about any attempts the rebels may have made to contact him."

Maya obeyed silently, rather glad to get away and think things over alone. When she had come to Mars as an agent of the Earth government, it had not occurred to her that there would be areas of information from which the local government would bar her. She recognized that such a prohibition was perfectly valid, but she was a little offended, nevertheless.

Her room was a spacious one on the ground level, and boasted one of Ultra Vires' few large windows. Maya unpacked her bag, and gratefully stripped off her boots and socks, her tunic and baggy trousers. In underpants, she went into the small bathroom, washed cosmetics from her face and brushed down her thick, short hair.

Donning her light sleeping garment, she sat down on the edge of her bed. She was very tired from the long drive and, almost without thinking, she did not get up to turn out the light. She thought at it.

The switch clicked and the light went out.

She felt foolish and a little frightened. She had never told Nuwell of this sort of thing. Can a woman ask her witch-hunting lover: "Do you think I'm a witch?"

With almost total recall, as though she heard it spoken, she remembered the summation speech Nuwell had made the first time she had seen him in action. He was prosecuting a man charged with conducting experiments similar to the historic and outlawed Rhine experiments of Earth.

"Gentlemen, we sit here in a public building and conduct certain necessary human affairs in a dignified and orderly manner. We follow a way of life we brought with us from distant Earth. Apparently, we are as safe here as we would be on Earth.

"I say 'apparently.' Sometimes we forget the thin barriers here that protect us against disaster, against extermination. A rent in this city's dome, a failure in our oxygen machinery, a clogging of our pumping system by the ever-present sand, and most of us would die before help could reach us from our nearest neighbors.

"We live here under certain restrictions that many of us do not like. Certainly, no one likes to be unable to step out under the open sky without wearing a bulky marsuit and an oxygen tank. Certainly, no one likes to be rationed on water and meat throughout the foreseeable future.

"But what we have to remember is that absolute discipline has always been a requirement for those courageous souls in the vanguard of human progress.

"Witchcraft—the practice of extrasensory perception, if you prefer the term—is forbidden on Mars because to practice it one must differ from his fellow men when the inexorable dangers of our frontier demand that we work

together. To practice it, one must devote time and mental effort to untried things when our thin margin of safety makes concentrated and combined effort necessary for survival. That is why witchcraft is forbidden on Mars.

"Let those who yet cling to the wistful liberalism of Earth label us conformists if they will. I say to you that until Mars is won for humanity, we cannot afford the luxury of nonconformity.

"Gentlemen, I give you the prosecution's case."

Maya stared out the window. This whole side of Ultra Vires was dark, except for a rectangle of light cast from a window a little distance away—the window of Goat Hennessey's study. In this rectangle, the red sand of the desert lay clear and stark.

Near the end of the rectangle lay an indistinct, crumpled, oblong figure. Puzzled, Maya studied it. It looked like a body to her.

In the study, Nuwell gazed at the skinny doctor with angry brown eyes.

"The bulletins sent to you, as well as other researchers, gave specific instructions that research was to be directed toward human utilization of certain foods now being developed," accused Nuwell.

"I thought this was more important," replied Goat.

"You thought! You're not on Earth, where scientists can get government grants and go jaunting off on wild research projects of their own."

"I still think this is more important," said Goat stubbornly. "I know that all of us are expected to co-operate and stick to tried and accepted lines so we won't be wasting time and material. Perhaps I was wrong in not doing that initially. But now I've proved that this line of research can be followed profitably, so its continuance now can't be looked on as a waste of time."

"Scientists should leave political direction to more experienced men," said Nuwell in an exasperated tone. "This is not merely a matter of time waste, or nonconformity. The Mars Corporation operates our sole supply line to Earth, Dr. Hennessey, and that supply line brings to man on Mars all the many things he needs to live here. The Earth-Mars run is an expensive operation, and it's important that it remain economically feasible for Marscorp to operate it.

"No matter how altruistic you may be about it, you get man to the point that he doesn't depend on atmospheric oxygen here, and domes, pressurized houses and groundcars, oxygen equipment—a great many things are going to be unnecessary. But there'll still be a lot of other things we'll have to have from Earth. Don't you realize what a disaster it would be if Marscorp decided to drop the only spaceship line to Earth because its cargo fell off to the point that it was economically unsound?"

Goat looked at him with shrewd blue eyes.

"I think I can jump to a conclusion," he remarked mildly. "Marscorp has some sort of control over the 'foods' you're trying to make practical for human consumption in the approved experiments, doesn't it?"

"Well, yes. Marscorp wants to make man gradually self-sufficient on Mars, and I think it's legitimate that Marscorp derive some economic benefits from its efforts in that direction."

"I've wondered for some time just how close Marscorp and the government were tied together," said Goat dryly. "Obviously, if I don't do as you say, my supplies here will be cut off. So I have no choice but to discontinue this work and turn my attention to the approved line."

"That isn't quite adequate now," said Nuwell. "You're going to have to leave here and come to Mars City where you can do your research under supervision. Your experimental humans here will be destroyed, of course."

"Destroyed?" There was an agonized note to Goat's voice. "All of them? How about the two mothers I have who haven't given birth yet?"

"You'd destroy them anyhow, as you have the others, not long after the births. And that brings up another thing. When you get to Mars City, watch your tongue. You almost revealed to Miss Cara Nome that the government has been kidnapping an expectant mother now and then for your experiments."

"Years of work, gone to waste," mourned Goat somberly. "When must I do this?"

"As soon as possible. You'll be expected in Mars City within two weeks. Now, I'd like to see these experimental humans."

A few moments later, they made their way together through a large dormitory in which all of Goat's charges were sleeping. Nuwell shuddered at the sight of the small, deformed bodies.

"I don't worry that you could ever take any of these to Mars City undetected. But," he said, pointing to Brute, "that one looks too near normal. I want to see him destroyed before I leave."

"Brute? But he's the most successful one I have left!"

"Exactly. That's why I want to see him destroyed, tonight."

Goat awoke Brute, and the monster man sleepily followed them back to the study.

Goat picked up the huge knife, still stained with Adam's blood, and looked Brute squarely in the face. Brute returned the gaze, no comprehension in his dull blue eyes.

"You think I can't kill you, Brute?" said Goat coldly. "I'll show you!"

With a surgeon's precision, Goat plunged the sharp point between Brute's ribs and into the heart.

Shock swept over Brute's mind.

Father kills me!

Reject! Reject!

Father, all kindness, all hope, all wisdom and love, wants me no more. Father rejects me! Father kills me!

Despair!

Reject! Reject!

Blackness swept fading through Brute's despairing brain.

One agonized note of pleading in the pale-blue eyes, and they closed in acceptance. Brute swayed and fell forward, crashing to the floor, driving the knife into his chest to the hilt.

Brute shuddered and rolled over on his back. He lay sprawled, arms flung out limply, the knife hilt protruding upward. He sighed, and his breathing stopped.

Goat stared down at him. He picked up Brute's wrist and held it. There was no pulse.

Shortly after dawn, Maya awoke. Remembering what she had seen dimly the night before, she went curiously to the window.

There were two of them now. They were bodies, human bodies, naked and unquestionably dead. In the night, the dry, vampirish Martian air had desiccated them. They were skeletons, parchment skin stretched tightly over the lifeless bones.

Even as she stood and looked, a group of figures appeared on the horizon and came slowly nearer. They were Martians— monstrous creatures, huge-chested, humpbacked, with tremendously long, thin legs and arms, their big-eyed, big-eared heads mere excrescences in front of their humps.

Trailing slowly through the desert toward Aurorae Sinus, they passed near the skeleton bodies. One of the Martians saw them. He boomed excitedly at the others, loudly enough for Maya to hear through the double window.

The Martians stopped and gathered around the bodies.

What, she wondered, could interest them in two corpses? There was no guessing. Martian motives and thought processes were alien and incomprehensible, even to one who had lived among them and communicated with them as a child.

One of the Martians picked up one of the corpses, and the whole group moved away toward the lowland, the Martian carrying the body easily with one long-fingered hand. Wisps of sandy dust trailed them as they dwindled and slowly vanished.

The second body lay where they had left it. A gaping wound in its throat seemed to mock her.

CHAPTER FOUR

Fancher Laddigan made his way down a long dim corridor in the rear portion of the Childress Barber College, in Mars City's eastern quarter. He stopped and hesitated, with some trepidation, before an unmarked door near the end of the corridor.

Completely bald, bespectacled and well up in years, Fancher looked like a clerk and he had the instincts of a clerk. Yet he utilized that appearance and those instincts in a perilous cause.

Fancher knocked timidly on the door. On receiving an indistinct invitation from inside, he pushed it open and entered.

Fancher had a tendency to shiver every time he had occasion to see the Chief, whose real name was unknown to Fancher and to most others here at the barber college.

Small as a child in body, wagging a thin-haired head larger than lifesize, the Chief surveyed Fancher with icy green eyes. The eyes were large and round as a child's, but there was nothing childlike about their expression. As though to deny his physical smallness, he smoked one of the fragrant, foot-long cigars produced only in the Hadriacum Lowlands.

"Sit down," commanded the Chief in a high, piping voice.

Fancher swallowed and sat, facing his superior across the big desk. The Chief opened a drawer, took out another of the long cigars, and handed it to Fancher. Fancher did not like cigars, but he had never dared say so to the Chief. He lit it gingerly, coughed at his first inhalation, and smoked at it dutifully and unhappily.

"You recognized this man certainly as Dark Kensington?" asked the Chief.

"Well…" Fancher began, and started coughing again. The Chief fixed him with an unwinking green stare. When the coughing spell ended, Fancher sat silent, his eyes stinging with tears, fumbling at what he wanted to say.

"You knew Dark Kensington before his disappearance twenty-five years ago," said the Chief, with a trace of impatience in his tone. "I am told that you saw this man and talked to him. You are qualified to recognize Dark Kensington. Is this man Dark Kensington, or not?"

"Well," said Fancher again, "the man was walking alone across the desert, and when someone picked him up he asked how he could find the Childress Barber College, and of course our men heard of it and went out to—"

"I have received a full report on the man's appearance and our initial contact with him. I asked you a question."

"Well, Chief, it's a peculiar thing. If this man, as he is now, had reappeared twenty-five years ago, I'd *know* it was Dark Kensington. But he looks exactly as Dark did when he disappeared, not one day older. And he doesn't remember a thing beyond his disappearance except events of the past two weeks, he says.

"Yet his memories of Dark's activities before his disappearance are unquestionably accurate and clear. It's as though Dark had been put on ice at the time of his disappearance and just now thawed out, without any aging or memory during the interim."

"Perhaps he was," said the Chief dryly. "But is it possible that this man, looking so much like Dark Kensington, could have studied Kensington's personality and activities carefully and be posing as Kensington?"

"No, sir," said Fancher promptly. "Dark and I were very close friends at one time. He remembers that, although he had difficulty recognizing me since I'm so much older. We went through some experiences together that I never told to anyone, and I'm sure he didn't. He remembers them in every detail. Like the way we trapped a sage-rabbit once when we'd run out of supplies out in Hadriacum."

Fancher chuckled.

"Then we couldn't eat the thing," he reminisced.

"Very well, if you're sure of his identity, that's all I wish to know," said the Chief. "I don't want to be trapped by a Marscorp trick with plastic surgery. But if this man is Dark Kensington, it's the best fortune the Phoenix has met with in a long time."

He fell silent, and busied himself with papers on his desk, paying no more attention to Fancher. Fancher waited, then concluded reasonably that the interview was at an end. And, since the long cigar agonized him, he rose and moved quietly toward the door.

"I have not given you permission to leave," said the Chief, without raising either his eyes or his voice. "Kensington is due to arrive in a few moments, and I want you here when I talk to him. If any of his words or actions appear inconsistent in any way to you, I want you to let me know."

Fancher sighed silently, returned to his chair and puffed disconsolately on the cigar.

Some five minutes passed. Then there was a firm rap on the door.

"Come in!" called the Chief in his reedy voice.

The door opened, and in walked a man whose entire presence radiated strength, confidence and the potentiality of instant violence. Dark Kensington was tall and broad-shouldered, clad in dark-blue tunic and baggy trousers. His face was darkly tanned, strong, handsome. His hair was black as midnight. His eyes were startlingly pale in the dark face; eyes of pale blue, remote and filled with light.

"I'm Dark Kensington," he said, striding up to the Chief's desk. "You're the man known as the Chief?"

"Yes," answered the Chief, and waited.

Dark nodded to Fancher. Fancher, feeling rather green about the gills, returned the greeting.

Dark turned his attention back to the Chief, and he, also, waited. There was a long silence. The Chief broke it first.

"What do you know about Dr. G. O. T. Hennessey—Goat Hennessey?" asked the Chief calmly.

Fancher blinked at this unexpected line of questioning. A cloud passed over Dark's face, as though the name had triggered something in him that he could not quite remember.

"He was a very good friend of mine," answered Dark, "although it seems that something happened between us that I can't quite recollect. He was one of the most brilliant geneticists of Earth, and came to Mars with an experimental group that was to try to develop a human type that could live more comfortably under Martian conditions. The project was backed by the government."

He stopped. It was the Chief who added:

"Then Marscorp stepped in."

The expression on Dark's face was blank.

"You don't know what Marscorp is, do you?" asked the Chief curiously.

"The name's familiar," replied Dark. "It's a spaceline, isn't it?"

"If your amnesia is genuine, you might very well react in such a fashion," said the Chief reflectively. "Marscorp is the Mars Corporation, and it's the only spaceline that serves Mars now. It's a giant combine on Earth which has a virtual monopoly on the spacelines and exports and imports between Earth and all the colonized planets.

"Marscorp is against any development of human beings who can live under natural extraterrestrial conditions, because that would end the colonies' dependence on Marscorp for supplies. As it is, the colonies literally can't live without Marscorp. Marscorp controls enough senators and delegates in the World Congress to block other important projects if the Earth government refuses to co-operate with it, so the government—that is to say, Marscorp—put a ban on the experiments by Hennessey and other scientists here."

"I remember the government ban on the projects, but I wasn't aware that Marscorp had anything to do with it," said Dark. "Goat Hennessey was one of a group of us who retired to the desert to continue work despite the government ban."

"Goat sold out," said the Chief. "Perhaps your memory doesn't include that important point, but Fancher remembers it well. It was a little before my time. Goat sold out, and betrayed the others to the government in return for assistance in carrying out more limited experiments. Some of the group escaped and formed the nucleus of the rebel movement which now is centered here at the Childress Barber College. We call ourselves the Order of the Phoenix."

The Chief allowed himself the luxury of a very faint smile.

"Marscorp and the government call us the Desert Rats," he said. "Very appropriate. They consider us in the same category as rats."

Dark had been standing, casually at ease, before the Chief's desk, with the air of a man who does not tire from standing. Now he did something Fancher would not have dared: without the Chief's invitation, Dark sat down in a comfortable chair, leaned back and stretched out his legs in relaxation.

"It's a little hard for me to realize there's a twenty-five-year gap in my memory," he said. "It seems to me that it has been less than a month ago that Goat and I were together, with other refugees from the government edict, in the Icaria Desert. Why did you ask me about Goat?"

"Because the government brought him back to Mars City not three months ago," answered the Chief. "None of us had any idea where he was, but it turns out that the government has had him working under surveillance some place in the Xanthe Desert north of Solis Lacus. Since it was not far from Solis Lacus that you were picked up, I wondered if you had had any contact with him."

"Not that I remember," said Dark. "Do you have another of those cigars?"

"Why, yes," answered the Chief, startled. He produced another Hadriacum cigar and handed it to Dark. Dark lit it and puffed the fragrant smoke with evident enjoyment.

"As I say, the last time I remember seeing Goat was in the Icaria Desert, in a dome we had set up there," said Dark. "The next thing I remember is waking up in the midst of some sort of cave in a different part of Icaria, surrounded by Martians.

"I could communicate with them in a fashion—something I was never able to do before—and they were able to write the name of the Childress Barber College so I could read it. But they evidently don't differentiate our dome cities by name. I had no idea the college was here in Mars City until your men contacted me; I just assumed it was at Solis Lacus."

"You'd have waged a merry search for it, clear on the other side of Mars," remarked the Chief. "What was your purpose in finding it?"

"I don't know that I had any specific purpose," replied Dark easily. "I gathered from the Martians that here I could find someone who concurred with my philosophy of resisting the government edict against seeking self-sufficiency on Mars, and this was more or less confirmed by your two men who contacted me at Solis Lacus."

"I'll see to it that in the future they're not quite so frank until they're sure of their man," said the Chief darkly. He looked quizzically at Fancher, and Fancher nodded slightly. "But it's true. As a matter of fact, the Phoenix follows the path toward self-sufficiency that you recommended, rather than the one sought by Goat Hennessey."

"That's the wrong way to approach it," said Dark promptly. "Goat and the other scientists were following a line offering valid possibilities in their genetic research. The only reason the rest of us chose to attempt the extrasensory powers—particularly teleportation—was that we were not qualified in genetic research and this seemed a field in which we stood a chance to contribute along alternate lines. The effort should be followed along both lines."

"The government managed to capture all the scientists at the time of your disappearance, and it was assumed that you had been captured, too," said the Chief. "We don't have any scientists in the Phoenix who are capable of doing Goat Hennessey's type of research."

"You say he's in Mars City? I wonder if it would do any good for me to contact him."

"I told you that he was the one who betrayed the whole thing to the government, and he's been working under government supervision these last twenty-five years. I wouldn't trust him."

The Chief surveyed Dark's strong face with speculative green eyes, then added:

"As a matter of fact, we've made a certain amount of progress following your line of research. Since there are probably a good many things you discovered in this work that we haven't stumbled on yet, we could use your help in developing it, if you're interested."

"Very definitely," answered Dark. "I'm interested in seeing what you've done, and I'll be glad to help in any way I can."

"There's one thing," said the Chief, measuring his words. "I've held this organization together despite some pretty severe reverses for more than fifteen years now. The reason I've been able to do it is that I expect and must insist on absolute obedience to my orders."

Dark smiled. "I said that I would be willing to help you," he replied gently. "I follow no man's orders."

The green eyes fixed themselves unwinkingly on the pale-blue ones for a long moment. The blue ones did not waver.

At last, to Fancher's utter amazement, the Chief nodded agreement.

CHAPTER FIVE

Maya Cara Nome looked from her furnished room through cracked shutters at the building across the street.

A barber college. The building at 49 Sage Avenue, Mars City, was a barber college.

That surprised her. She didn't know exactly what she had expected: a hospital, perhaps, or even a kindergarten. But a barber college!

But the source of the information she had received that 49 Sage Avenue was the address she sought was unimpeachable. She had ferreted it out, after a long time and through devious ways, and she was sure she could trust it.

"The Childress Barber College" read the neatly lettered sign above the door. Maya's landlady, moon-faced Mrs. Chan, had pointed out Oxvane Childress to her as he left the building one day: a big man, comfortably stomached, with a heavy brown beard which, even at that distance, she could see was shot with gray.

As innocent as you please. Childress came out and went in, the students went in and came out. Still, it was the address she had been given.

Maya had to gain entrance to the building. She could learn nothing watching it from outside. She was established here as a tourist from Earth; besides, the position and activities of women were prescribed rigidly by Martian colonial convention, and women did not study to become barbers on Mars.

She would have to have help. She, thought at once of Nuwell, and as immediately rejected him.

"Maya, I don't see why you insist on working alone," he had complained. "I can set the whole machinery of government in motion to help you, whenever you need it."

"Primarily because you're well known and your activities are observed," she had answered. "Your whole government machinery hasn't been effective in tracking down the rebel headquarters yet, and it's reasonable to assume that the rebels have a fairly effective intelligence network. My job is to find that headquarters, and if I were seen very often with you or tried to utilize your government machinery, they'd have me pinpointed pretty soon."

She left the window, filled a tiny basin with precious water, shrugged out of her negligee and sponged her small, perfect body. She donned form-fitting tunic, briefs and short skirt, pulled on knee-length socks and laced up Martian walking shoes. She spent some time preparing her hair and face.

Then she left the room and the house and walked uptown. The walk was about a kilometer, along sidewalks bordered by cubical, functional houses and trim lawns of terrestrial grass and small trees. Above the city, its dome was opalescent in the morning sun.

The small houses gave way to larger business buildings, also cubical, and the lawns dwindled and vanished. Farther down, the buildings were even larger and the streets were wider and busier; but she was not going into the heart of Mars City.

She turned into an office building, and studied the directory in the lobby. The offices were those of doctors and lawyers. On the directory she found "Charlworth Scion, Attorney-at-Law, Room 207."

There was no elevator. Maya walked up the stairs and down a corridor, finding a door that had nothing on it but the number. She turned the knob and went in.

The small outer office was uninhabited. It was carpeted and desked, with two straight chairs against a wall, for clients. Through a door, she could see part of the inner office, cluttered and stacked with papers and books.

She stood there, hesitating. The outer door clicked shut behind her. At the sound, a gray-haired, preoccupied man with spectacles and stooped shoulders peered from the inner office.

"Oh!" he said. "I'm sorry, my secretary went to lunch a bit early today. Can I help you, Miss?"

"I'm looking for Mr. Scion," she said.

"I'm Charlworth Scion."

"Terra outshines the Sun," said Maya.

Scion's eyes were suddenly wary behind the spectacles.

"Well, well," he murmured. "Come in, please."

She went into the cluttered inner office, and Scion closed and locked the door.

"And you are...?" said Scion behind his desk, his pale hands fumbling aimlessly with papers.

"Maya Cara Nome," she said.

Scion found a paper and scanned it. He apparently found her name there.

"I'm surprised to see you here," he admitted. "Our information was that you would be working entirely alone."

"I am," said Maya. "Or I was. I was told not to contact you unless I had to, Mr. Scion, but it seems I'm going to need some help."

Scion inclined his head, but said nothing.

"As you may or may not know, my specific assignment is to locate the nerve center of rebellious activity," said Maya. "It seems that the rebels have an intelligence network about as effective as the government's, and it was felt that a woman tourist from Earth might be successful where any unusual probing by local agents might arouse suspicion."

"That's true," conceded Scion. "I doubt that they're really sure of the identity of more than a few of our agents, but sometimes I think they have a card file on every person on Mars. We have to be very careful that movements of our agents are consistent with their pretended occupations."

"I have a reliable tip that their nerve center is the Childress Barber College here," she said. "I can't find out anything, though, unless I get into the building over a period of time. As a woman, I can't very well apply to study barbering."

"No," said Scion. "I see your problem."

He turned to a filing cabinet, unlocked it and searched through it, whistling tunelessly. He found a folder, pulled it out and studied it.

"If it is, they've certainly kept it well covered," he said. "There's not a mark of suspicion entered against the Childress Barber College. But here's a possibility for getting you in. The barber college employs one secretary, female. Now, if you could take her place..."

Maya smiled.

"I might as well apply as a barber student," she said. "You propose to remove a trusted member of their own group from their midst and replace her with a complete unknown?"

"We don't know that she's a rebel," answered Scion. "If she isn't, she can be lured away to another job at a much better salary. If she is, and can't be lured...well, there are other methods. The Mars City Employment Agency is operated by one of our agents, and you'll be the only secretary available when the barber college asks for a woman to fill her place.

"Believe me, Miss Cara Nome, as easy as it is for a woman to get married on Mars, it is difficult to find women to do any sort of business work. It won't seem at all strange that you're the only one available."

"The only trouble is that I'm known in the neighborhood as a tourist from Earth," objected Maya.

"Well," said Scion, "things have been more expensive than you planned for on Mars. You've run short of money. You have to work for a while to pay living expenses here until the next ship leaves for Earth."

"My account at the bank?"

"It will vanish quietly from the records," said Scion with a smile. "The bank is a government institution."

"Very well," said Maya, taking her purse from his desk. "Let me know when I'm to apply."

"You won't hear from me again," said Scion, shaking his head. "The employment agency will notify you to appear at the barber college for an interview."

Maya knew of Scion only as her emergency contact on Mars. She did not know what position he held in that underground network of terrestrial agents which was largely unknown even to Nuwell Eli, the government prosecutor. But, whatever his position, he got things done in a hurry.

Within two weeks, Maya was typing up applications, examination reports and supply orders in the Childress Barber College, joking and flirting with barber students between classes, and naively declaiming to her ostensible employer, phlegmatic Oxvane Childress, how lucky it was for her that she was able to get a job right across the street from her rooming house.

"The work's easy," rumbled Childress, explaining her tasks to her. "Any time you want to take a coffee break with any of the young men, or go uptown shopping, go ahead, as long as the work gets done. Just one thing: you have to stay up here in the front of the building, and don't ever go back in the classrooms. The instructors are mighty strict about that, and that's one rule I won't stand to be violated."

This significant restriction convinced Maya she was on the right track. But she needed to move cautiously, if she was not to arouse immediate suspicion. So she adhered strictly to her role for nearly a month, keeping her eyes open.

If it was a rebel operation, it was almost perfectly disguised. Childress performed the duties of the administrative head of a barber college, and nothing more. The students, about fifty of them, went in and out at regular school hours, and she became casually acquainted with a good many of them. The half-dozen instructors, whom she also came to know, were less regular in their movements, but she could detect nothing suspicious about them.

"We cut the hair of Mars," was the college's motto, and she learned that it was the larger of only two barber colleges on the planet. Apparently, it actually did supply graduate barbers to all the dome cities. It took in customers for the students to practice on, and, although many of them were strangers, some of them were prominent Mars City citizens whom she knew by sight.

There was no question about it: partially, at least, it was a legitimate barber college, whatever other activities it might mask. The only thing noticeably unusual on the surface was that it was extremely selective in its approval of students who applied for courses in barbering. She discerned that through her processing of the applications.

If she was going to find out anything definite, she would have to get into the forbidden rear portion of the building. But obviously there were legitimate classrooms there, in addition to the activities she suspected, and if she were caught nosing around the classrooms she would be discharged at once for violation of the rules, without finding out what she sought. She would have to hit it right the first time.

Biding her time and watching, she was able to learn, almost intuitively, from the movements of students, customers and instructors, that the classrooms in which barbering was actually taught were all concentrated on the western side of the building. If there were any more sinister activities, they occurred on the opposite side. Having determined this, she planned her course of action.

Near the end of her first month at work, she chose her time one day when Childress was downtown, leaving her alone in the business office. The afternoon classes were in full swing.

Taking along a filled-out order form as an excuse, Maya walked quickly down the corridor that stretched across the front of the building. Carefully and quietly, she pushed open the door at the extreme end of the corridor—a little surprised, as a matter of fact, to find it unlocked.

She was in another corridor, that struck straight back to the rear of the building.

She hesitated. There were doors spaced all along both sides of this corridor. Did she dare attempt to open one, on the chance that the room behind it was unoccupied?

Then she saw that one door, a little way down, stood half open. Quietly she walked down the hall, not quite to the door, but near enough to it to be able to see a large area of the room behind it.

There were people in there. In the part she was able to see, there were half a dozen students seated, and one of the instructors standing among them. Fortunately, their backs were to her.

Whatever they were studying, it was not barbering. There was an occasional murmur of voices, but she could not make out the words.

Then she saw! On the table at the front of the room, which the students faced, there was a big barber's basin.

As she watched, the basin slowly raised off the table and moved upward a few inches. No one was near it, but it floated there, quivering and tilting a little, in the air. And then, from it, slowly, the water itself came up in a weird fountain, moved completely free of the basin and hung above it in the air, gradually assuming the form of a globe.

Telekinesis! This was a class in telekinesis! The students were concentrating on the basin and water, and lifting them into the air by the power of their minds.

This was indeed the heart of the rebel movement. She had found what she sought.

"Aren't you where you shouldn't be, young lady?" asked a calm masculine voice behind her.

Shocked, terrified, she whirled. A tall, handsome, dark-haired man she had never seen before was standing there, observing her quizzically. His pale eyes seemed to look through her and beyond her.

She forced herself to casual composure.

"I don't believe I've met you," she said. "Are you one of the instructors?"

"I'm Dark Kensington, one of the supervisors," he replied. "And you're Miss Cara Nome, the secretary, who shouldn't be back here."

Had he noticed that she saw the telekinetic action? She glanced back at the classroom. The basin was now comfortably ensconced back on the table, full of water.

"I had this order, which I thought was of an emergency nature," she said, offering it to him. "Mr. Childress wasn't in, and I thought I'd better find one of the instructors so it could be approved and go out right away."

Dark took it and glanced at it.

"I doubt that its emergency nature is as grave as you may have thought," he said soberly. "However, Mr. Childress would be better qualified to judge that. You understand that I shall have to report this infraction of the rules to him."

Suddenly, Maya was overwhelmed by an utterly terrifying sensation. It seemed that these pale-blue eyes were looking into her mind, searching, seeking to determine her thoughts and her true intention.

Instinctively, not knowing how she did it, she veiled her thoughts with a psychic barrier. And, instinctively, she recognized that he detected the barrier and could not penetrate it.

Telepathy? Why not, if they were experimenting successfully with telekinesis?

"I'm sorry," she murmured hurriedly, and brushed past him. He did not try to detain her.

She hurried back to the office. She hurried, but as she hurried down first the one corridor and then the other, she discovered that her steps were slowing involuntarily. A powerful force seemed to be detaining her, attempting to draw her back.

Frightened but curious, she attempted to analyze this force even as she struggled against it. She could not be sure—it was disturbing, either way, but she could not be sure whether it was a telepathic thing or merely the magnetic force of this man's powerful masculine personality that pulled at her.

In a state of mental turmoil, she reached the office. Childress was not yet back.

Should she wait for him?

Then, as suddenly as she had sensed Dark Kensington's telepathic probing, she sensed something else. Somewhere in the back of the building, he was talking to another man she had not seen before, and within ten minutes Dark Kensington would be in this office. And the prospect was far more serious than mere discharge for infringement of company rules.

She had to get in touch with Nuwell at once. She recognized that if she could get out of this building and across the street to her rooming house, she would be safe for a little while. She could telephone Nuwell from there.

Grabbing her purse, she hastened out of the office

CHAPTER SIX

The three men who stood by a table in the back lobby of the Childress Barber College and checked off the departure of the men at regularly spaced intervals were as completely different in appearance as they were in their positions in the Order of the Phoenix.

Oxvane Childress, big and bearded, was the "front," and directed the very necessary task of administering the Childress Barber College as a genuine barber college. Childress was a prominent member of two of Mars City's civic and social clubs, and careful examination of his activities over a period of years would have thrown no suspicion on him.

The Chief, whose real name perhaps Childress knew but never spoke, was a huge-headed midget who directed the far-flung activities of the Order of the Phoenix as an underground rebel organization. He never left the building, but reports were brought in to him from all over Mars. He knew a great deal at any time about what the government and Marscorp were doing, and he gave the orders for those moves aimed at maintaining the secrecy of the Phoenix.

Dark Kensington, tall and pale-eyed, had moved at once into the natural position of guiding the experimental work of the organization in extrasensory perception and telekinesis. He was able to add his knowledge of earlier work to the progress that had been made since his disappearance, and coordinated the studies in the various dome cities.

A little behind the three stood Fancher Laddigan, doing the actual checking with a pencil on a list in his hand.

"I think it's all unnecessary," rumbled Childress unhappily. "I watched the girl carefully while she was here, and the usual checks were made into her background. It's true she had some social contacts with Nuwell Eli when she first came to Mars, but there's nothing sinister about that association and it seems the last thing a Marscorp agent would do openly. As far as I could determine, she just realized she'd violated a rule and would be discharged for it, so she left before she could be discharged."

"She hasn't returned to her rooming house," remarked the Chief in his high, thin voice.

"Looking for another job, or maybe just on a trip," said Childress. "After all, she's a terrestrial tourist. If this is all a false alarm, how am I going to explain suspending operation of the college for a period?"

"Remodeling," replied the Chief. "Work out the details and put a sign up as soon as evacuation has progressed far enough."

"It may be unnecessary, Oxvane," said Dark, "but it's best not to take chances. This telepathy is a very uncertain thing, and sometimes it's hard to differentiate true telepathic communication from one's own hopes or fears. But it seemed to me that I had the very definite sense that Miss Cara Nome was seeking something with hostile intent, and it's entirely possible that she saw part of one of the experiments through that open door."

Two students appeared, gave their names to Fancher in an undertone, and sauntered out the back door of the building.

"What's the status now?" asked the Chief.

"They were nineteen and twenty," answered Fancher precisely. "They're part of Group C, which is going to Hesperidum. Group A goes to Regina, Group B to Charax, Group D to Nuba and Group E to Ismenius."

"None to Solis?" asked Childress in surprise.

"No, sir, nor to Phoenicis, either," answered Fancher. "They're both so far, and Solis is a resort, where they might be easier to detect. We're using both public transport and private groundcars. All of them so far have reported safely through the flower shop, except these last two, so the government evidently hasn't thrown a ring around the building yet."

"And I don't think they will, either," growled Childress. "I tell you, it's all unnecessary."

"Are things going smoothly here?" asked the Chief.

"Yes, sir," replied Fancher. "The last five men scheduled to leave are taking care of any customers who come in, and the rest of them are packing supplies into the trucks. As soon as I get word from the flower shop that the last pair has cleared, I give another pair the word to leave."

"It seems to be moving along well," said the Chief, and he turned his green eyes upon Childress. "Is the business office manned?"

"Why—why, there's no one there right now," said Childress, taken aback.

"I think it would look extremely peculiar to any investigator if you weren't there, frantically trying to locate a new secretary," said the Chief quietly.

Childress left, in confusion. The Chief turned to Dark.

"I think Fancher's handling this very well without my help," he said. "You know where your groundcar is, if we all have to make a run for it?"

"Yes," answered Dark. "We won't be going together?"

"No," replied the Chief, and his lips twisted in a faint smile. "I have my own method of exit, which should give them other things to think about."

He left, moving with quick, short steps. Dark stayed for a few moments more, then he too went back into the building to help with packing.

The Lowland Flower Shop, on the other side of Mars City, near the west airlock, was the clearance point for the evacuees. The flower shop was operated by a Phoenix agent, and each pair that left the barber college passed through there before leaving the city to let those behind know that they had not been stopped by government men. Other Phoenix agents watched the heliport and bus station for any evidence that the government was trying to block these routes out of Mars City.

The evacuation moved steadily, and it began to appear that Childress was right. Singly, the first two of the five trucks moved out, and all of the ESP instructors and thirty-two of the students had reported back safe clearance from the flower shop, when...

Dark was moving a stack of charts from one of the classrooms to the basement when bells all over the building set up a tremendous clangor. Immediately the quiet evacuation dissolved into an uproar, with men running and shouting and the bell ringing incessantly.

Dark knew what had happened. Childress, in the front office, had seen government agents approaching, or perhaps they had actually entered the building. He had pressed the alarm bell, then sought to delay them with the righteous indignation suitable to the administrative head of a barber college which is invaded by government officials.

The bells stopped suddenly, and the scattered shouting sounded strange and thin in the comparative silence. Then the piping voice of the Chief came over the loudspeakers spread throughout the building.

"Attention!" said the Chief. "We are temporarily safe. The alarm automatically sealed all doors to the building behind the front corridor.

"Kensington, please come to my office. The rest of you, tie up the customers still here and leave them unharmed, and then leave the building by the emergency exits. Scatter, and make your way by whatever private transportation methods you can to the rendezvous assigned to your respective group. Do not use public transportation, because Marscorp will undoubtedly be checking public transport now."

Dark set the charts down on the stairs and made his way back to the Chief's office. The Chief was sitting, tiny behind his big desk, his face as serene as ever. He was puffing casually on one of the long Hadriacum cigars.

Dark laughed.

"You don't have another of those cigars, do you?" he asked.

For the first time since he had been here, Dark saw the Chief's mouth break into a full, broad smile.

"I think so," said the Chief, an undertone of delight bubbling in his voice. He reached into the desk and pulled one out. Dark accepted it gravely, and lit it.

"The last two evacuees haven't reported to the flower shop, and they're overdue," said the Chief, his face getting serious. "Childress hasn't reported back here by telephone, either, so the Marscorp gang probably had already entered the building before he detected them and sounded the alarm."

"What about Childress?" asked Dark. "What will happen to him?"

"He'll take the rap," answered the Chief. "His defense will be that if there were any Phoenix activities going on here he didn't know about it. He was just running a barber college in good faith. I don't think they can prove otherwise."

"Do we have any idea what our situation is?" asked Dark.

"A very accurate idea. We have observers posted in the two houses at the ends of our emergency exits, and they've been reporting to Fancher, in the next room, by telephone. There's a force of about a hundred Mars City policemen and plain-clothes agents in the streets all around the building. They saw a squad go into the front, but evidently they didn't have enough warning to let Childress know in time."

"Will the doors hold?"

The Chief's mouth quirked.

"They'll need demolition equipment to break them down," he said. "All these have are heatguns and tear gas. One of the observers farther downtown said he saw a tank heading this way, but if they don't already know there are innocent customers in here, Childress will tell them."

"Then everybody gets away but Childress?"

"We hope. They're not going to ignore these surrounding houses, especially with men drifting out of them and moving away. That's why I want to stress the importance of one thing to you, Kensington: you're too important for us to lose at this juncture, with your knowledge of the original work done. That house at the end of your exit will have a dozen or so of our men in it, waiting to drift away one by one, but you can't afford to worry about them. I want you to get in that groundcar, alone, and take off like Phobos rising."

"You're going out the other emergency exit?"

"That's none of your business. But, as a matter of fact, no. If you want to see something that will throw consternation into this Marscorp outfit, watch the roof of this building. Now, get moving, Kensington, and good luck. Fancher and I will be leaving as soon as he gets all the records packed."

The Chief held out his tiny hand, and Dark shook hands with him. Then Dark left, went down into the basement and entered an underground door in its eastern wall. He had to crawl through the tunnel driven through the sand under the street.

He emerged in the basement of a house across the street, which ostensibly was owned by Manfall Kingron, a retired space engineer. He went upstairs.

About half the personnel of the barber college who had not been caught by the alarm were roaming the rooms of the small house, drifting singly out the back door at ten-minute intervals.

Dark went to the front window and looked across the street at the barber college.

The street was full of men carrying heat pistols, moving restlessly, facing the barber college. Some of them were in police uniform. Squads of them moved about on the college grounds, and a few were in the yards of houses on this side of the street.

Dark watched the roof.

As he did so, from its center a helicopter rose into the air, hovering over the building, moving upward slowly.

So that was the Chief's escape method. He had smuggled a helicopter into the domed city itself! But how was he to get out of the city in it?

The appearance of the copter threw the men outside into confused excitement. They ran about, aiming their short-range heat beams futilely up at the rising copter.

A military tank, undoubtedly the one the Chief had been told about, spun around the corner. It stopped, and its guns swung upward toward the copter. But they remained silent. Heavy heat beams or artillery could puncture the city's protecting dome.

The copter went straight up, gathering speed. Up, and up, and it did not stop!

It hit the plastic dome near its zenith. It tilted and staggered. It ripped through the dome and vanished.

Immediately, sirens began to wail throughout the city. Doors clanged shut automatically everywhere. Lights and warning signs flashed at every street corner, advising citizens to run for the nearest airtight shelter.

The dome was punctured!

Emergency crews would be up within minutes to repair the break, and very little of the city's air would hiss away. But, in the meantime, every activity in Mars City was snarled by the necessity to seek shelter. The Chief had, indeed, created a situation of consternation in which it would be easier for the Phoenix men to elude their enemies.

The armed men of the government forces were already running for the houses in this area. Some of them were headed for the house from which Dark watched.

The Phoenix men were donning marsuits. They would admit the refugees, after requiring them to lay down their arms, and then leave the house in their marsuits.

Dark grinned happily, and walked quickly through the house to the attached garage. He climbed into the groundcar, started the engine, and opened the garage door by the remote control mechanism on the dashboard.

Accelerating at full power, Dark drove the groundcar out of the garage and spun into the street. The men afoot, seeking entrance to the houses, paid no attention. The tank began to turn ponderously in his direction, but by the time it was in a position to bring its guns to bear, Dark's groundcar had reached the corner and raced around it into the broad thoroughfare leading to Mars City's east airlock.

The airlock was only a dozen blocks away. The Chief's theory had been that the government, depending on surprise in its move to surround the Childress Barber College, would not attempt the complicated task of checking all traffic passing through the airlock until it was realized that some of the Phoenix men had escaped from the trap at the college.

Dark reached the airlock in minutes. The Chief's theory proved correct. There were no police at the airlock, and the maintenance employee stationed there did not even look up as Dark's approach activated the inner door.

He drove the groundcar into the airlock. The inner door closed behind him. The outer door opened, and Dark drove out onto the highway that struck straight across the Syrtis Major Lowland toward the Aeria Desert and Edom. It was as simple as that.

About ten miles out was the circular bypass highway that surrounded Mars City, and Dark proposed to turn right on that, for his destination was Hesperidum. The highway he was on would take him eastward, and Hesperidum was about 8,000 kilometers southwest of Mars City—a little better than two-days' drive at groundcar speed on the straight, flat highways.

Dark reached over and set the groundcar's radio dial on the frequency which had been agreed on for emergency Phoenix broadcasts during this operation. If government monitors caught the broadcasts and jammed them, there were alternate channels chosen. With only about two dozen radio stations on all Mars, plus the official aircraft and groundcar band, there was plenty of free room in the air.

There was nothing on the Phoenix frequency now but a little disconsolate static.

The country through which he drove here was uninhabited lowland. The human life on Mars, agricultural, industrial and commercial, was concentrated under the domes of the cities. Except for a few tiny individual domes at the edge of Mars City, there were no human structures close to it except the airport and the spaceport, and these were west and north of the city, respectively.

The highway struck straight and lonely through a faintly rippling sea of gray-green canal sage, spotted occasionally with the tall trunk of a canal cactus, rising above it. Later he would see infrequent dome farms, but he could expect no more than two or three score of these in the entire long drive to Hesperidum.

Dark slowed and entered the cloverleaf that took him onto the bypass expressway. Even as he did so, the radio crackled and the thin voice of the Chief sounded over the groundcar loudspeaker.

"Attention, Phoenix," said the Chief intensely. "Attention, Phoenix. Emergency instructions. We have monitored reports that the government is checking airlocks at all cities. Repeat: the government is checking airlocks at all cities.

"Some Phoenix have been captured attempting to leave Mars City. Instructions: those in Mars City do not attempt to leave but find shelter with Phoenix friends. Those beyond dome without credentials, go to assigned emergency rendezvous spots *outside* dome cities. Repeat instructions: those…"

Swearing under his breath, Dark pulled the groundcar to a stop beside the highway. It was so simple! They should have foreseen that the government would take such a step as soon as it was realized that the Phoenix men were leaving Mars City. He himself evidently had gotten through the airlock just in time.

But he had been assigned no outside rendezvous! Whether it was an oversight or not, he did not know, but the only place he had been instructed to go was Hesperidum. The only Phoenix contact he knew was the South Ausonia Art Shop in Hesperidum; and now he could not enter the city without being captured.

He had only one alternative: the Martians, in the Icaria Desert, halfway around Mars. They would remember him and shelter him, and he was sure he could find the spot.

He looked at his fuel gauge. The tank was full. It would not take him quite there, but he could chance refueling at Solis Lacus, some 20,000 kilometers from Mars City. He could take the highway, turning out into the desert to go around Edom, Aram and Ophir.

He put the groundcar in drive again, and made a U-turn in the highway. He entered the cloverleaf and was halfway through it when he saw the copter.

It was a red-and-white government copter, and it was descending at a shallow angle toward him from the direction of Mars City. Dark switched his radio to the official channel.

"…await check. Repeat: groundcar in cloverleaf, stop at once and await check."

Dark braked the groundcar to a stop. As soon as the copter grounded, he could accelerate and escape.

But the copter did not ground. It hovered, directly over him. Then Dark realized it was awaiting a patrol car from Mars City to check and take him in custody if necessary.

Immediately, he put the groundcar in drive and whipped out of the cloverleaf under full acceleration. If he could only achieve top speed, 350 kilometers-an-hour, the copter couldn't match it.

But the copter was on his tail at once as he swerved out of the tight curve. Its guns spat fire.

There was a terrific impact, and the groundcar dome shattered above him. Unprotected, he felt the air explode from the groundcar, from his lungs. Oxygenless death poured in through the broken dome.

It all happened in an instant. Even as the dome shattered under the copter's shell and Dark recognized the imminence of death, the groundcar twisted out of control and careened from the highway. He felt it spinning over and over, and then blackness closed in around him.

CHAPTER SEVEN

Maya had never seen Nuwell in such a state of sustained rage.

He strode back and forth in the private dining room of the Syrtis Major Club, near the western edge of Mars City, slapping his fist into his hand. His face usually was engaging and boyish, the wave of his dark hair setting it off handsomely, but now it was flushed like that of a petulant child and the lock of hair hung down over his forehead. Maya, the only other person in the room, sat quietly and watched him pace.

"They had plenty of time and all the information they needed," stormed Nuwell, "and yet they didn't get a single one of the key men! Most of the rebels slipped out easily, right under their noses!"

Maya watched him detachedly. This was the man she had promised to marry, and, as she had once or twice before, she was undergoing pangs of doubt. After all, she had known Nuwell Eli only during the few months she had been on Mars.

She had fallen in love with him for his charm, his intelligence, his good-humored gentleness, but she did not like this display of temper. It was not a controlled anger, but had something of the irrational in it.

"Childress was captured," she reminded him.

"Childress! A figurehead! He says he didn't know about the rebel activities going on in the college, and he's so stupid I may not be able to make a case against him."

Maya recognized that this element, the success of his prosecution, was a very important factor to Nuwell.

"Are the twelve I identified the only ones captured?" asked Maya.

"Yes. Twelve captured, seven killed, and every one of them small fry. The leaders undoubtedly got away in that copter. We blockaded the airlocks fast, so most of the others are probably still in the city, but we don't have any idea where to look for them."

"I may be able to help in that, when I get back from my swing around the other cities," said Maya.

"I don't want you to go on that jaunt, Maya!" exclaimed Nuwell, swinging around to face her with fierce emphasis. "You said when you had found the headquarters, you'd resign the service and marry me. Now you want to go all over Mars looking for rebels!"

"Nuwell, I can identify almost all of those who were at the barber college," Maya remonstrated. "They've picked up some men at the airlocks and others on the roads at several cities, and even Martian law won't permit you to uproot those people and send them to Mars City just on suspicion. They can't be sent here for me to identify: I'll have to go there."

"We can work out some charges to get them extradited to Mars City," snapped Nuwell angrily. "I don't want you to go, Maya. I want you to stay here and marry me, immediately."

"Aren't you being a little dictatorial, Nuwell?" she suggested coolly.

The warning implied in her remoteness seemed to trigger a polarized reaction in Nuwell. The furious dark eyes melted suddenly, the stubborn anger of the face altered on the instant to a sentimental, wistful smile of appeal.

"Don't be angry, Maya," he pleaded, half-ruefully, half-humorously. "It's just that I love you so much. It's just that I'm impatient for you to be my wife."

Changeability is attributed to the feminine, but Maya was not able to shift her mood as facilely as her fiancé.

"If I'm worth marrying, I'm worth waiting for a little longer," she said, with an edge to her voice. She was angry at Nuwell for acting so like a spoiled child. "I'm going to see this job finished. I'm leaving for Solis Lacus on the jetliner tonight."

"Solis Lacus!" he exclaimed in astonishment. "Why, Maya, that's halfway around Mars!"

"That's exactly why the rebels might be more likely to go there. In spite of the patrols, you know they haven't picked up all of the rebels who escaped Mars City by groundcar. Any of them who headed for Solis Lacus will be arriving there within the next two or three days. Then I'll make a swing around and spend as much time as necessary at each of the dome cities before coming back here."

The angry, stubborn expression swept across Nuwell's face again.

"Maya, I won't—" he began.

But at that moment, their guests began arriving. As the judge of Mars City's superior court and his wife entered the room, Nuwell cut himself off sharp and turned to greet them. His face cleared instantly, his lips curved into a delighted smile and he welcomed them with such natural, innocent charm that one would have thought he was incapable of frowning.

The presence of the guests seemed to intoxicate him with good-humor, and when he had to leave in the midst of the party to drive Maya to the airport he did not resume his argument. He merely kissed her good-bye tenderly before she boarded the plane and begged her with melting eyes to hurry back because he would be lonely every moment she was away.

So it was that Maya stretched in a reclining chair on the sundeck of the Chateau Nectaris the next afternoon and permitted herself to be disgusted with the entire planet Mars.

Maya's small, perfect body was kept minimally modest by one of those scanty Martian sunsuits. A huge straw hat, woven of dried canal sage, hid her beautiful face.

A disappointing resort area for an Earthwoman, this Solis Lacus Lowland. No swimming, no boating, no skiing. No water and no snow. Just a vast expanse of salty ground, blanketed with gray-green canal sage and dotted with the plastic domes of the resort chateaus. Nothing to do but hike in a marsuit or sun oneself under a dome.

She had chosen the Chateau Nectaris because it was the largest of the resort spots, and therefore the most likely one to be chosen by men who sought to hide out for a while. She had contacted the managers of all the resort chateaus and all had agreed to let her know of the arrival of any new guests.

There had been three of them during the morning, two arriving by groundcar and one by copter, at three different chateaus. She had driven to each one and circumspectly inspected the new guest, but none had been anyone she recognized from the Childress Barber College.

In a way, she wished she had yielded to Nuwell's importunities. There was much more of interest to do in Mars City. And Nuwell *was* charming and intelligent and rather dashing, and she did love him, and she did want to marry him. But...

But she was right in wanting to help identify those rebels who had been captured before she considered her task finished. And perhaps Nuwell had been right in his implied disagreement with her idea of coming first to Solis Lacus, so far from Mars City. Logically, would it not be harder to lose oneself in a fashionable resort area than in a good-sized city? But something within her had urged her to come here first. It was a hunch, and she intended to play it.

With a sigh, Maya pushed the hat off her face and stared with exotically slanted black eyes at the shining blur of the dome hundreds of feet above her. She sat up, hugging her knees with her arms.

A score of other guests were sunning themselves here also. At her movement, the unmarried men turned their eyes on her frankly; the married ones did so furtively, to be promptly yanked back to attention by their wives.

Maya's onyx eyes surveyed this dullness aloofly, then lifted over the nearby parapet and across the sparse terrestrial lawn which would grow only under the dome. The far cliffs of the Thaumasia Foelix Desert loomed darkly, distorted through the dome's sides.

The dome's airlock opened to admit a groundcar. She watched it, interestedly, as it scurried like a huge, glassy bug along the curving road and disappeared under the parapet in front of the chateau. Mail from Mars City, perhaps, or supplies. Maybe even a new guest.

Something struck her, now that the groundcar was no longer in sight. It had been a little too far away to discern its details clearly, but there was something strange about the appearance of that groundcar. A glassy bug, but not entirely sleek and shiny. Rather like a bug that had come out second best in an argument with another bug.

Maya arose, purposefully. She stretched lithely, to the delight of the assembled viewers, and padded gracefully toward the chateau's second-floor entrance, trailing the huge hat in one hand.

She walked lightly along the balcony over the lobby, toward her room. As she turned its corner, passing the grand stairway, she could see the chateau entrance and the registration desk.

The groundcar had brought a new guest. He was signing the registration book, a tall, broad-shouldered man in a marsuit, holding his marshelmet under his arm. Why would he be wearing a marsuit in a groundcar?

As she looked, he laid down the pen and turned. His face was darkly tanned, strong, handsome. His hair was black as midnight, his eyes startlingly pale in the dark face.

His gaze lifted to the balcony, and Maya ducked behind the big hat just in time.

Dark Kensington!

Triumph swept through her. She had been right in coming here! This was Dark Kensington, the man she had met once, just before the raid on the college. This was one of the leaders!

The hat held casually to conceal her face, Maya walked on to her room.

The telephone was ringing as she entered. She dropped the hat on the bed, and answered it.

"Miss Cara Nome, this is Quelman Gren, the manager," said the male voice on the line. "You asked me to notify you about any new guests. One has just registered."

"I saw him," she said. "What can you tell me about him?"

"He is registered as D. Kensington, from Hesperidum," answered Gren. "He is just staying overnight. His groundcar dome was broken in an accident, and he wants to have it replaced and the groundcar refueled."

"Thank you," said Maya. "Now, please put in a call for me to S. Nuwell Eli in Mars City."

She had bathed and dressed for dinner by the time the call came through.

"Nuwell," she said, when he had identified himself on the other end of the line, "I knew I was right in coming here. One of the rebel leaders just registered."

"Are you sure?" he asked excitedly.

"Certainly I am. He was one of those who stayed hidden in the back of the barber college, and I saw him for the first time the day of the raid. He identified himself then as a supervisor. But he's just staying overnight."

"That's long enough! I'll get a jet and be up in a few hours. Get the police to take him in custody and hold him for me."

"Darling, there aren't any police at Solis Lacus," Maya reminded him. "This is a private resort area. The nearest police are at Ophir."

There was a silence while Nuwell digested this.

"You say he's staying overnight?" Nuwell said then. "I can be there before midnight with some men to take him in custody."

"I'm a trained agent," said Maya. "I can take him in custody for you."

"You'll do no such thing!" squawked Nuwell in alarm. "It's, too dangerous! Now you listen to me, Maya. You stay out of sight of this man and wait till I get there!"

"All right, darling, I'll use my own judgment," replied Maya demurely, and hung up.

She sat and cogitated for a time. She was dressed for dinner, and she had been looking forward to appearing in the dining room in the somewhat sensational moulded, flame-red gown she had bought recently in Mars City. She didn't relish the idea of having dinner sent to her room, and sitting up here alone to eat it.

With sudden decision, she arose. She donned dark glasses and tossed a powder-red veil over her dark hair. Kensington had only seen her once and would not be expecting to see her here. If he saw her now, he wouldn't recognize her.

Fifteen minutes later, she was sipping an extremely expensive martini in the dining room when she raised her eyes to see Dark Kensington enter, wearing a dark-red, form-fitting evening suit.

He paused just inside the door and stood there, slowly surveying the room. His eyes fell on Maya and paused. Then he walked straight to her table.

"May I join you, Miss Cara Nome?" he asked in a deep, controlled voice, a rather sardonic smile on his lips.

She felt trapped, and irrationally angry at him for recognizing her.

"I'm afraid you've made a mistake," she said coldly. "That isn't my name."

At this juncture, a helpful waiter appeared at Maya's elbow and asked in an appallingly distinct tone:

"Would you care for another drink, Miss Cara Nome, or do you wish to eat now?"

"An understandable mistake, since it's such a common name," said Dark, sitting down opposite her. He turned pale-blue eyes, remote and filled with light, on the waiter, and added: "She'll have another drink, and bring me one of the same."

The waiter left, and Maya removed her dark glasses to level furious black eyes at Dark.

"I could call the manager and complain that you're annoying me, you know," she said.

"You could," he agreed somberly. "You seem to be a very efficient tattletale. Or are you going to try to pretend that you weren't the one responsible for the raid on the college?"

She recognized that she was well in for it. He was not going to play a game of pretense. Well, she had tried—partly, anyway—to do as Nuwell wanted.

Very deliberately, she opened her purse, realizing that Dark was watching her closely, all his muscles tense. She took out a cigarette case and a lighter, laying them side by side on the table, and he relaxed visibly.

Maya extracted a cigarette and placed it between her lips casually. She picked up the lighter and balanced it in her hand.

"I assume that you're not armed, Mr. Kensington," she said.

He shrugged and smiled, revealing strong white teeth.

"Hardly, in this suit," he replied. "I'm glad to see you've decided to recognize me."

"I am," she said grimly. "Armed, I mean. This is not a cigarette lighter, but a very efficient and deadly heatgun. You're under arrest, Mr. Kensington, so I suppose you're having dinner with me whether you like it or not. Now, do you mind being a gentleman and lighting my cigarette, since this is not very good for the purpose?"

He looked at her face, then dropped his eyes to the lighter, still smiling.

"You'd better take my word for it," she advised. "I don't want to kill you, Mr. Kensington, but I won't hesitate. I'm an agent of the terrestrial government."

Dark shrugged again. He produced a lighter and leaned forward to light her cigarette, without a tremor.

The waiter returned with their drinks and an announcement.

"There's a telephone call for you from Mars City, Miss Cara Nome," he said.

Maya kept her eyes on Dark.

"Can you bring a telephone to the table?" she asked the waiter.

"Certainly, Miss," he replied. He left, and returned a moment later with a telephone. He set it before her and plugged it in under the table.

Juggling the lighter-gun gently in one hand, Maya picked up the phone. As soon as she answered it, her ears were assailed by Nuwell's agonized voice.

"Maya, I can't get up there tonight!" he said. "There aren't any jets here, and these idiots refuse to bring one in from Hesperidum or Cynia for me to use. I'll have to come up by groundcar."

Maya sat silent, stunned. It had not seemed too great a feat to her to hold Dark captive with her disguised heatgun when she was anticipating Nuwell's arrival within hours. But suddenly she felt like a hunter who has snared a lion in a rabbit trap.

"Maya, are you there?" demanded Nuwell querulously. "We'll spell each other at the wheel and drive up without stopping, but it will still take two and a half days to get there."

Maya took a deep breath.

"Come ahead," she said in a steady voice. "I'll have your man waiting for you when you get here."

"You'll what? But I thought you said he was only staying overnight! Maya, don't you do anything rash!"

"I'm afraid I already have," she said, a little ruefully. "I have him under arrest right now."

The noise at the other end of the line sounded like a dismayed shriek.

"You little fool!" he shrilled. "I told you not to do anything like that! How can you hold a man like that for two days, single-handed? Call in the police!"

"It seems to me that I already mentioned there aren't any around here," she reminded him patiently.

There was a long silence on the other end of the line. Then Nuwell said, with forced calm:

"I'm leaving immediately. In the name of space, Maya, be careful!"

Maya put the telephone quietly back in its cradle and looked across the table at the Tartar she had caught. Dark smiled at her, easily.

"So the reinforcements you were expecting won't get here tonight, after all," he remarked softly.

"He didn't say that at all!" she retorted, too quickly.

"There's hardly any point in trying to deceive me about it is there?" he pointed out. "I can tell a great deal from your conversation and the expression on your face, and I'd estimate that your help is going to have to come from Mars City by groundcar— a trip I've just made, so I know exactly how long it takes. Do you plan for us to spend these two nights in your room, or mine?"

She looked at him silently, stricken.

"I see our waiter returning," said Dark equably. "I trust you'll enjoy your meal as much as I'm going to enjoy mine, Miss Cara Nome."

CHAPTER EIGHT

The waiter unplugged the telephone and lifted it from their table.

"We're ready to order now," Maya said to him. "And please ask Mr. Gren to come in here."

A few moments after the waiter left, the manager came to their table. Quelman Gren was dark and thin-faced, with sleek, oily hair.

"When I told you I was here in an official capacity for the government, Mr. Gren, you said you would co-operate with me in every way possible," said Maya.

"Yes, Miss Cara Nome, I have made every effort to do so," replied Gren. "Is there some way I can help you now?"

"Yes, there is," she said. "This man is my prisoner, and I'm going to have to keep him in custody here for two days and a half, until help arrives from Mars City. I'd like for you to arm a couple of dependable men with heatguns and assign them to help me guard him."

Gren shook his head.

"I'm sorry, Miss Cara Nome, but none of the employees of the Chateau Nectaris was employed for that sort of work, and I'm not going to ask them to do it. What you should have is police help."

"As you know very well, there are no police nearer than Ophir," she said in an exasperated tone. "Surely, you have some semi-official officers employed in the chateau in case of trouble among the guests."

"I have a house detective, but his duties are to intervene only when some crime has been committed against a guest or against the chateau. You told me that you were seeking political rebels, and I assume that that is your charge against Mr. Kensington. My house detective has no authority to act in such cases, and I do not intend to get the chateau mixed up in these affairs.

"I've co-operated with you to the extent of giving you information you wanted, Miss Cara Nome, and I'll continue to co-operate insofar as I am not asked to do something I have no authority to do. It occurs to me that if you came here seeking rebels, you should have come equipped to handle them if you found them."

"It occurs to me that you act very much as though you were in sympathy with the rebel cause," retorted Maya angrily.

"My sympathies are not the government's affair, as long as I take no illegal actions," said Gren. "Good evening, Miss Cara Nome."

Maya gazed after him furiously as he left the dining room. Dark, sitting completely relaxed, smiled pleasantly at her.

"Please be assured," he said, "that I'm going to try to avoid injuring you in any way when I escape your custody."

"I'm not worried, because you aren't going to escape," she said. "But I appreciate the thought. You seem to be a very mild-mannered person, for…"

She stopped.

"For a rebel?" he finished for her. "I really don't know what sort of indoctrination you must have had, Maya—if I may call you Maya, and there's no point in being formal under the circumstances. The students at the barber college were all rebels, and the reports I received were that you got along nicely with most of them."

"Yes, I did. I don't suppose it should surprise me to find that rebels are human beings, too."

"Merely a matter of a difference in orientation. And a question for you to consider is, which orientation actually is correct?"

Maya did not like the direction the conversation was taking. She was relieved by the appearance of the waiter with their meals of thick, steaming steaks, with all the necessary trimmings.

"It will be a long time before we can be served anything like this by teleportation," she said, laughing. "But, Mr. Kensington—"

"Dark, if you don't mind."

"Very well. Dark, you say that you drove here from Mars City. How did you avoid the copter patrols that were out trying to intercept the escaping rebels?"

"As a matter of fact, I didn't, and that's a very peculiar thing," he said thoughtfully. "One of them got me just outside Mars City and blasted the dome of my groundcar."

"I noticed you were wearing a marsuit when you registered here, and Gren said you were having the dome repaired."

"That's what's peculiar about it. I wasn't wearing the marsuit when the copter broke my dome. I didn't have any protection at all. The groundcar went off the road and overturned. I don't know how long I was unconscious, but it was evidently long enough for the copter to look me over, decide I was dead, and move on out of sight. What I can't understand is why I didn't asphyxiate."

"You mean that you were protected by no oxygen equipment at all?"

"None. I returned to consciousness and I was lying there with the dome broken wide open and my face bare to the Martian air. I got into my marsuit right away, of course, but that took a few minutes in addition to the time I was unconscious. And I didn't feel restricted by the lack of air. I wasn't even breathing. And I felt that I didn't need to!"

"That is peculiar," she said meditatively. "Tell me, do you know a man named Goat Hennessey?"

"You're the second person who's asked me that recently," said Dark. "I knew him well, many years ago, but I haven't seen him in years. Why do you ask?"

"Because the only case I've heard about of any human being able to live without oxygen in the Martian atmosphere involved some genetic experiments of Goat Hennessey, before the government made him stop them and destroy the creatures he'd been experimenting with."

Dark laughed.

"I can assure you I'm not one of Goat's genetic experiments," he said. "Goat and I were colleagues in this rebel movement twenty-five years ago, before I was hit by a period of amnesia that I've just come out of."

She stared at him.

"A twenty-five year period of amnesia? Impossible! You're not more than twenty-five years old," she said positively.

"If what people tell me is correct, I'm nearer sixty," said Dark. "Terrestrial years, of course."

"Of course. But I don't believe it."

Dark shrugged, and cut another bite of steak. He seemed to be enjoying his meal quite as much as though he were not her prisoner and she his captor—as, indeed, she was, too.

They chatted pleasantly throughout the meal and Maya found, somewhat to her surprise, that she was talking about herself a great deal to this pale-eyed man. She told him of her childhood on Mars, among the Martians, and of going to Earth to live with her uncle, a World Senator who had had close and profitable connections with Marscorp.

She went on to tell of her decision to become an agent of the terrestrial government, despite her uncle's objections but as a result of his often-expressed enthusiasm for the government's role in developing the planetary colonies; and of her assignment to Mars to ferret out a rebel headquarters which had eluded the best efforts of the Martian government. She even told him how she had met Nuwell and fallen in love with him.

Some time after the meal's conclusion, she suddenly stopped in mid-sentence.

"What's the matter?" asked Dark.

"I just realized that you're my prisoner," she answered, smiling at him. "Frankly, I'm not sure what to do with you. We can't just sit here in the dining room all night."

"Why not go out and sit on the terrace?" he suggested. "They say that Solis Lacus is a beautiful sight when Phobos is up and moving."

"And a shadowed terrace is a very convenient place from which to attempt an escape," she countered.

"Look," he said, "there's no point in making the evening more difficult than it is. I very definitely intend to get away from you and get out of here during the next two days if I can, but I'm enjoying this conversation. If I promise that I won't attempt an escape in the next two hours, are you willing to go up on the terrace for a while?"

She studied his face carefully. It was a handsome, earnest face, full of strength, full of wisdom, with a touch of weariness.

"All right," she said at last. "But I warn you that if my trust is misplaced and you do attempt to escape, I'll burn you down without compunction."

They went up together, quite as casually as might any two guests relaxing at the resort, and found chairs in the semi-darkness overlooking the moonlit lowland.

Deimos hung near the zenith, a tiny globe of light, virtually stationary. Phobos, larger and brighter, was not long risen, and it moved swiftly and smoothly across the sky, like the cold searchlight of some giant aircraft. Touched and transformed by the shifting shadows, Maya and Dark sat and chatted like old friends.

Dark talked now, and he told her of his past life, of his coming to Mars, of his joining the rebel movement upon realizing how the government was holding back man's progress toward Martian self-sufficiency. He spoke soberly, with intense conviction, and Maya, listening, began to realize that there was another side to this conflict than the one she had been taught.

She began to waver and to wonder, for the grave voice of this man was like a deep music she had never heard before but seemed to remember from some time before there was hearing, a music that touched the depths of her being.

Then his arm slid around her waist and he drew her gently toward him. For an instant, she responded, turning her face upward.

And, on that instant, she remembered.

With a lightning twist, she was free, and on her feet before him. She stepped back, and the lighter-gun was in her hand.

"I thought you said I could trust you," she said coldly. "Evidently, I was foolish to do so."

He looked up at her, and there was nothing but surprise on his face. Then, slowly, he smiled at her.

"It depends on your interpretation of the word," he said. "I was merely attempting to kiss you, my dear."

She let her hand sag, feeling rather foolish.

"Well, don't," she said, her sharpness covering her confusion. "We aren't lovers, Mr. Kensington."

"No," he said, quite seriously. "And I find that I rather regret that we aren't."

She stood looking at him, fighting off a sneaking regret of her own that he hadn't succeeded in his intention.

"I think this moonlight has had an unfortunate effect on us both," she said. "We'd better go inside. Besides, if I'm to keep watch over you all night, I want to get into something more practical than an evening gown."

Without protest, Dark preceded her inside. They went to the manager's office, and Maya issued instructions to Gren.

"Have a maid move my things from my third-floor room to a room on the top floor," she ordered. "We'll wait here until it's done."

When the maid brought Maya the key to the new room, she and Dark took the elevator to it. As soon as they were inside, she locked the door behind them.

"I'm going into the bathroom to change clothes," she said precisely. "The window to this room is six floors above a stone courtyard and I don't think you can jump that far without being killed, even on Mars. Since these windows don't open, I'll hear you if you break it to get out, and I can burn you long before you can climb down the face of the wall."

The lighter-gun in her hand, she went into the bathroom and closed the door behind her.

She had just stripped off the evening gown when she heard the bathroom door lock from the outside. A moment later, there was the crashing sound of breaking glass.

Calmly, Maya burned off the lock of the bathroom door with the little heatgun. She pushed it open and went out into the room in her underwear. Dark was in the process of gingerly climbing through the broken window.

"It's a long fall, Dark," she said.

He looked back over his shoulder. He smiled ruefully, and came back into the room.

"Well, it was worth a try," he said philosophically.

He surveyed her with frankly admiring eyes and added:

"And it was worth failing, for the view."

She turned pink. But, without taking her eyes off him, she reached back into the bathroom, got the tunic and trousers she had laid out, and slipped them on.

"I think it would be better if we go down and sit in the middle of the lobby," she said, unlocking the door to the room. "That way, you'll have farther to run if you try to get away."

They went down and found comfortable seats. They sat there, talking, to all casual appearance two of the chateau's guests. Gradually, the conversation moved back to its earlier informal and friendly terms.

How long they sat chatting, Maya did not know, for she was wrapped up in her enjoyment of the things Dark said and his attitude toward life. But after a time she realized that no more guests were sitting in the lobby or moving through it. They were the only ones there, except for Gren, sitting morosely behind the registration desk.

"Just how do you propose to get any sleep and watch me at the same time?" asked Dark.

"I don't," she answered, smiling. "If you can stay awake for two nights, so can I."

"You forget, young lady," he retorted. "I don't have to."

With that, he stretched out unceremoniously on the sofa on which he had been sitting, clasped his hands behind his head and closed his eyes. Within a very short time, he was obviously and genuinely sound asleep.

Maya sat and watched him, piqued and a little nonplussed. She could hardly afford to go to sleep, too. Her only course was to stay awake, to sit there and watch him sleeping comfortably and soundly. It was not a pleasant prospect, for two nights.

She sat, heavy-eyed, and racked her brain for some solution, and silently cursed Gren for refusing to give her the help she needed. Dark slept on, and a faint smile touched his lips. Then Maya found herself thinking pleasantly over the things they had talked about during the long evening, and admiring this man and liking him...

She woke up.

With a start, she woke up, realizing that she had been asleep. She was not sitting in the chair any more, but curled up comfortably on a sofa, her head pillowed like a child's against—against what?

Against Dark's chest! He was awake, sitting up, smiling down at her, and she was cradled in the curve of his arm. And the little lighter-gun was no longer in her hand.

She did not react violently to the sudden realization. She sighed, almost happily, and murmured to him:

"So you win, after all. I think I'm glad, Dark. Now you can go, if you want to."

He shook his head.

"I'm glad you feel that way about it, Maya, but I'm afraid it's too late. I really shouldn't have stayed around to serve as your pillow till you awoke."

There was something in his face that caused her to sit up suddenly.

Two uniformed men stood there in the lobby before them, relaxed but watchful, regulation heatguns dangling from their hands. As she sat up, one of them touched his cap and spoke to her:

"We're police officers from Ophir, Miss Cara Nome. Mr. Eli called from Mars City and directed us to drive over here and help you guard the prisoner until his arrival."

She rose angrily.

"I didn't ask for your help, so you may go," she said, aware of Dark's surprised gaze on her. "I made a mistake in identification."

The policeman who had spoken shook his head.

"I'm sorry," he said. "We're acting on Mr. Eli's orders, not yours. We'll have to hold Mr. Kensington until Mr. Eli arrives."

She glared at them. The one who had spoken was big and burly and efficient-looking. The other was sallow and silent, with a deadly cast to his thin face.

Then she saw her lighter-gun, lying on the lobby floor beside the chair in which she had gone to sleep.

She bent down, casually, and picked it up. She straightened, the little instrument ready in her hand.

"This is not a cigarette lighter, but a heatgun," she said flatly. "I'm in charge here, and I say Mr. Kensington is to be permitted to go free. If any effort is made to stop him, I'll burn you down."

Both police heatguns swung up in short arcs and trained on her. The burly policeman spoke gently.

"I'm sorry, Miss Cara Nome, but we're under orders from Mr. Eli, and we intend to follow them," he said. "I'd hate to see you injured, but if you blast either of us the other one will burn off your hand."

"No, Maya!" exclaimed Dark, getting to his feet. "Don't! There's no point in your getting hurt for my sake."

She ignored him.

"Drop those heatguns, both of you, or I blast!" she snapped, almost hysterically.

Then Dark hurled himself bodily at the two men.

The thin-faced man swung his heatgun around to meet Dark's charge. Maya twisted the lighter-gun toward him, and at the same moment the burly policeman threw himself against her. Her heat beam singed the thin-faced one's shoulder, then she collapsed under the impact of the other's body.

As she fell, she saw the almost invisible beam of the thin-faced policeman's heatgun strike Dark directly in the stomach, burning away the cloth, burning a great gaping hole in his abdomen. Dark slid to the floor, writhing, gasping, clutching his stomach.

Her lighter-gun knocked from her hand, Maya struggled, half-dazed, to her feet. The burly policeman had swung his own gun on the prostrate Dark, but the other one, grimacing with the pain of his wounded shoulder, stopped him.

"Let him be," he said. "I like to watch them die."

With a wail, Maya dropped to Dark's side. She cradled his head against her breast and sobbed as he died in her arms.

CHAPTER NINE

From the time she saw Dark Kensington die until Nuwell's arrival at the Chateau Nectaris a day later, Maya remained in her room, half in shock, half in an agony of sorrow and remorse.

She was so exhausted by her ordeal that she did sleep, but it was fitfully and without genuine rest. She had her meals sent up to her room, and ate automatically, not tasting the food.

Rationally, she could in no way blame herself for Dark's death, but that did not prevent her feeling strongly that her insistence on tracking down the fugitives from the Childress Barber College had made her, directly, his slayer. Her feeling of distress was much deeper and more personal than normal regret at having brought about the death of a friendly enemy while in pursuit of her duty.

Maya realized that in those few hours she had been with Dark and talked to him, something had taken root and flowered that had changed her whole outlook on existence. She did not want to call it love; she was a very practical young woman and did not believe in love on such short notice. But, in examining her feelings, she was at a loss as to what else to call it.

She had felt a powerful attraction to this man, a tremendous admiration and liking for him, a feeling of *belonging* in his presence. She had sensed his strength. It had appalled her when she had had to oppose herself to him in keeping him captive, but in other circumstances she felt it was the sort of strength she could depend on. Willingly, she thought now, she, could have dispensed with everything else in her life, and followed Dark Kensington wherever he chose to wander, a fugitive, among the deserts and lowlands.

And Nuwell? Her feeling for him had not changed. She was still attracted to him and she still admired him. But the admiration she had felt for his sharp, sardonic handling of his opponents in a court of law seemed a little shallow and a little immature in comparison to the sudden onrush of what she sensed about Dark.

Since her early teens, she had been an eager enemy of those rebels whom she conceived to be disrupting the orderly settlement of Mars, and her desire to contribute to the defeat of those rebels had been a disciplining, integrating force in her personality. Yet, in only a few short hours of quiet talk, Dark had cut the foundation from that force and dissipated it.

If only she had not delayed, if only she had made up her mind decisively to what she felt now… Dark need not have died, she could have freed him, and together they could have left Solis Lacus. With him, she would have fought as hard for the rebel cause as, in the past, she had fought against it.

But now it was too late. And, moping tearfully in her room, she found that she didn't care any more, one way or another, about the struggle between Marscorp and the rebels.

By the time Nuwell arrived from Mars City, she had regained control over her feelings. When he telephoned her in her room, she went down to the lobby to meet him, pale but composed.

She had a strange feeling as she came out into the big lobby, arching up above its balconies, a feeling as though she had been away in a distant land for a very long time and was just returning to the world she had known all her life. In this returning, she looked upon things with new ideas, and they did not appear the same as before.

This was the same spacious lobby across which she had walked to register when she came to Solis Lacus from Mars City a few days ago. It was the same lobby in which, looking down from the balcony, she had seen Dark Kensington arriving. It was the same lobby in which she had sat with Dark and talked for so long. But it seemed a strange place, a different place, one that looked like the lobby she remembered but in which she had never walked before.

Nuwell was standing across the lobby with the two police officers from Ophir, beside a long wooden box that rested on the floor next to the registration counter. Behind the counter, Quelman Gren, the manager of Chateau Nectaris, was sorting the day's mail.

Nuwell saw her, detached himself from the others and came across the lobby to meet her. As he approached, she experienced the same feeling toward him that she had felt toward the lobby: he was like someone she had known, but a different person.

There was a worried frown on Nuwell's face, and he managed to get something of disapproval in his greeting kiss.

"It's lucky I called Ophir and had those men sent over here," were his first words. "If they hadn't gotten here when they did, that rebel might have killed you and escaped. I told you, Maya, not to try to handle a situation like that."

"It was very astute of you to send them over," answered Maya dryly. "I should have thought of it myself."

"That's exactly why you shouldn't try to handle such things alone," said Nuwell, apparently somewhat mollified.

Maya looked into his face, a handsome, youthful face bearing a slightly peeved expression, and she thought two things: she thought of the long and intensive training she had undergone as a terrestrial agent, and she contemplated just how effectively Nuwell might have handled Dark's capture, had Nuwell been in her place.

"Come on, Maya, let's clear this up, so we can get out of here and get back to Mars City," said Nuwell, and led her across the lobby to the two policemen and the wooden box.

The two men from Ophir greeted her with a certain embarrassment, and seemed relieved when she smiled wanly at them.

"These men have told me how the rebel had turned the tables and gained the advantage of you before their arrival," said Nuwell. "They say that before he was killed, he confessed to them that he was Dark Kensington, one of the major rebel leaders who escaped from the Childress Barber College. I believe that coincides with your identification of him, doesn't it?"

"Yes," answered Maya in a low voice. "He was Dark Kensington. I saw him once at the college, and he identified himself to me then as a supervisor."

She did not feel called on to say anything more, and to tell Nuwell what Dark himself had told her about the rebellion and his part in it.

"Very good," said Nuwell with satisfaction. "We've captured the Chief, the peculiar-looking individual who escaped by driving his copter through the city dome. All the indications are that he and Kensington were the two top figures in the rebellion. I think all that's needed now is for you to identify the body positively as Kensington, Maya."

He indicated the wooden box, which lay, lidless, on the floor. Reluctantly, Maya stepped up to it, and looked down into it.

The pain which distorted Dark's face when he lay writhing from the heatgun blast was gone from his features. They were calm and peaceful in death.

Maya gazed down at his face wistfully, sorrowfully, then turned away.

"Well?" asked Nuwell impatiently.

"Yes," she murmured. "That's Dark Kensington."

"Very good," said Nuwell, and turned to the two men. "We'll take the body to the hydroponic farm for the vats," he said.

"There'll be others after the trials and executions of the rebels we've captured."

"Do you have to do that?" protested Maya. "Why can't you give the man a decent burial out here in the lowland?"

"Don't interfere in matters which are none of your affair," replied Nuwell brusquely. "Bodies of criminals are always sent to the vats. They're constantly short of bodies, as it is, and we can't very well send them corpses of law-abiding citizens."

He turned away. As Maya accompanied him across the corridor, the two men from Ophir began nailing the lid on the wooden box that contained Dark Kensington's remains.

At the elevator, Nuwell said:

"Get your things packed as soon as you can. I want to go back to Mars City right away by copter. I have some things I want to talk to you about, very seriously, but they can wait until we're airborne."

"Why by copter?" asked Maya. "Groundcar is faster."

For the first time, Nuwell's face broke into a genuine smile, and his ordinary charming self shone through.

"Because," he replied drolly, "I've just made that trip by groundcar, and every bone in my body aches. It may be slower, but I want to go back by air, where there aren't as many bumps!"

Maya was able to laugh at this. She went up to her room.

It did not take her long to pack, and to dress in a tunic and trousers for travel. When she came back down to the lobby, Nuwell was waiting, and they took a groundcar from the chateau to the dome airlock.

The three government agents who had come with Nuwell from Mars City had the helicopter ready for them on the flat lowland just beyond the airlock. As the groundcar emerged onto the sage-covered plain, the men were helping the two policemen from Ophir unload the box containing Dark Kensington's remains from another groundcar and load it into the baggage bay of the copter.

Nuwell and Maya slipped into their marsuits, secured the helmets and climbed out of the groundcar. Nuwell gave his men some final instructions to follow before returning to Mars City by groundcar. Then he and Maya went aboard the copter.

They strapped themselves in the seats. Nuwell sealed the copter door, and released oxygen from the tanks into the interior. When the dials showed the air to be breathable, he and Maya removed their helmets, Nuwell started the motor and the craft lifted slowly and smoothly into the air above the Solis Lacus Lowland.

Nuwell headed the copter northwestward. As soon as they were well on course, he turned to Maya with a stern expression on his face.

"There's one thing I can't understand at all," he said severely. "What madness possessed you to resist those men I sent over from Ophir, and attempt to help Kensington escape?"

She looked at him steadily without replying.

What should she answer? Could she say, "I discovered that I had fallen in love with Dark Kensington. I found that his reasons for the rebellion made sense to me, and that you and the government and Marscorp are wrong"?

What would Nuwell's reaction be if she told this truth?

But it could do no good to say that. It could do the rebels no good, because now they were scattered and defeated. It could do Dark no good, because he was dead. She did not think she would suffer personally from such a revelation, but it could only hurt Nuwell, who loved her.

So, at last, she said:

"Nuwell, I'd rather not talk about that. I didn't succeed, so can we forget it?"

"I think it's best that we do," agreed Nuwell. "The only thing I can think is that you were slightly hysterical over Kensington's having gained the upper hand, after the strain of guarding him for so long, and your action was an unconscious expression of resentment at their having to take over his custody where you had failed. But we might have learned a great deal through questioning the man at length, and that action of yours made it necessary for them to kill him."

Nuwell could not know how deeply those words struck her. She turned her face away from him, and the tears came to her eyes.

"At any rate," went on Nuwell, unaware, "I think this demonstrates that these espionage activities have been far too much of a strain for you, and I think it's time you stopped. We have one of the two major leaders captured and the other one dead, and I don't think they're going to give us much more trouble even if we don't locate all the fugitives. So I want you to give up this idea of wandering around from city to city, helping identify rebels."

"I think you're right," she agreed in a choked voice. She had no more interest now, certainly, in tracking down rebels.

"And," continued Nuwell, even more firmly, "marry me when we get back to Mars City."

Well, why not? Nuwell loved her. What else was there for her?

"Yes, I'll do that, too," she said. "As soon as we get back, I'll make out my report, and send my resignation with it back on the first ship to Earth. Then I'll marry you, Nuwell."

His face was radiant and triumphant as he turned to her. He put his arm around her shoulders, drew her to him and kissed her.

The helicopter flew northwestward. Passing over the Solis Lacus Lowland, it crossed the Thaumasia Desert and the Tithonius Lacus Lowland, and whirred above the Desert of Candor. Ahead of it, after a time, there rose on the horizon the white stone forms of a distant group of buildings.

Nuwell dropped the helicopter lower. He angled it down, and in a short time landed it on the desert near one of the four buildings of the Canfell Hydroponic Farm.

As he and Maya donned their marshelmets, a group of marsuited men emerged from the building's airlock and came across the sand toward them.

Maya stared curiously out the copter window. She had heard of this government experimental station, but had not visited it before.

"This is another reason I wanted to take a copter," explained Nuwell, releasing the air from the copter's interior. "There aren't any roads to this place, and I didn't want to drive a groundcar across the desert to bring Kensington's body here."

They emerged from the copter as the group from the building approached. Nuwell greeted the five of them and introduced them to Maya. Four of them were strangers to her, but the fifth she remembered: Goat Hennessey, white-bearded and watery-eyed.

"How are you adjusting to your new work here, Dr. Hennessey?" Nuwell asked him.

"Very well," answered Goat in his cracked voice. "They're using a different approach from mine, but I find it extremely interesting."

Remembering Goat's earlier experiments at Ultra Vires, it occurred to Maya to be grateful that Dark had not fallen alive into the hands of these people at the Canfell Hydroponic Farm.

Their entire stop lasted only a few minutes. Nuwell refused an invitation to remain overnight, explaining that he was anxious to get on to Mars City. The others unloaded Dark's coffin and moved with it back toward the building. Nuwell and Maya climbed back into the copter, and shortly they were airborne again and the buildings of the Canfell Hydroponic Farm were receding behind and below them.

Nuwell guided the copter almost straight westward now. It passed over Candor and buzzed out over the broad Xanthe Desert.

And here trouble developed. Without warning, the engine coughed and stopped. Nuwell worked frantically at the controls, to no avail. As the big blades slowed in their rotation, the copter sank, slowly at first, then ever more swiftly, to the surface of the desert. They donned marshelmets hurriedly.

It struck with a terrific crash, which would have hurled them through the windows had they not been strapped down. The entire body of the copter crumpled in on itself, and it came to rest, a collapsed wreck, with the two of them sitting in its midst, miraculously uninjured.

There was no question of trying to start the engines or fly the machine. It was a total wreck. Nuwell tried the radio without success.

"What in space went wrong with the thing?" he demanded angrily. "I know it wasn't short of fuel. There's nothing left for us to do but walk, I'm afraid, Maya."

"Back to the hydroponic farm?"

"No, we've come too far. By my chart, we're not far from Ultra Vires. I think we'd better try to make it for the night, and if Goat left his radio equipment in working order we'll call for help. If not, the only thing I know to do is to head for Ophir."

Ultra Vires—Maya remembered it with a shudder. The grim, black bastion in the desert where Goat Hennessey had worked with grotesque, twisted caricatures of humans.

They fumbled about the wreck to find the minimum emergency supplies they thought they would need, and started westward on foot.

CHAPTER TEN

Happy Thurbelow finished sweeping the long barracks and leaned wearily on his broom. That is, he didn't lean on it, or it would have collapsed him to the floor, but he made the gesture. Why, he wondered, didn't the Masters make the Toughs sweep their own barracks? Perhaps the Toughs couldn't be made, or perhaps the Masters did it just from an excess of cruelty.

Happy's monstrously bloated body sagged, and his skin felt dangerously dry and tight. Happy was so adipose that his hands engulfed the broom handle like a toothpick; under the transparent skin, his flesh was clear and translucent, and there could be seen the tiny red lines of the branching veins. Happy was like a jellyfish, in huge human form.

"Shadow!" he called in a high, grating voice. "I'm going below."

Shadow appeared disconcertingly, ten feet away. Dark-skinned Shadow looked at him silently with white-rimmed eyes. Then Shadow turned and disappeared, as only Shadow could.

Hanging up the broom, Happy waddled to the iron-barred gate that prevented entrance to a downward-plunging ramp. He pressed a button beside it and waited.

He looked out the window beside the gate. The sands of the Desert of Candor stretched orange and bleak under the bronze sky. Somewhere out there to the south, across those sands, under that sky, lay the shining dome of Ophir.

The window would be easily broken, and it was large enough for even Happy's bulky body to pass through. But the oxygen-scant air of Mars would sear his lungs to quick death without a helmet; and even if it would not, Happy's skin would dry and crack in a few hours of that outside air, and he would die in slower agony.

"What is the purpose of your call?" asked an impersonal voice from the loudspeaker beside the barred gate.

"I have finished my task, Master," said Happy, puffing a little. "I seek your grace to go below."

The loudspeaker said no more, but after a moment the gate stirred and lifted into the ceiling. Happy went through it gratefully, and waddled down the gently sloping ramp. The gate descended behind him.

Happy did not know whether Shadow had come through the open gate with him, but it didn't matter. Shadow could slip easily through the bars when he wished.

At the foot of the ramp was a vast, low cavern, stretching out of sight in all directions. It was dim, shading into the darkness of distance. Its floor was water, flat water, subdivided into large rectangular vats. In most of the vats vegetation grew in various stages, greening under the ultraviolet rays that radiated from the low roof. Between the vats ran straight, narrow walkways of packed earth.

Happy waddled along one of the walkways until he found an empty vat. He lowered himself over its edge and sank happily into the still, cool water, like a hippopotamus submerging. He immersed himself completely, then lay back in the water, with only his face floating barely above the surface.

Shadow appeared, apparently out of nowhere, and sat down on the edge of the vat, letting his flat legs dangle into the water.

"Nothing like it," proclaimed Happy, splashing a little. "Nothing on Mars like it. You ought to come on in, Shadow. As flat as you are, you ought to float on the surface without any trouble at all."

Shadow nodded silently, but made no move.

"I don't see why the Toughs can't take care of their own barracks," complained Happy, returning to the subject closest to his displeasure. "You reckon the Toughs are actually the rebels, and the Masters can't make them do anything?"

Shadow shook his head, but whether in negation or disclaimer of knowledge, Happy could not interpret.

Happy flinched, and shifted in the vat.

"There's still part of a skeleton in here," he announced. "I thought this was an empty one."

Moving, he flinched again. With purpose, he aroused himself and ploughed to the edge of the vat.

"I've got to find another vat," he said. "I can't take a nap if I'm going to get punched in the fanny with bones every five minutes."

He heaved himself over the edge onto the walkway with difficulty, and got slowly to his feet. Shadow lifted his feet out of the vat, stood up and vanished.

Happy knew how Shadow was able to disappear so suddenly, and it did not disturb him. Seen directly from front or rear, Shadow had the dimensions of a normal, black-skinned man. But Shadow was flat, no thicker than half an inch. When Shadow turned sidewise, he vanished to the sight.

Occasionally, Happy wondered how Shadow happened to be, and why he was here in the caverns, but it was not the sort of thing to bother his mind for very long.

Happy moved along the walkways, peering into the vats which appeared to be empty. He assumed Shadow was following him; Shadow always did.

Around corners, he came upon blubbery creatures like himself, tending the plants. They nodded greeting at him, and Happy nodded back.

His search was discouraging. All the vats not filled with plants seemed to have corpses in them, in varying stages of decomposition.

Around one corner, Happy came upon a Tough, lounging in the walkway. The Tough was a compact, muscular youth, with bullet head, sullen eyes and hard mouth. He looked as though he lounged with hands in pockets, but, like Happy and all the others, he was naked, so that was just an impression.

Happy stopped. He and his soft kind avoided the Toughs when they could. The Tough looked at him with disinterested eyes, then looked away.

Happy was uncertain what to do or say. His impulse was to turn and go back, but he did not quite dare.

"Are you a rebel, Tough?" he burbled the first thing in his mind, for lack of something else to say.

The Tough looked at him contemptuously. Then, suddenly, the Tough's hard eyes flared with savage excitement and he moved swiftly on Happy. As he began to turn in panic, Happy saw from the corner of his eye another Tough racing around the corner of the walkway to come upon him from behind.

The Tough in front of him reached him and began pummeling him viciously with his fists, the hard fists sinking like painful hammers deep into Happy's flesh with every blow. Happy bleated in fright and distress, trying ineffectually to ward off his attacker.

Then, out of nowhere, Shadow flashed in like a lightning bolt on the other Tough as he had almost reached Happy. There was a brief, squalling tangle and the Tough pitched headlong into a plant-choked vat.

Shadow vanished and reappeared, intermittently, like a flashing light. The first Tough, seeing what had happened to his cohort, ceased pummeling Happy abruptly and took to his heels. He vanished around a corner.

The vanquished Tough climbed out of the vat, sputtering and cursing, and fled in the other direction.

"Oh, my! Oh, my!" exclaimed Happy to the now-invisible Shadow. "What wicked creatures!"

Sore and shaken, he moved on down the walkway, his search now intensified by the need for wetness to soothe his injured flesh.

He came upon a vat without vegetation and, at first joyous glance, thought it empty. Then, disappointment, a comparatively fresh body floated in it, just under the surface.

It was the body of a man. Naked, it was smooth and plump with the water that had seeped into its tissues, and it was a uniform dead-white all over, like the belly of a fish. The face and lips were monochrome white, the hair was bleached, and when it opened its eyes, they were so colorless that the action was almost unnoticeable.

Realizing, Happy was paralyzed with shock.

The dead creature's eyes moved from side to side, then stopped, fixing on Happy. Its chest began to rise and fall slowly, with breathing—*under water.*

"Shadow!" squeaked Happy helplessly.

Shadow appeared beside him.

"Shadow, it's alive," whispered Happy, desperately frightened.

The two stood side by side, staring breathlessly down into the water. The creature in the vat moved its hands tentatively, it opened its mouth and closed it. Then it stirred with purpose, turned and climbed up over the side of the vat, dripping like a weird creature from the depths of the sea.

It stood up before them, dripping.

The man bent slightly and belched forth a great quantity of water from his lungs. He straightened, and breathed in the air in great, satisfied gasps.

"I'm Dark Kensington," he said in a rusty voice. "Where is this?"

At his words, Shadow disappeared.

Dark Kensington. Had Maya seen him now, she could not possibly have recognized him. The muscular body and dark, handsome face were bloated and pale. The black hair was bleached to pale seaweed, and the blue eyes were completely colorless now.

"This is the Canfell Hydroponic Farm," answered Happy, gaining a little courage. "Under the surface of the Desert of Candor."

"The Desert of Candor?" repeated Dark, and the pale lips twisted in a smile. "They hauled me quite a way. I was at Solis Lacus."

"How did you get here?" asked Happy with sudden eagerness. "Only dead people are thrown in the vats, to make chemicals for the plants. How could you stay alive under water?"

"I imagine I can breathe water for the same reason I can still live after a heat beam burned my guts out, but I don't know what that reason is. I imagine that the first step in finding out is to get out of this place."

"You can't get away from here," said Happy positively. "Nobody ever has."

"We'll see," said Dark confidently. "I gather you and your companion are some sort of prisoners."

"Slaves," corrected Happy with unaccustomed bitterness. "The Jellies are slaves, to work in the vats. I don't know if the Toughs are slaves, too, but the Masters let them sleep in barracks on the surface. Shadow's not either a Jelly or a Tough, and I don't know if he's a slave. Shadow's just Shadow."

"Before you go on," interrupted Dark, "I seem to be extraordinarily hungry."

Happy twittered and quivered. He moved hurriedly around a corner to one of the storage vats, and returned in a moment with a supply of the tasteless gelatin that was their food here. Dark fell to greedily, and Happy, his tongue loosed by this new companionship, started feeding him information in a steady stream.

"I don't know how they get us here," said Happy. "We aren't born here, but something happens to our memories. We can't stay up in the dry air very long, or our skin cracks and our flesh collapses. You see, our tissues are mostly water.

"Everybody down here's like me. Everybody but the Toughs. You'll see them. I don't know how they got here, either, or what use they are. They don't work like we do.

"And Shadow. He's different. Shadow likes me. He stays with me all the time. And then there's Old Beard. He hides down here, and I don't think the Masters know he's here. He's very old and very wise."

"Who are the Masters?" asked Dark curiously, between mouthfuls. "And what sort of work do you do for them?"

"They're the people who run the hydroponic farm. They're normal men, like you—I mean, like you would be if you weren't swollen up and pale like the bodies that are thrown in the vats.

"Old Beard knows; he's very wise. He calls the Masters 'Marscorp.' I don't know why, but it seems that before I lost my memory I knew a language where *corp* meant *body*. Like *corpse*, you know. Maybe it has something to do with the bodies they put in the vats.

"Old Beard says that the Masters are developing Martian foods that we can eat without dying, and he must be right, because sometimes they bring down some hard foods and make some of us eat them instead of gelatin. But those who eat the hard foods always die, so I don't suppose they've succeeded yet, except some of the Toughs. Some of the Toughs have eaten the hard food without dying, sometimes, but they got pretty sick. And then—"

"Hold on! Wait a minute!" exclaimed Dark, holding up a restraining hand. "I know what Marscorp is, and I'm not surprised they're behind it. But I'm trying to digest all this you're throwing at me."

Happy fell silent, reluctantly, and Dark cogitated deeply.

Happy fidgeted, anxious to speak but afraid to interrupt Dark's thoughts.

And then Shadow reappeared. Shadow appeared out of nowhere, and made gestures at Happy. Happy glanced at Dark, timidly. At last, he gained courage to speak.

"Shadow tells me—" he began, then cringed when Dark looked up in surprise. Dark gestured to him to go on.

"Shadow tells me," said Happy, "that Old Beard wants to see you. Will you go with us to Old Beard?"

"Certainly," agreed Dark. "From what you tell me, I'm rather anxious to meet Old Beard, too."

He followed Happy and the alternately visible and invisible Shadow along the paths that twisted among the vats for some distance. At last they ducked into some luxuriant foliage that hung over to form a bower above the space between two vats.

Old Beard sat there, in a corner of the dimness, pale eyes fixed silently on the trio. Old Beard was not so very old. He appeared to be in robust middle age, although his skin was very pale from long existence underground. His hair and heavy beard were long and untrimmed, and were a deep iron-gray.

"Thank you for coming," said Old Beard in a deep, resonant voice that bespoke strength and bore an undertone of bitter determination. "It is safer for me not to move around too much in the open except at certain hours."

"I was glad to come, because I'm sure you can help me and I may be able to help you, too," said Dark. "I'm Dark Kensington."

"So Shadow told me. I find this extremely interesting."

"You've heard of me, then?" asked Dark.

Old Beard laughed, deeply.

"More interesting than that," he said. "Once, before I was marooned here and Happy's people came to know me as Old Beard, I had a name of my own."

He stroked his beard, and favored Dark with a shrewd look from his pale eyes.

"Yes," said Old Beard, "I've heard of Dark Kensington, and there never was but one Dark Kensington, as far as I knew. That's why I find it so interesting. You see, I'm Dark Kensington!"

CHAPTER ELEVEN

The Xanthe Desert stretched red and barren on all sides of the plodding couple, the sands unbroken by the form of plant or stone or any living thing, all the way to the tight horizon of Mars. Above them, the small, glittering sun slid down the copper-hued sky slowly toward the west.

It was remarkable, thought Maya, how smooth and flat the desert looked from the air, and how rough and rolling it was when one had to walk across the packed sand. They had been walking for hours and, despite the gentle gravity of Mars, she was getting very tired.

"It's farther than I thought," said Nuwell, his voice distorted by the marshelmet speaker. "Distances on the chart are deceptive. We may not reach Ultra Vires by night."

Maya did not answer. Again, as she had many weeks before, she was in the grip of a sensation that this desert through which they walked was only a surface thing, a shimmering mask to the reality which lay behind it. That reality seemed very deep, very significant, and she felt that she was on the verge of comprehending it, but could not quite grasp it.

She was a little irritated at Nuwell for speaking when he did. If his voice had not interrupted her probing emotions, she felt, she might have broken through to that reality she sensed.

"Nuwell," she said, giving it up, "I'm going to have to rest a while. If we don't make it by night, we don't make it. There's always tomorrow, and I'm tired."

Reluctantly, he consented, and they sat down together on the sand. Nuwell pulled a chart out of his marsuit pocket and began to study it. Maya lay back, clasped her hands behind her helmet and closed her eyes, gratefully feeling the tired muscles relax and the perspiration that bathed her begin to dissolve in the gentle circulation of the marsuit's temperature-control system.

"Maya!" exclaimed Nuwell suddenly. "Look! We're going to be rescued!"

She sat up and looked in the direction of his pointing finger. On the horizon to the northeast was a cloud of dust, too placid and stationary to be a sandstorm.

They stood up, and Nuwell spoke hastily into his helmet radio on the conventional emergency band.

"Attention, groundcar! Attention, groundcar! We're afoot and in trouble. We're afoot, due southwest from your position. Help, please. Attention, groundcar!"

There was no radio reply in the ensuing silence. But all at once it was as though a deep and alien voice spoke within the depths of Maya's mind:

"We see you."

Startled, she looked curiously at Nuwell. But he evidently had not had the same experience. He was chattering into the radio frantically again.

"They're evidently not tuned in on the emergency band, Nuwell," she said to him. "But they're coming almost directly toward us. They're bound to see us soon, if they haven't already."

"That's true," said Nuwell, and added sourly: "But they ought to be tuned in. It's required by law."

The dust cloud moved closer slowly, too slowly for a groundcar. They were able to discern a dark nucleus below and in front of it. Then Nuwell said:

"In the name of space! It isn't a groundcar, Maya. It's a band of Martians! Let's get out of here!"

He started to walk on swiftly, but Maya stood her ground.

"Don't be silly," she said. "Martians won't hurt us. I was raised among them."

Nuwell stopped and returned reluctantly to her side.

"They may not hurt us, but why wait for them?" he demanded, and there was a touch of hysterical fright to his tone. "Let's go on, Maya!"

"We may very well have gotten off course in trying to go straight to Ultra Vires," replied Maya logically. "That may be why we've not sighted it yet. The Martians will know where it is, and meeting them may prevent us from getting lost in the desert."

Nuwell subsided, but she could see from the expression on his face that he was in a blue funk. This puzzled her. She could not understand why anyone would be afraid of Martians. They were huge, and ugly, and alien, but they were not inimical to humans.

When the Martians came near enough, Maya waved her arms at them and started off to meet them, Nuwell following her at a little distance. The Martians changed course slightly and came toward them.

Maya called childhood memories to her aid. She turned her helmet speaker to its maximum volume, and spoke to them in their own language, in the deepest tones possible to her.

"Children of the past, we seek that place in the desert which is called 'Ultra Vires' by humans," she said. "Can you show us the direction in which we must travel?"

The Martians gathered around her, towering over her. There were four of them. Their huge chests moved slowly, mixing oxygen from their great humps with the surrounding air. Their thin arms hung limp at their sides, and their big ears were pricked forward toward her. Their huge, dark eyes seemed to look through her and beyond her.

"The sun moves toward this place, but there are no humans there now," boomed one of the Martians. "Nothing lives there now except small animals in the walls and corridors."

"This we know," answered Maya. "We wish to go there that we may communicate with other humans and have them come and get us."

She wanted to say that the supplies of oxygen in their marsuit tanks were inadequate to take them anywhere other than Ultra Vires, but she did not know how to say this properly in the Martian language.

But, to her astonishment, the Martian answered as though she had said it.

"If the breathing chemicals which you carry are at such a depleted stage, you cannot chance going astray," said the creature. "Rather than tell you the direction of this place, we shall accompany you there."

Throughout this conversation, Nuwell had been standing at Maya's side, his face bearing an expression of mingled curiosity, irritation and awe. Maya turned to him.

"The Martians say they will go with us to Ultra Vires, so we won't get lost," she told him.

"No!" he exclaimed vehemently. "Tell them we don't want them along. Tell them just to show us the way, and we'll go alone."

"Don't be ridiculous," replied Maya coldly, and indicated to the Martian that they were ready to accompany the group.

They moved off together toward the west, the four Martians and the two humans. Maya, feeling somewhat relieved that now they had expert help in reaching their goal, attempted to talk to Nuwell, but he refused to answer except in monosyllables. He was angry that she had agreed for the Martians to accompany them, and obviously was still very nervous at their presence.

So she talked instead with the Martian who had acted as spokesman for the group. Its name, she learned, was Qril.

"The place to which you go lies under an evil atmosphere," said Qril. "The human who abode there many years attempted to do things wrongly."

"We were there in the season before this one," answered Maya. "This was just before that human left."

"I already had read this in you," said Qril. "I also read in you that, as a child, you lived among us who are children of the past. Therefore, perhaps you knew before I spoke that an evil atmosphere remains at this place and has not yet been washed away by time."

"No, I was not taught such matters as a child," answered Maya. "But tell me, it is true that this man tried to do evil things, by human standards, but were Goat Hennessey's genetic experiments also evil by Martian standards?"

"You do not read what I have said quite correctly," replied Qril. "The evil atmosphere is left by the man, because what he did was evil by his own standards. I said only that he attempted to do things wrongly."

"What do you mean?" asked Maya.

"To explain to you, I must speak to you about things about which you already know partially," answered Qril. "Before you were born, the human you call Goat was one of a group of humans who sought ways to make humans independent of the spaceships which bring materials from Earth to Mars and create small islands of terrestrial conditions in the midst of the Martian environment. When they met the natural resistance of those humans who gain material advantage through operation of the spaceships, they came into the desert to be free to work.

"Seeking to get far from the men who resisted their work, this group of humans went to that area which you know as the Icaria Desert. Some of us who are children of the past live at that place sometimes, and these humans sought our help, knowing that we possess many remnants of the knowledge that our forefathers had.

"But we had difficulty helping them. They were attempting to follow two courses simultaneously, and both of them were wrong."

"I know something of those two courses," said Maya. "Some of them were trying to develop human extrasensory powers so that materials could be teleported from Earth, and the others were trying to change the human body physiologically so that humans could live under Martian conditions. But you say they were both wrong?"

"In each way that they followed, they sought to make humans partly like us, the children of the past," said Qril. "We have the power to communicate with our minds over a distance, and some of us are able to transport things with our minds over a distance. We do not need your rich terrestrial air, because we take oxygen directly from the soil and store it in our bodies for combustion purposes.

"But humans and the children of the past are different forms of life, and they cannot be made so much alike. It is possible for humans to develop mental powers similar to ours, but this course would leave them dependent upon importing materials from Earth, even though this would be by mind transmission instead of by spaceship. The other course they followed could not succeed, because the human body cannot be altered so that it is able to take oxygen from the soil and store it for later use."

"But you're wrong!" exclaimed Maya. "Goat Hennessey had succeeded in developing some humans who could live without oxygen in the air for a time. His experiments were imperfect, it's true, but they were able to do that."

"The imperfect humans that the human called Goat had developed were not what he thought," replied Qril. "We tried to help the humans to find the right course, but they could not understand us well. We tried to show them, by charts and example, that the proper way to adapt a human to Martian conditions was a different way.

"Because Earth is nearer the Sun, humans have a possibility that we do not have. What we tried to show these humans was a method whereby they could change the embryonic physiology so that the adult human would be able to use the energy of solar radiations directly, instead of depending on the energy of combustion of those chemicals you call oxygen and carbon. This makes the body independent of both air and food, and has the advantage also of giving a far superior regenerative power to the bodily tissues.

"The human, Goat, for reasons that are not known, stole some of our charts and two of the pregnant female humans, and continued his work at this place to which we are going. But he thought he was still attempting to change the physiology so that oxygen could be stored, and therefore his experiments went wrongly."

"But he had your charts," objected Maya. "Even though he was not making the alterations he thought he was, how could he go wrong if he followed the charts?"

"The charts showed the changes to be made in the embryonic cells, but they could not show the method whereby the changes are made," replied Qril. "The human, Goat, attempted to make these changes by mechanical, surgical methods but these are too crude to be successful. The method we utilize to make such changes, which is the only right method, is to focus the mental forces upon the embryo. I believe you would call it psychokinesis."

Maya was vastly excited at this revelation.

"Then Goat's oldest experiments, the ones he called Brute and Adam, were actually the ones on whom you children of the past had performed the embryonic changes!" she exclaimed. "They must have been the sons of the pregnant women he kidnapped. That's why they were more successful than the others!"

"That is true," said Qril. "We had completed the change on only one of the two, therefore only that one would develop into an adult who could live in complete independence of air and food, if necessary. The other one would never be able to do it for more than a short period without returning to terrestrial conditions."

The party now came over a long low ridge, and the mass of Ultra Vires rose from the desert ahead of them. The sun was near setting, and the black walls of the stronghold huddled sullenly under its crimson rays.

The Martians left them here, and Nuwell and Maya went on alone toward their goal. Nuwell expelled an audible sigh of relief.

"I'm glad we're free of those monsters," he said. "I don't understand how you could carry on a conversation with such creatures, Maya. It sounded like a series of animal grunts and cries to me. I caught an occasional word, like 'oxygen' and 'psychokinesis.' What were you talking about?"

"He was telling me about Goat Hennessey's experiments, and how they differed from the rebels' experiments before Goat came to Ultra Vires," answered Maya.

"That kind of talk serves no good purpose," said Nuwell irritably. "The rebel movement has been broken now, and there's no point in thinking about the illegal things they tried to do."

They came down the slope and approached the southern airlock of Ultra Vires. The airlock was still sealed. Nuwell activated it, and they went through it into the big building.

It was dark inside. Nuwell fumbled around a wall and found a light switch. He pressed it, but nothing happened.

"The electrical system isn't operating," he said. "We'll have to use our marsuit torches."

He switched on his flashlight. It cast a long beam down the dusty corridor. Far ahead of them, a small animal scurried across the faint light and vanished into the darkness.

Nuwell checked his atmosphere dial.

"The oxygen in here is all right," he said. "The air has been maintained, anyhow. We can take off our helmets."

They took off the marshelmets and walked down the corridor. They checked each side door, looking for the communications room, but found only empty chambers or abandoned rooms in which books, papers and broken furniture were scattered in complete disorganization.

It took them nearly an hour to find the communications room. And there they met disappointment.

Ultra Vires' radio transmitter and receiver had been dismantled. There was nothing there but a jumble of broken tubes, discarded parts and bare wire ends dangling from the walls. Nothing but an overturned table and two bent metal chairs.

"That settles that," said Nuwell, more philosophically then Maya would have expected. "Our only hope is to find a groundcar."

That necessitated another search, but at last they found the motor pool. And there were three groundcars, all in various stages of breakdown or dismantlement.

"It looks like we'll have to walk, Nuwell," said Maya.

Nuwell shook his head.

"I checked the chart carefully," he said. "The oxygen supply of a marsuit won't take us either back to the Canfell Farm or to Ophir, even with extra tanks. We're just going to have to cannibalize two of these machines and repair us a groundcar."

"But, Nuwell, how long will that take?"

"I don't know," he admitted. "It looks like it may be quite a job. I expect it will take two or three weeks, but that's the only way we're going to get out of here."

He looked at her speculatively.

"It's a shame we aren't already married," he said. "This would provide us with a honeymoon, of a sort, out here by ourselves in the desert."

"Well, we aren't," she said flatly. "And we won't be until we get back to Mars City."

"That's true," he said. "Well, the only thing we can do for tonight is to have supper and find the rooms that Goat assigned us when we were here before. I hope he left some beds intact in those, or some of the other rooms. If not, we may have some uncomfortable nights ahead of us."

CHAPTER TWELVE

The two Dark Kensingtons and Happy Thurbelow walked along one of the pathways between the vats, Happy trailing a bit behind. Somewhere near them, they knew, Shadow accompanied them.

The place was dim, with the moist dimness of a swamp. The source of the light that filtered through the faint mist and seemed to permeate the air was not discernible, and the roof of this underground world was lost in the darkness above them. The placid surface of the water gleamed vaguely in the vats they passed, and the pale-green tangle of vegetation rose above and around them, sometimes drooping over the paths like skinny arms that sought to detain them.

"What I don't understand," said Dark the younger, "is that our memories coincide exactly, up to a point which you say is a time twenty-five years ago. My memories are just as genuine as you say yours are; they aren't something someone told me, but real memories of things that happened to me, things I felt and did. If they're both genuine sets of memories, how can it be explained? Are we the same person, who was somehow split into two distinct individuals?"

"I can only guess at the explanation, but I have a theory," answered Old Beard. "You are much younger than I am. I would estimate that you're twenty-five years younger than I am. My memories are consecutive and complete: I remember not only the earlier things you say you remember, but the events of these past twenty-five years, without a break. You say you suffered a period of amnesia, and your next consecutive memory is of being with Martians in the Icaria Desert."

"That would appear to give you an advantage in claiming to be the real Dark Kensington," agreed Dark with a smile. "But, if you are, who am I? How is it that I remember being Dark Kensington?"

"It's entirely possible that, for some reason, my earlier memories were grafted onto you as your own," replied Old Beard. "I don't know how this would be done, perhaps through very deep and extensive hypnosis. The Martians, as well as we can tell anything about them at all, are experts in such mental fields, a relic of the ancient science they're legended to have had when their civilizations covered Mars.

"I worked with Martians very closely for long periods during the early days of the rebellion—the Phoenix, as you say they call it now—and they may very well have recorded my memory pattern through some means I don't know anything about and for reasons I can't imagine."

"That sounds reasonable," conceded Dark. "But that still leaves unanswered the questions: Who am I, and what's happened to my memories of the past twenty-five years?"

"I'm afraid I can't answer that," replied Old Beard.

In the dimness ahead of them, they discerned a group of nude Toughs approaching, swaggering down the path. They turned aside and found a recess in the vegetation in which they could wait until the Toughs passed and went on their way. The Toughs were aggressive, and insensately brutal, and a meeting with them could only mean trouble.

"Happy's explained the situation here, as well as he could, but I'm afraid it wasn't a very adequate explanation," said Dark as they huddled in the shadowed recess. "Could you tell me more about it, and explain how you happen to be here?"

"Happy is very intelligent, for a Jelly, but none of the Jellies are exceptionally bright," answered Old Beard, with a touch of affection in his voice. "I'll outline it to you as briefly as I can.

"As your memories—or transplanted memories—indicate, I was one of a group of Martian colonists who joined forces to work at what, at first, appeared to be a theoretical and fantastic project: the development of the ability to live under natural Martian conditions, without dependence on the regular importation of extremely expensive imports from Earth. As you know, this project very shortly began to lose its fantastic qualities and appear to be definitely within the realm of possible realization.

"Because of the differing background and orientation of those of us who attempted this project, two approaches were adopted. One, based on advancing terrestrial research into the field of extrasensory perception, was aimed at developing telepathic and telekinetic powers so that food, oxygen, machinery and other essentials could be teleported directly from Earth into the Martian domes without dependence on the spacelines. The other, based on more orthodox science, was aimed at genetic development of a human type that could live *without* these importations, on native Martian food and in the Martian atmosphere.

"As you know, the government banned these experiments and we retreated into the desert to carry them on despite the ban. From what you tell me of the extent of your memories, what you do not know is the reason behind the ban, which we discovered— or, at least, I did—only after we had been betrayed and the government had raided and broken up our experimental colony.

"The spacelines, as one might have guessed, were responsible. They saw that the success of the experiments would destroy their lucrative business. These spacelines, led by the Mars Corporation, which later absorbed the others and gained a monopoly, brought political pressure to bear and got the project banned.

"I had heard reports that a great many of my colleagues escaped and formed a rebel organization that carried on the work secretly and illegally, but I was never able to learn details of it until you came and told me of the activities in which you have been engaged. You see, I haven't been out of these caves in a quarter of a century."

Shadow appeared at the recess to report to them that the Toughs had passed on. How he did it, Dark was unable to determine surely, for he could hear no words spoken. Either Shadow communicated by subtle gestures or by tones beyond Dark's powers of hearing, but both Old Beard and Happy seemed to understand him readily.

"How do you happen to be here, Old Beard?" asked Dark as they left the recess and resumed their progress down the walkways.

"I was captured when the government broke up the experimental groups," answered Old Beard. "I was the leader of the section of the experiments dealing with extrasensory perception, and, instead of executing me at once, they tried to persuade me to continue this work for the government along specific lines and under supervision. I refused, because I knew that anything I helped them develop would not be used for the benefit of the Martian colonists, but for greater profits for the spacelines.

"At last I was able to escape into these underground caverns where they grow food plants hydroponically and sell them to supplement the produce of the dome farms and the gardens in the dome cities. These caverns are extensive and, with the friendship and help of the Jellies, I've evaded discovery for twenty-five years."

"Just who and what are the Jellies?" asked Dark. "I haven't been able to get a very satisfactory answer to that question from Happy."

"They're human experimental animals," answered Old Beard. "The terrestrial food plants grown hydroponically and sold in the dome cities actually are a supplemental sideline to the real purpose of this place. Marscorp is conducting its own experiments here, with a crew of expert geneticists.

"What Marscorp is trying to do is to breed native Martian plants, that will grow in the open lowlands without expensive oxygenation and irrigation, that are not poisonous to humans and can be used for food. At the same time, they're approaching the problem from the other side, and the Jellies are men and women whose glandular structure has been altered in an effort to make their physiology more receptive to native Martian vegetation. If they succeed, of course, Marscorp has just as complete a monopoly over such a food supply as it does over imports from Earth, but at considerably less expense."

"And the Toughs?"

"They're human experimental animals, too, based on a different type of glandular alteration. They're neither as docile nor as intelligent as the Jellies, so they can't be used for slave labor as the Jellies can. About the only way they're ever used is as occasional goon squads to terrorize the Jellies and keep them in line."

"You've been here twenty-five years and have never been able to escape?" asked Dark incredulously.

"This place isn't guarded," replied Old Beard, with a wry smile. "They don't have to guard it. All they have to guard are the supply room where the marsuits are kept and the motor pool of groundcars. This place is in the middle of the Desert of Candor, and no one can live in the Martian desert without oxygen."

They came now to one of the walls of the underground cavern, and Old Beard led them suddenly into a fissure that was well concealed from the walkways by a tangled screen of vegetation. They stumbled along a narrow passageway for a few feet, and emerged into a rude shaft, around the walls of which a roughly-chiseled and steep stairway led upward into pitch darkness. Here Old Beard halted.

"When I told you there's no way of escape here, it was not that I haven't tried many times," he said to Dark.

"This shaft leads up into the walls of the structure above—above, although it is still underground—and I have been up there often at night. It has long been my hope that I might be able to get a marsuit or a groundcar and make my escape, but they are kept locked up and always guarded, against the Jellies and the Toughs.

"I want to take you up and give you an idea of the place now, and later perhaps you will have some ideas to contribute. Happy and Shadow will stay down here until we get back."

Old Beard mounted the steep steps slowly, and Dark followed at his heels. Although the bottom of the "well" was lighted with the same dim light as that which spread throughout the entire underground area, there was no light at all higher up, and they had to feel their way carefully lest they fall off the narrow steps.

At the top, Old Beard stopped and Dark bumped sharply into him.

"I'm going to move down the space between the walls," Old Beard whispered. "Hold onto my hand and follow me. But don't say anything or make any more noise than you can help, because anyone beyond the wall may be able to hear you."

They moved ahead. The way was very narrow, very dark and very difficult, and frequently was choked with ventilator pipes or tangles of wiring. They had gone some forty or fifty feet, when Old Beard stopped.

By Old Beard's movements, Dark knew he was working at something. Then a section of ventilator pipe came away from a ventilator grill, and faint light illuminated the space in which they crouched. In this dimness, Old Beard gestured to Dark to look through the ventilator.

Peering out, Dark saw that they were near the ceiling of a large, high-ceilinged room. In it, under glaring lights, a group of half a dozen white-clad men were working with knives and other instruments on the body of a man, either anaesthetized or dead, which lay on a surgical table.

Old Beard put his face against the grill next to Dark's, and the two men watched the scene below for a few moments. Then one of the men around the table raised his head, revealing a thin face, with watery blue eyes and a straggly goatee.

The two men inside the wall gasped as one man.

"*Father!*"

The single loud word was torn from Dark's throat without his volition, without his actually realizing he had spoken.

The heads of the men in the room jerked up at the cry, and they looked around and at each other, with puzzled expressions. Old Beard clapped a firm hand over Dark's mouth and hissed in his ear:

"Fool! Let's get out of here!"

As quietly as possible, they made their way back. Through the ventilator behind them came the murmur of querulous voices.

When they had climbed back down the stairs and, with Happy and Shadow, made their way back through the fissure, Old Beard fixed penetrating eyes on Dark and said:

"I told you to keep quiet up there! What was that exclamation all about?"

"It's something very strange," murmured Dark, his face thoughtful and bemused. "But you evidently recognized that man, too. Who is he?"

"Yes, I know him very well," answered Old Beard, with deep bitterness in his tone. "That's Goat Hennessey. But that's the first time I've seen him in twenty-five years. He must have just come here recently."

"Goat Hennessey? I heard of him when I was in Mars City."

"Goat Hennessey was one of my most trusted friends," said Old Beard. "If you bear my earlier memories, I'm surprised you didn't recognize him as Goat Hennessey, too."

"I recognized him as someone else," said Dark in a low voice.

"We worked together," went on Old Beard. "I was a leader in the effort to solve our problem through extrasensory perception, and he was the major scientist in the group attempting to solve it by genetic change. We worked together and we went into the desert together with the others when the government banned our experiments.

"But Goat was the man who sold out. He betrayed us to the government—for what price I don't know. And when government agents raided us and broke up our organization and captured me, Goat Hennessey kidnapped my young and pregnant wife, and I never saw her again.

"I'm glad Goat Hennessey is here, because now I can get to him. And when I can reach him, I'm going to kill him. I'd like to kill him as slowly and painfully as he killed the heart inside of me!"

As Old Beard spoke these last words, his face was tense, his fists clenched and a somber fire burned in his pale eyes. Then, slowly, the fire died out and he turned his eyes, once more cool and rational, a little quizzical, on Dark.

"Didn't you call him 'father'?" he asked.

"Yes," said Dark in a low voice. "But I'd rather not talk about it right now."

He looked at Old Beard, and seemed to be ridding himself, with an effort, of a deep introversion.

"There's one thing that I've remembered as a result of seeing Goat Hennessey," said Dark in a firmer voice. "This place isn't too far from a place in the Xanthe Desert where Goat conducted some significant experiments. If he left any of his records there—and I'm thinking of some in particular—they might go a long way toward solving the problem we've all be working on for so long. So now I know what to do next: I'm going to Ultra Vires."

Old Beard smiled sadly.

"Have you forgotten we can't get out of this place?" he reminded. "We can't get at either the marsuits or the groundcars."

It was Dark's turn to smile.

"I believe you said there aren't any guards on the airlocks to stop one from walking out at night?" he said.

"That's true, but—"

"There's something you don't know," continued Dark. "You were wondering at the basis of the regenerative power that permitted me to revive here after being shot in the stomach with a heatgun. I don't know what it is, but whatever it is, it's something that also permits me to live without oxygen.

"Happy can testify that I was fully alive and conscious underwater. I discovered, before I was shot, that I can operate just as well outside, in the Martian atmosphere, without a helmet. And that's why Goat's records may solve our problem.

"So tonight I'll leave this place and go to Ultra Vires. If there are any marsuits and groundcars left there, I'll come back here with them, and you and Happy and Shadow can escape with me. If not, you may have to wait a while longer.

"But I'll be back!"

CHAPTER THIRTEEN

Brute Hennessey plodded westward through the Xanthe Desert, naked, wearing no marsuit, his head bare to the thin, oxygen-poor Martian air. The two small moons shone in the star-spangled sky above the lone figure, casting fantastic shadows on the sands.

But this was not the stupid, shambling Brute Hennessey of a few months past. He walked surely and proudly, and the light of intelligence shone in his eyes.

He called himself, now, Dark Kensington.

Dark's muscular body had not regained, quite, the firmness and tone it had had before he was shot down at Solis Lacus, but he had recovered greatly from the bloated flabbiness of a few days ago. Most of that had been water in his tissues, and resumption of normal physical activity had wrung it out in short order.

As he plodded through the Martian night toward Ultra Vires, Dark was remembering, with something of awe, that emotional explosion within him that had occurred on his first sight of Goat Hennessey at the Canfell Hydroponic Farm. It was this sudden, overwhelming recognition that had wrung from his lips the cry: "*Father!*"

In that moment, memory had returned with terrible impact and he had been overwhelmed by the re-experience of those moments when he had stood before the man he admired and loved as his father and had seen the bitter realization of rejection by that man written with the point of a knife.

Now he remembered it all. He remembered his childhood at Ultra Vires, he remembered Adam and their experiences together, he remembered their treks through the desert at Goat Hennessey's command, he remembered his slaying of Adam and his acceptance of death at Goat's hands. He remembered that he, Dark Kensington, was Brute Hennessey, somehow brought to life once before in the Icaria Desert even as he had himself regained life a second time in the vats of the Canfell Hydroponic Farm.

So Goat Hennessey was his father, apparently. And Old Beard, the real Dark Kensington, vowed vengeance on Goat. Dark was able to view this with equanimity. He no longer felt any admiration or affection for Goat, whatever relationship might exist between them.

But, since he was Brute Hennessey and thus not old enough to be the real Dark Kensington, how and why had he acquired the memories of Dark Kensington? That question remained unanswered.

Phobos was setting for the first time that night when Dark reached the great hulk of Ultra Vires, manipulated one of the airlocks and entered its dark corridors. There was no light, and a test of the light switch proved that the electrical system was no longer operating. But Dark knew every inch of this place from early childhood. He felt his way through the pitch darkness to Goat Hennessey's old bedroom.

Probing about in the darkness, he discovered that Goat's bed was still supplied with mattress and crumpled blankets. This surprised him somewhat, as any item of cloth on Mars had to be imported from Earth and was far too valuable to abandon. But, apparently, these things had been left temporarily in Goat's abandonment of Ultra Vires and would be picked up by truck later.

Deriving a certain humorous satisfaction from taking over the master's chamber, Dark curled up on Goat's bed and went to sleep.

He awoke the next morning with the glare of the desert sunlight reflected into the room. He arose, stretched and yawned. The room was a mess. Goat had left the bed clothing intact, but he had turned everything else upside down in packing his personal effects to leave the place.

There was still water in the reservoir, and Ultra Vires' plumbing system was still in operation. Dark bathed. He felt ruefully at the thick stubble of beard that had overgrown his face in the past few days, but Goat had left no shaving equipment behind.

Dark made his way down to the big kitchen. There were supplies of canned food there, and he found utensils and ate. He was hungry, but not ravenous, and this surprised him a little, because he had had no food since he started out afoot from the Canfell Hydroponic Farm, four nights ago. But he was no hungrier than he would normally be after a night's sleep.

As he ate, his eye fell on dishes stacked beside the sink. He was startled to notice that water still sparkled on them.

He arose and checked them. Yes, they were still wet.

There were remnants of fresh food in the garbage can.

People, here? Camping out? Or, more likely, someone passing through the desert who had taken shelter here for the night? But he thought he would have heard the roar of a groundcar leaving.

Thoughtfully, Dark finished his breakfast. It occurred to him that perhaps some members of the Phoenix had taken refuge here after fleeing Mars City. But most of them did not even know of the existence of Ultra Vires, much less its location.

At any rate, there was no reason to assume that anyone who happened to be here would be unfriendly to him, in case they met by chance. He saw no reason to worry about it.

Finishing breakfast, Dark went down to the storeroom and picked out three marsuits, for Old Beard, Happy and Shadow. There was a large-sized suit there that he thought might accommodate Happy's bulk, but he wondered how Shadow, with his flat build, was going to manage one.

Nakedness felt quite natural to Dark, especially since he remembered his identity as Brute, but it occurred to him that it would look peculiar to anyone he might meet before leaving Ultra Vires—or, for that matter, on his way back to the Canfell Hydroponic Farm. So he donned a marsuit himself, leaving off the helmet.

Carrying the other three marsuits, he went down the corridor to the motor pool.

Dark remembered that Goat had always kept four groundcars on hand. There were three here now, all in advanced stages of dismantlement.

At one of them, a small figure in black tunic and loose trousers was bending over, head and arms plunged into the bowels of the engine.

Dark hesitated. He had found his intruder, perhaps a traveler who had run into engine trouble in the desert and had fortuitously been near enough to take shelter here while making repairs. But, again, there was no reason to anticipate unfriendliness.

Carrying his marsuits, Dark walked up to the groundcar, overhearing a muffled bit of profanity as he approached. The unfortunate mechanic evidently heard his footsteps, because he was greeted with:

"I wish to Phobos you'd stay down here and *try* to help me, instead of spending all your time snooping around this deserted shack!"

The voice was muffled, but it was definitely feminine and definitely irritated. Dark grinned and replied drolly:

"I'm sorry, but this is the first time you've asked me to help you."

With an audible gasp, the woman disentangled herself, in dangerous haste, from the groundcar engine and faced Dark.

They stared at each other, in mutual shocked recognition.

There was Dark Kensington, bearded, his arms full of marsuits, and there was Maya Cara Nome, sleeves rolled up, her lovely face streaked with grease.

Dark's jaw dropped. Maya's lips formed a round, astonished O.

Then, with a squeal, she hurled herself on him, throwing her arms around his neck. Dark staggered back, overwhelmed by marsuits, an abundance of wriggling femininity and a babble of happy and-completely unintelligible words gushed against his bearded cheek.

He managed to disentangle himself by the dual process of dropping the marsuits and holding Maya forcibly at arm's length. She gazed up into his face, her own awed and radiant, and was able to reduce her own words to connected sentences.

"You're not here," she said positively. "You can't be here. You're dead. I saw you killed. You must be one of the ghosts of Ultra Vires."

She wriggled free and threw her arms around his neck again, announcing happily, "But you're a solid, *comfortable* ghost, and I love you!"

Again, Dark managed to get her at arm's length and looked down seriously into her face.

"Did I hear you correctly?" he asked soberly. "Did you say you love me?"

"I did. And I mean it. Oh, Dark, how I mean it!"

He pulled her to him. He kissed her gravely. Then he held her close in his arms, while she rested her head contentedly against his shoulder.

"What," he asked at last, "are you doing here, tinkering with a groundcar?"

"Nuwell and I were on our way to Mars City by helicopter, when it failed and crashed," she explained. "This was the only place near enough for us to make it afoot, and the marsuit radios don't have the range to call for help. We've been here more than two weeks now, trying to repair these groundcars."

She looked at the machine she had been working on and shook her head ruefully.

"I don't think any of them can be fixed," she said. "Nuwell, it turns out, doesn't know a damn thing about machinery, but I was taught a good deal about mechanics when I was trained as a terrestrial agent. Even with three groundcars to supply parts, there are some things missing that I don't think I can jury-rig substitutes for."

She turned back to Dark.

"But you're dead!" she exclaimed. "I know you are, because we carried your body with us to the Canfell Hydroponic Farm. How in space can you be here, alive and kissing, when you made such a beautiful corpse?"

Dark explained the circumstances to her; how he had awakened in the vat, how he had been able to breathe underwater, how the sight of Goat Hennessey had revived in him the memory of his identity as Brute, how he had been able to walk across the desert without a marsuit.

"If you're Brute Hennessey, I know why you aren't dead," she said when he had finished. "We fell in with a party of Martians on our way here, and they told me about certain embryonic changes they made on you and Adam before Goat kidnapped your mothers and brought them to Ultra Vires. Qril—he's the Martian I talked to—said that these alterations not only permit you to live in a free Martian environment, but give you extraordinary regenerative powers."

"They must be extraordinary, if they permit me to come to life again after being stabbed in the heart and having my belly burned out with a heatgun," observed Dark.

"That's because your tissues aren't dependent on oxygen-carbon combustion," explained Maya. "According to Qril, when oxygen is no longer available to you, your cells utilize direct solar energy. That would prevent your tissues from dying while the damaged area of your body is under repair."

She looked at him in sudden awed realization.

"It would seem, darling, that you're virtually indestructible!" she said.

Dark laughed.

"Perhaps so," he said. "But I don't hanker to experiment along those lines any more than necessary. Dying is a very unpleasant experience, even if I do come to life again."

"Oh, Dark," said Maya, remembering. "I'd like for Qril to see you, and maybe he'll give us some more information. They came back here three days ago and, for some reason, have just been hanging around outside, under the walls. Let me get on a marsuit, and I'll take you to him."

"Here, put on one of these," suggested Dark, picking up the one he had selected for Old Beard.

Maya wriggled into it. The Martians, she said, were on the other side of Ultra Vires, so they left the motor pool and walked down one of the long corridors together, Maya clinging to Dark's arm with one hand and carrying her marshelmet under her other arm.

They were halfway across the big building when Nuwell Eli appeared around a corner about thirty feet ahead of them. He stopped, staring, at the sight of Maya's companion.

"Maya," he began, as they neared him. "Who…?"

Then he recognized Dark.

With a terrified yelp, Nuwell turned and raced back down the side corridor at top speed. They heard the clack-clack of his heels on the stone floor, fading in the distance.

Dark and Maya stopped and looked at each other.

"It must have been quite a shock to him, too, to see you risen from the dead," she said. "I don't believe he's as happy to see you as I was, Dark."

"No, his joy seemed considerably mitigated," replied Dark gravely. "But, Maya, this raises a rather serious question which hadn't occurred to me before, in the happiness of our reunion."

"What's that, darling?"

"You're a terrestrial agent and, as such, you put me under arrest. It's true, you tried to free me later. But didn't you tell me that night that you were engaged to marry this man, Nuwell Eli?"

"Yes," she admitted in a small voice. "But—"

"I haven't had the pleasure of meeting the gentleman before," continued Dark, still in the same grave tone. "But you and he were going back to Mars City together, and, for some reason, it occurs to me that you and he planned to be married as soon as you could get there."

Maya was somewhat stunned at this evidence of mind reading.

"That's true," she said in a very small voice.

"Now," said Dark, "you tell me that you love me. You must admit that the question raised by this is rather serious. Does this declaration of love—which, I assure you, is reciprocated completely—imply a radical change in your past course of action? Or, since you're still a terrestrial agent, can I expect to be arrested again as a preliminary to your joining Mr. Eli in the holy state of matrimony?"

Maya looked up into his face, and burst out laughing.

"I may have put it jokingly," protested Dark, a little taken aback, "but I'm serious, Maya."

"I know you are!" she giggled. "That's what makes it so funny. Answering you in the same vein, Mr. Kensington, I don't intend to put you in double jeopardy!"

Dark raised his eyebrows quizzically.

"I arrested you and you were killed resisting arrest," she explained mischievously. "I've discharged that duty as a terrestrial agent, so I don't think I'm either required or entitled to arrest you again. And as for the other, well, I am a little sorry for Nuwell, but I do love you, and I won't marry Nuwell, since you're alive. But I can't marry you, Dark."

Dark was stunned at this.

"Why not, Maya? You mean, because you're a terrestrial agent?"

"No, it isn't that. I'm planning to resign as an agent, as soon as I get back to Mars City, and that wouldn't stop me, anyway. The reason I can't marry you is simply that you haven't asked me."

Dark laughed, a rollicking, relieved laugh, and swept her into his arms.

"Maya, darling, I ask you now!" he exclaimed. "Will you marry me?"

"Yes, Dark," she answered demurely.

She leaned back in the circle of his arms and looked up into his face, seriously.

"Whither thou goest, I will go," she said, very quietly. "If you're a rebel, Dark, I'll be a rebel, too. I want to be with you, and help you in whatever you do.

CHAPTER FOURTEEN

Dark and Maya sat with their backs against the wall of Ultra Vires, and Qril squatted before them, towering huge above them. A little distance away the other three Martians were grouped, playing some sort of game, doing some sort of work or participating in some sort of joint demonstration. Dark could not be sure which.

Qril boomed out a long, rolling sentence and Maya broke into laughter. She turned to Dark and translated:

"He said he didn't understand why I'm wearing a helmet, when you aren't. I explained that I have to wear a helmet to breathe, and he said that, since you and I are alike, it appears that we'd dress alike. So you see, darling, even the Martians recognize that we're made for each other."

Dark shook his head in wonderment.

"No human has ever been able to figure out Martian thinking processes, and I doubt that one ever will," he remarked. "This is the Martian who explained to you the physiological structure that permits me to live without oxygen, and yet he asks a question like that!"

"There's one thing that puzzles me," said Maya curiously. "Without a helmet, you can't use your marsuit heater, and you said you walked here naked. But the temperature out here right now is well below freezing. Aren't you cold?"

"No," answered Dark. "I get cold in temperatures that are uncomfortable to anyone else when I'm in a dome or a building and breathing. But out here, when I'm not breathing, I'm aware of temperature changes but they don't cause me any discomfort. It must be that switching to direct utilization of solar power alters my reactions to temperature."

"Well," said Maya, "I can understand that utilization of solar power when you're in the sunshine. But how can you keep operating when you're in shadow, or at night, and not breathing?"

"I don't know. Maybe Qril does."

Maya asked the Martian, and relayed his answer to Dark:

"Qril says that you store excess energy in the tissues, very much as the Martians store oxygen. In a sense, direct sunlight's your generator, and it charges your batteries for power when it isn't operating. Now, Dark, why don't you ask him anything you want to know about your origin, and I'll act as translator."

"All right," agreed Dark. "But first, it was among Martians that I awoke when I returned to life the first time in the Icaria Desert. That's pretty far away, but I understand Martians have a weird sort of sympathetic communication among themselves. Does he know anything about how I got there?"

Maya talked with Qril and translated:

"Qril is one of the Martians I saw come by here and pick up your body the morning after Goat killed you and threw your body out in the desert. Qril says they recognized you from your genetic pattern—and don't ask me how they did this!—as being the one they had completed embryonic alteration on years before, so they picked you up and took you with them to give you a chance to regenerate and revive."

"But how and why did I turn up after my revival with Dark Kensington's memories?"

"He says they gave you a memory pattern by a deep telepathic process," answered Maya after talking with Qril, "because your memory pattern as Brute was of no value to you in meeting a new environment. It seems that there was some blockage in the operation of your brain as Brute, because of a slight fault in the embryonic alteration, and they corrected that before you revived."

"But why Dark Kensington's memory pattern?" asked Dark. "It turned out to be a valuable one for me, but I've met the real Dark Kensington since then, and he's a much older man. Why did they choose his memory pattern?"

Maya talked with Qril.

"He says names mean very little to them," she said then. "That's something I learned as a child: that Martians often interchange their names, and the names evidently refer to a state of experience and being rather than to a specific individual. But he says that the memory pattern they chose to give you was that of your father!"

Dark stared at her, stunned.

"Then," he said slowly, "Old Beard is my father. I should have known! I think I felt it."

"I'm not surprised if you did," said Maya. "From what Qril tells me, Dark, this prenatal alteration they performed on you gave you even more extensive powers than we realized. He says that you have extraordinary extrasensory ability, if you would only make an effort to use it."

"Oh, I do, do I?" murmured Dark thoughtfully.

He looked over at the other Martians, seated in a circle in the morning sunshine. They were taking turns tossing some small polygons, and evidently the objective of whatever they were doing lay in the way the polygons fell.

Dark felt a sudden surge of power in his brain. He concentrated it, he focused it, and one of the polygons rose slowly from the ground and drifted into the air above the Martians' heads.

Dark could feel the strength that went out and raised the polygon, like an invisible extension of himself. Then he felt another force seize the polygon, and it was drawn back firmly and without hesitation to its former place.

Dark turned his head back to look into Qril's huge eyes, and at once he was in mental contact with the Martian.

Qril was laughing at him. There was no change of expression on Qril's face, but in his mind was the atmosphere of high humor. Qril's thoughts came to him without words, in no language, silently but clearly:

You have not practiced your power. Experience will be necessary before you can compete with the simplest effort of one of our race.

Dark turned to Maya.

"He's right," said Dark. "I do have extrasensory powers, but they'll need some development."

"I know," said Maya. "The telepathic voltage in the atmosphere must be very high right now, because even I sensed your effort in lifting that object, and I understood Qril's communication to you."

Maya and Dark took their leave of Qril, and went back into Ultra Vires. As they did so, Qril and the other Martians arose and began to drift away into the desert, as though they had had a mission in staying here, which was now accomplished.

"I hope you know something about mechanics," said Maya as they walked down the corridor together. "Because if you don't, it looks like we're stuck here for a while. At least I am, unless you can run one of these groundcars with psychokinetic power."

"No, apparently I'm not that good at it yet," said Dark. "Maybe I could teleport in any parts you need. No wait! I just remembered something! Come with me."

They turned off into a side corridor, found stairs and climbed to the top floor of the building. There they followed another corridor until Dark stopped and opened a door.

It was the door to a small airlock. Dark led Maya through it into a huge room.

A helicopter stood in its center.

"Goat *did* leave it here!" exclaimed Dark joyfully. "I'd forgotten that he had this. He must have just packed the most necessary things when he left the place, planning to send trucks and a crew back and clean it out later at his leisure. Now, if this copter's only in good flying shape, we're set."

He checked the machine over. Everything was in order.

"How do we get it out of here?" asked Maya curiously, looking around the room. "That little airlock's too small for a copter to go through it."

"The roof rolls back," said Dark. "Put on your helmet, and I'll show you."

Maya donned her marshelmet. Dark went to the wall and pulled a switch. Nothing happened.

"I forgot," he said. "The electricity's off. Well, let's try something."

Dark concentrated his mind intensely on the movable ceiling. For a moment, there was resistance, then, very slowly, it began to open. A crack appeared in its center, and the air of the room hissed out with the swish of a minor tempest. After that, it was easier. The crack widened swiftly, and the roof rolled back to the walls, leaving the room open to the heavens.

"All we have to do now is to climb into it and go," said Dark with satisfaction. "You fill the fuel tanks, and I'll run down to the motor pool and pick up those other two marsuits. One of them is for my friend Happy, who is very fat, and he couldn't wear either of the emergency suits in the copter."

Maya uncoiled the hose from one of the fuel drums in the room and poked it into the copter's tank. Dark left the room, walked down the corridor and descended the stairs.

He made his way to the motor pool. Maya was wearing one of the three marsuits he had brought down, but the other two were still lying on the floor. He picked them up and started back.

He was walking down the first floor corridor, carrying the marsuits, when there crashed in on his mind a terrifying, silent scream:

Help!

Dark stopped, appalled. It took him a moment to realize that he was still standing in the corridor. It took him a moment to realize that he actually had heard nothing.

The corridor stretched away ahead of him, dim and dusty. There was no movement in it, no sound. It was utterly silent. He stood there, in a dim, dusty corridor, in waiting silence, holding two marsuits under his arms.

Help!

It was a cry that shrieked in his mind, reverberated in his mind, touching nothing around him, touching not the silent corridor.

Maya!

Dark's mind went out to her, rode up on swift wings to the room above where she had waited for his return.

He was there, in that room, and there was the helicopter. There was no Maya there.

But there were figures in the copter, moving.

He was in the copter, and there was Maya, struggling and writhing, as Nuwell Eli, in a furious concentration of savage energy, bound her into one of its seats with a length of rope.

Dark touched her mind, and her mind grasped his, desperately.

Dark, he followed us up here, and hid until you left. He crept up behind me and seized me. Hurry, Dark, he's taking me away!

Hurry? Down those corridors, up those steps, when Nuwell already was sliding into the pilot's seat of the copter?

Frantically, Dark grasped at his only chance of reaching her in time. Teleportation.

He clamped down with his mind on himself. With a frenzied burst of strength, he sought to lift himself bodily, to be there in the copter with them. He put every ounce of energy he possessed into the effort.

And he failed.

He was standing in the dim, dusty corridor, two marsuits under his arm, straining futilely toward a place he could not reach. And now he actually heard, with his ears, the muted vibration above him as the copter's engines roared to life.

Dark started running.

He dropped the marsuits, and ran down the corridor. He leaped up the stairs, two and three at a time. Breathless, his heart pounding, he staggered down the upper corridor and impatiently went through the seemingly interminable process of negotiating the airlock.

He emerged into the big room.

It was empty.

The ceiling was open to the Martian sky. The sunlight poured into the roofless room.

In the sky, a small, teetering object rose and moved away from Ultra Vires, its blades whirring a sparkling circle in the thin air.

Dark reached out to it with his mind, and again he was in the copter. Nuwell sat tensely at the controls, guiding it. Maya was in the other seat, her arms bound down by her sides, her expression agonized.

Nuwell was unaware of Dark's mental presence. Maya sensed it and her mind turned toward him.

Dark, Dark, what can we do? I should have been watching for him. I should have known, after he saw us together, that he would do something.

Dark: *It was my fault, Maya. I shouldn't have left you alone. I just didn't consider him a factor to be reckoned with, and I should have known better.*

Maya: *What can we do?*

Nuwell turned to Maya, and his face was bitter and sullen. His brown eyes were flat with anger.

"You treacherous witch, I should have known better than to trust you after that trick of trying to help Kensington escape. I wanted to give you a chance, because I thought that, with him dead, you might have recovered from your madness," he said.

A change came over his face: a mixture of fear, disbelief and utter lack of comprehension.

"He *was* dead," said Nuwell, a hysterical note underlying his tone. "I saw him. You saw him dead, too, didn't you, Maya? How could he be back there with you?"

Maya's only answer was a defiant smile.

"There's some explanation for this," said Nuwell, more positively. "I don't know what it is, but I'll find it. That man back there isn't Dark Kensington, because Kensington's dead. Maya, I promise you, I'm going to find out what the answer is, but first I'm going to make sure that you don't cause me any more trouble."

Dark touched Maya's mind.

Maya, I'm going to try something here.

He moved back. He was outside the copter, near it, keeping pace with it as it flew. It was tilted slightly forward, falling forward through the sky at the pull of its blades.

Dark seized the copter with his mind. He tried to drag it back.

It hesitated. It quivered. Then it jerked forward and went on. He felt his mental grasp slipping from it.

Suddenly he was completely in the big room in Ultra Vires, the room with its roof open to the sky. He could no longer touch the copter. He could no longer be in it. He could no longer touch Maya's mind.

He tried. He reached out again. But he failed. He was where he was.

He realized he was almost exhausted. The tremendous drain of his efforts on his energy told on him at last. He no longer had the strength to try any more, and Nuwell and Maya were gone away from him into the Martian sky.

Wearily, he turned back and went through the airlock, down the corridor and down the stairs.

There was nothing more he could do now. Nuwell undoubtedly would take Maya to Mars City. And then?

Maya would refuse to marry Nuwell now, and Dark doubted that Nuwell could force her. What Nuwell would do with her, he did not know. Probably some sort of confinement, eventually perhaps a trial. But Nuwell had no ground or reason to do her any real harm.

He would have to try to get to Maya as soon as he could, and that meant intensification of his efforts. But there was only one course he could hope to follow successfully, and that was the course he had planned when he started out for Ultra Vires.

Only now he *could* speed it up.

He had to have some rest. Then he would pick up three marsuits and walk back across the desert to the Canfell Hydroponic Farm

CHAPTER FIFTEEN

Dark walked across the desert toward the Canfell Hydroponic Farm.

He had discarded the marsuit he had been wearing, and substituted for it a light loincloth torn from one of Goat Hennessey's sheets. This reverse reaction, in a temperature that would be uncomfortably chilly for a fully clothed man and descended far below zero at night, resulted from his recognition that he gained a tremendously greater direct influx of energy from the total exposure of his skin to the sunlight. He could feel the energy penetrating his flesh, building up in him. And, with this energy, the low temperature did not bother him.

Behind him, by a rope, he dragged a little two-wheeled cart he had constructed from groundcar parts. It rolled and bumped over the sandy terrain, containing all the marsuits and all the seven heatguns that he had been able to find at Ultra Vires.

It also contained a supply of water, in cans. Dark had found that, while he was operating directly on solar energy, he did not need food at all and he did not need as much water as he did under ordinary circumstances. He probably could have survived two weeks without any water at all. But some water did make him much more efficient. His independence of food and oxygen did not prevent the slow desiccation if his tissues in the dry Martian air.

As he walked, only part of his mind was devoted to the routine task of moving across the desert. The remainder of it was free of the limitation of distance, touching and interacting with the minds of three other men.

These men were members of the Phoenix. At the Childress Barber College, they had been among the instructors, struggling to develop the ESP potentialities of their students so that a psychic community of purpose and action might be developed toward the goal of teleporting materials from Earth to Mars.

These were the men whose ability at telepathy and psychokinesis had been most fully developed, to the point of practical demonstration. Now, newly aware of the extent of his own inner powers, Dark had conceived a bold plan of action to which these men's comparable abilities was a necessary contribution.

There were three of them: Mantar Falusaine at Hesperidum, Pietro Corrallani at Mars City and Cheng I K'an at Ophir. Among them, by a vast intangible network of communication, they discussed strategy and the situation on which it was based.

Mantar: *We knew of the existence of the Canfell Hydroponic Farm. It was on our charts as a Marscorp industry, supported by the government. But we thought it was only an industry, producing food. We did not know it was an experimental center.*

Cheng: *We did not know Marscorp was conducting genetic experiments at all, except those of Goat Hennessey. We kept a casual observation on Goat's work. Our intention was that, if he ever succeeded completely in what he was trying to do, we would make a fast raid with a task force and appropriate his work to our own purposes.*

Dark chuckled.

Dark: *That would have dismayed Marscorp! But it appears that, as things have developed, this sort of raid must be directed now at the Canfell Hydroponic Farm, to free my father and the Marscorp slaves there. Old Beard is, after all, the real leader of the Phoenix. If we succeed in kidnapping Goat, we can put him to work for us, but that is not the primary objective.*

Pietro: *Do you plan to take over the Canfell Hydroponic Farm, and make it our base of operation?*

Dark: *No. When we attack the Farm, they will radio Mars City for help and we don't possess the force to fight off an all-out government counterattack. I have been in communication with a Martian friend, Qril, and I am informed that the domes in the Icaria Desert, which were used by the original rebels a quarter of a century ago, are still usable, although they will have to be supplied with oxygen, food and water. I intend for the Phoenix to congregate there and utilize the help of the Martians in carrying out the embryonic changes which will make your children and mine as I am. A new race, capable of living in the natural Martian environment.*

Pietro: *Will these characteristics of which you speak be inherited, or must the embryonic changes be made in each generation?*

Dark: *They will be inherited, because they are changes of the genetic structure. The changes will have to be made on each individual embryo of your children, but their children will be born with these qualities naturally.*

Cheng: *What are your instructions?*

Dark: *How many Phoenix are at each of your places?*

Cheng: *Twelve at Ophir.*

Mantar: *I would have to count. About twice that many at Hesperidum.*

Pietro: *About seventy-five here, as well as the wives of most of the Phoenix who are married.*

Dark: *Seventy-five! That's more than we had in school!*

Pietro: *Don't forget that the school was there for a long time before you came, and it had many graduates. The government captured between a third* and a half of us who were in the school at that time, but there are still probably three to four hundred Phoenix scattered about Mars.

Dark: *Where are the other three instructors, whom I was unable to contact with this telepathic call?*

Pietro: *They are at Charax, Nuba and Ismenius. Their telepathic powers are not as well developed as ours, and they would not hear you unless they were expecting the call.*

Dark: *Cheng, I thought your group was to go to Regina.*

Cheng: *It was, but the Regina airlocks were more effectively blockaded to us than at the other cities. Those who went to the other cities, except those who were caught, had identification establishing them as legitimate residents of those cities. Regina has a peculiar social structure which makes this virtually impossible, except for the Phoenix who are already there and have been for a long time. We thought of stopping at Zur, but there were no arrangements to care for us there. We went to a dome farm operated by a friend of the Phoenix in Pandorae Fretum, and stayed there until we could trickle gradually into Ophir.*

Dark: *You had quite an odyssey. Cheng, I want you to bring your twelve in groundcars, with what weapons you can get, and attack the Canfell Hydroponic Farm. I'll try to break it open from inside.*

Pietro: *Shall I bring my group from Mars City as reinforcements?*

Dark: *No, twelve will be enough, and the conquest of the farm will depend on speed. Before you can get there with your group by groundcar, the government will have a well-armed force there by jet. I want you to load trucks with supplies, gather all the wives and go straight to the Icaria Desert to establish our colony. I'll direct you telepathically when you reach Icaria, if we aren't already there. Cut across the deserts and lowlands, and stay away from the roads and cities.*

Pietro: *Very well. But we'll have to leave the city vehicle by vehicle, and rendezvous somewhere in the lowland. It will take some time.*

Dark: *Whatever is necessary. Do you know where the Chief is?*

Pietro: *He's here in jail in Mars City. His trial is due in twenty days, and we had planned to rescue him sometime during the trial.*

Dark: *Leave a few good men there to rescue him as soon as you've cleared Mars City and are on the way to Icaria. Has Nuwell Eli gotten back to Mars City yet?*

Pietro: *I don't know. We can find out.*

Dark: *He has Maya Cara Nome with him. She's the girl who was the secretary at the barber college when it was raided, and she's one of the Phoenix now. I want her rescued, at the same time, if possible. If not, I'll go to Mars City and do it myself later, but I want to get all of you cleared of the city first.*

Mantar: *What do you want me to do?*

Dark: *The most difficult thing of all. I want you to stay in Hesperidum, and send out all the Phoenix you have with you to contact those in other Martian cities. They are to rendezvous at Hesperidum, and then you will gather supplies and form another caravan to join the rest of us in Icaria.*

Cheng: *When shall I move out?*

Dark: *As soon as you can gather your men and material together. But stay out of sight of the farm and don't attack until you hear from me. I should be there within the next forty-eight hours.*

The instructions given, the telepathic conference faded out, and Dark was a solitary man plodding across the desert, pulling a loaded cart behind him.

He came in sight of the Canfell Hydroponic Farm in just about the time that he had predicted to Cheng, but waited until nightfall to approach it. Phobos was abroad in the east at sunset, so Dark waited a little longer, until the nearer moon plunged beneath the eastern horizon. Deimos was not in the sky this night, and Phobos' disappearance left it near pitch-dark.

Dark moved across the starlit desert, pulling his cart, to the walls of the farm. The farm was not a massive, sprawling fortress like Ultra Vires, because most of it was underground. The upper floor, in which Happy's "Masters" lived and worked, was just below the ground level and the underground vats were below it, extending considerably beyond it in all directions. The only parts of the farm that projected above ground were its four entrances, small buildings of white stone, each with its own airlock.

Dark went through the airlock of the nearest one. These entrance buildings were the barracks of the Toughs, in which they slept at night, secure from the possibility of escape because no marsuits were available to them. Dark had moved quietly through a barracks of sleeping Toughs the night he had left the farm for Ultra Vires, but this time he had his cart with him.

There was no alternative but a bold course. Spearing the light of an electric torch before him, he walked down the aisle toward the barred gate leading into the regions below, pulling the metal-wheeled cart across the stone floor behind him.

Its clatter brought the whole barracks awake. On all sides of him arose an angry growling and shouting, an upsurge from many throats of the animal noises that were the Toughs' nearest approach to human language. Dark moved forward steadily, keeping a telepathic "radar" out to warn him of any impending attack.

The very boldness of his action paid off. Its openness apparently convinced the Toughs that this was merely another, unusually noisy case of one of the Masters returning to the farm at night—as Dark sensed had occurred often before. Dark was not molested.

The barred gate had no controls on this side. Dark operated it psychokinetically. It raised slowly, he pulled his cart through, and he lowered it behind him and went on down the ramp into the underground cavern.

He went straight to Old Beard's hiding place, and awoke him. Old Beard greeted him joyously.

"I was afraid something had happened to you, you were gone so long," said Old Beard.

"I had to walk back," said Dark. "None of the groundcars at Ultra Vires was in operating condition."

"Then there's no chance of the rest of us escaping," said Old Beard disappointedly. "We can't get at the groundcars here, and the marsuits you brought won't help. The oxygen supply of a marsuit isn't adequate to take us from here to the nearest civilization."

"I think we can get to the groundcars," answered Dark confidently. "I brought heatguns, as well as marsuits. Besides, I have a larger plan now than merely escape."

He related to Old Beard all the things that had happened, including the fact that Old Beard was his father.

"I am very happy," said Old Beard simply, tears in his pale eyes. "I liked you very much from the first, Dark, and I'm glad that you can bear the name of Dark Kensington rightfully."

When Dark told him of the plan for the conquest of the farm, Old Beard stroked his beard thoughtfully.

"I'm afraid that the attack from within will depend largely on you and me, although Shadow probably will be able to help effectively," said Old Beard. "The Jellies aren't very aggressive and, even with a few heatguns, I'm afraid they won't be of much use."

"How about the Toughs?"

"The Toughs would be fine, if you want to wipe out all the Masters and all the Jellies, and possibly us, too. They're vicious and unintelligent, and they can't be disciplined or depended upon."

"With the attack from the outside timed right, the three of us can handle it," said Dark. "How many of the Masters are there?"

"Only ten," answered Old Beard. "And they aren't soldiers, but scientists. But they do have weapons, and they know how to handle them. They have to, in order to keep the Toughs from getting out of line."

"Perhaps we can whip the Jellies up to the point of causing a good deal of initial trouble and confusion, and then the three of us move in at the proper moment after the attack from outside is under way," said Dark. "We might even turn the Toughs loose on them, without weapons."

Old Beard gave him a stare from beneath bushy eyebrows.

"I don't think we want to use the Toughs," he said slowly. "I said there are ten Masters, and that is correct. But they have a visitor who arrived by copter several days ago. A visitor and a prisoner."

"A prisoner?"

"Yes, a prisoner who wasn't sent down to the vats, but is kept on the upper floor. This prisoner is a black-haired, black-eyed woman."

"Maya!"

"Yes, I think the visitor is Nuwell Eli and the prisoner is your friend, Maya."

CHAPTER SIXTEEN

Nuwell Eli sat with Placer Viceroy, director of the Canfell Hydroponic Farm, in its large underground dining room, eating lunch. This meal was not the tasteless, gelatin-like food that was fed to the Jellies and Toughs and sold on the Martian market. It was a meal of thick, juicy steaks from the dome farms around Hesperidum and vegetables from the gardens inside the Mars City dome.

"We've been here better than a week, and she's still stubborn," Nuwell said morosely. "Surely she has the intelligence to realize how ridiculous and impractical is her sudden conversion to a lost rebel cause. I'm half convinced that this Kensington fellow put her under some sort of a hypnotic spell."

"You've been very gentle in your methods of conversion," said Placer. "It isn't like you, Nuwell. If you want quick results, we could turn her over to the Toughs for a while."

"No, I don't want her hurt. I love the woman and intend to marry her. The whippings and humiliations are as far as I'm willing to go."

"A peculiar sort of love, if you don't mind my saying so," remarked Placer.

Nuwell stared at him coldly.

"I do mind your saying so," he said. "My personal emotions are not subject to your interpretation. But Martian wives are expected to obey their husbands with deference and, by Saturn, I'm going to break her of that liberal terrestrial training!"

"You'd have the legal right to take the steps necessary for that, if she were married to you," Placer pointed out.

"But the little fool refuses to marry me now!" exclaimed Nuwell in exasperation. "If she hadn't refused, do you think I'd have brought her here? But I couldn't take her to one of the cities, except as a prisoner to be tried for sedition and treason, as long as she expresses this violent and open support of the rebel cause. Whether you consider it love or not, I want the woman for myself. I don't want her imprisoned or executed."

"Perhaps if she were presented with that alternative, she'd be more reasonable about it," murmured Placer.

"Don't you think I've threatened her with it? She just says that she'd rather die or go to prison than go back on her convictions and knuckle under to me. If she could only forget that she'd ever met that man Kensington!"

"Well, as for that, it might not be so hard to arrange," suggested Placer quietly.

Nuwell stared at him.

"What do you mean?" he asked.

"You're not familiar with the details of our work here, are you, Nuwell?"

"I thought I was, pretty well. But what you just said doesn't strike a chord."

"As you know, the Toughs and Jellies are originally criminals and vagabonds you have smuggled to us for experimental purposes. One major effect of our initial glandular experiments with them, which makes them into Toughs and Jellies, is that they lose all memory of their past."

"I don't want a flabby woman, like a Jelly!" exclaimed Nuwell with a shudder.

"I think we could eliminate the memory, permanently, without any physical changes at all," said Placer. "There are some pretty good scientists here. I expect the operation would cut down her thinking ability pretty heavily, though. I think it would still be slightly higher than that of the Jellies, but you couldn't ever expect her again to get above the intellectual level of a child of six or eight terrestrial years."

"I don't care anything about an intelligent woman," answered Nuwell ruthlessly. "If she weren't so proud of her intelligence now, I wouldn't have so much trouble with her. I want her as a beautiful woman, which is all a woman has a right to expect from a man, and if she were less intelligent and more tractable I might be able to train her to become the sort of wife a man of my profession and position requires."

Placer speared a bite of steak, casually, with his fork.

"Any time you say the word," he said carelessly.

"I'll give her the rest of today," said Nuwell with decision. "I'll work her over again with the whip this afternoon, and if she doesn't break I'll tell her what she can expect. Then, if that doesn't do the trick, I'll turn her over to you the first thing tomorrow."

"Tonight would be better," suggested Placer. "The initial surgery takes only about thirty minutes, and she'd do better to rest a night after that. It alone will remove a great deal of her volitional power. The entire series of operations will require about three days."

"Tonight it is, then," said Nuwell, "if she doesn't break this afternoon."

Maya sat in her locked room, her tunic and trousers covering the red welts on her back and legs. The tasteless gelatin which had been her only food since their arrival almost gagged her with every spoonful, but she had eaten all her lunch. She needed all the strength she could get to maintain her defiance.

She was in the grip of dull, unrelenting pain, physically and emotionally. Her flesh ached from yesterday's beating, and she was sick at heart at the revelation of Nuwell's essential brutality and callousness. She had thought him a sensitive and intelligent man, and she had admired him for this even after some of his exhibitions of childish temper had disillusioned her as to the glowing nobility which she had at first attributed to him.

She had felt a warm attraction to him and, when she thought Dark was dead, she had been willing to marry him on the basis, not of the passionate love she now felt for Dark, but of a mellow tenderness which she conceived a sound basis for an understanding life together.

But now! She shuddered at the thought that she might have married him, and perhaps lived all her life with him, thinking him to be gentle and kind. Whatever happened to her, she felt fortunate that this crisis had brought to her view the hidden side of him, that heretofore had been seen only by his partners in political manipulation and by the unfortunate victims of his prosecution.

Her shoulders drooped wearily. She stared across the room. It was as bare as a prison cell, which intrinsically it was.

There was a glass on the washbasin. It was made of heavy metal, with no sharp edges. Did Nuwell think she would commit suicide? Not as long as she knew Dark was alive!

Her mind touched the glass. It quivered. It tilted and fell to the floor with a clang.

She looked at it with mild curiosity as it rolled into a corner. She hadn't done that for a long time, not since she suppressed it because of Nuwell's hatred of witchcraft.

It was telekinesis. She had had the power since she was a child. It seemed that she remembered using it often, and in rather startling ways, when she was a small child with the Martians. But when she went to Earth, she gradually stopped playing with it, except in small ways when she was alone, because it seemed to make her elders very uncomfortable.

Telekinesis was ESP. It did not mean that she had any other ESP powers. But there was her experience in the copter...

Her mind reached out. At once, like a shock, she was in contact with Dark. His mind turned to hers at once.

Dark: *Maya! Where are you?*

Maya: *Come into my room, darling. I'm at the Canfell Hydroponic Farm. Are you still at Ultra Vires?*

Dark: *No, I'm in the vats below you. I knew you were here, but I didn't know where. I can see your room now, though, and its place in the building.*

Maya: *Can you free me?*

Dark: *Not now. There are four Toughs outside your door, guarding it. I can't attack them without arousing the Masters. Soon, though.*

Maya: *I don't know how I'm doing this. I didn't know I had telepathic powers.*

Dark: *A good many people have them, potentially. They don't have to have been "changed," as I was. But they usually require development.*

Maya: *I'm just glad I can, to know that you're here.*

Dark: *Maya, why are you in pain?*

Maya: *Nuwell has been whipping me, to try to get me to recant on my expressions of support for the rebel cause.*

There was a white-hot explosion in her brain that almost literally seared her mind. Staggered at its impact, she recognized it as the explosion of Dark's sudden anger. Then she was no longer in contact with him.

A hundred feet away, in another room, Nuwell pulled on a pair of black gloves and picked up a short, thick-lashed whip. Coiling the whip, he stepped out into the corridor, and turned toward Maya's room.

He met Placer, walking in the opposite direction.

"You're going to make your last try, now?" asked Placer.

"Yes," replied Nuwell. "I hope it works. Actually, her spirit and quick wit are among the reasons I like the girl. But I don't intend to be defied in this."

He proceeded on down the hall.

As he started past the barred gate to one of the ramps leading down into the vats below, the buzzer beside it sounded. A Jelly was standing behind the gate, fat, pathetic face pressed against the bars.

Nuwell stopped. No one else was in sight in the corridor.

"What do you want?" he asked the Jelly.

"Master, I seek entry in answer to the summons," replied the Jelly in a voice that quavered with fright.

"What summons?"

"It was ordered that one of us come above and do a task for the Masters," replied the Jelly. "I am one of those who must work today, and I have come in answer to the summons."

Nuwell looked up and down the corridor. He saw no one.

"What sort of task?" he asked, reluctant to accept the responsibility of admitting the Jelly.

"I don't know, Master."

"Look," said Nuwell, "I'm not a Master. I don't know anything about the summons. Someone else will have to let you in."

"If I'm late, they'll let the Toughs whip me!" wailed the Jelly pathetically. "Please let me in, Master!"

Nuwell, the whip coiled in his hand, impatient to get to Maya's room, was moved to pity at the creature's plight. Besides, the Jellies were harmless, and this one certainly wouldn't be seeking admittance without having been called.

"All right, then," said Nuwell, and flipped the switch.

The bars grated open and the Jelly came into the corridor. But as Nuwell reached out to activate the switch and close the gate, the Jelly, with surprising agility, slipped between him and the switch.

"What in space?" growled Nuwell. "Get out of the way!"

The Jelly did not move.

"I said get out of the way!" snapped Nuwell, shaking out the whip.

The Jelly cringed and its eyes were terrified, but it still stood against the switch, its huge, translucent body barring Nuwell.

"No, Master," it whimpered. "Don't shut the gate!"

Viciously, Nuwell slashed the whip across its naked shoulders, and the Jelly squealed with pain. Nuwell raised the whip again.

But then through the open gate there poured a solid mass of translucent flesh, a horde of naked Jellies. Silently, they tumbled into the corridor, filling it from wall to wall, and others behind them pushed to enter as they paused.

Wide-eyed, Nuwell stared at them for the briefest of moments. Then he dropped the whip and fled back up the hall, shouting at the top of his voice.

The door at the end of the corridor opened as Nuwell neared it, and Placer appeared in it. He held up a restraining hand.

"Don't make so much noise!" he snapped. "There's a conference going on in there. What's the—"

Voiceless now, Nuwell grasped Placer's arm and pointed, trembling, back down the corridor.

"What in space?" demanded Placer irritably, peering at the mass of Jellies pouring out of the gate and beginning to move hesitantly along the corridor in both directions.

"Jellies!" croaked Nuwell. "The Jellies are loose! They're attacking us!"

"Soft hunks of blubber!" said Placer contemptuously. "They can't hurt anybody. I wonder what idiot left that gate open?"

"I did," admitted Nuwell. "I mean, one of them wanted in and I let him in, and then he backed up against the switch so I couldn't close it, until the others came in."

"I don't know what sort of harebrained idea has gotten into their feeble minds," said Placer. "But I can take care of it in short order."

He stepped back into the room, and Nuwell heard him apologizing to the others for the disturbance. Then Placer reappeared, two whips in his hand, and closed the door behind him. He handed one of the whips to Nuwell.

"They're a lot more tractable than that woman of yours," said Placer. "Let's go."

Placer moved down the corridor toward the slowly advancing Jellies, and Nuwell followed reluctantly, at a respectable distance.

"Get back below!" shouted Placer at the Jellies as he neared them. "You know better than to come up here without permission!"

They stopped and milled as he approached them relentlessly, those in front trying to hold back and those behind them pushing them on. Placer moved straight up to them and began slashing right and left with his whip.

There was a sudden surge forward of the Jellies and Placer was engulfed. He vanished in a mass of seething, translucent flesh. Nuwell stopped, appalled, and began to edge backward.

There was a flurry of movement in the forefront of the Jellies, and Placer burst out of the group, his hair awry, his clothing torn, his whip gone. He staggered toward Nuwell at a half run.

"Get back to the room!" cried Placer. "I don't know what's stirred them up, but they can't be frightened back with whips!"

The two men ran back down the corridor and burst through the door, startling a conference group of five of the other Masters.

"Heatguns!" snapped Placer. "Something's stirred the Jellies up, and they're up here causing trouble! I'll turn the Toughs loose on them."

While two of the others hurried out another door for weapons and a third bolted the door through which the two men had just come, Placer picked up a microphone and switched on the amplifier system that covered every area of all levels of the Canfell Hydroponic Farm.

Into the microphone, he gave an animal call, a cry that started out on a low crooning note and rose in volume and intensity until it hurt the ears. He repeated this three times. Then he set the microphone down and turned back to his colleagues, an expression of satisfaction on his face.

"That releases the Toughs," he said. "Every Tough in the place is free to maim or kill any Jelly he sees, without fear of restraint or punishment. That should bring them to heel pretty quickly!"

CHAPTER SEVENTEEN

Behind the locked door of the conference room, one of the Masters passed out heatguns to Nuwell, Placer and the other four.

"If we use these on them at half intensity, I think we can calm them down without killing any of them," said Placer. "We'll probably have more trouble beating down the Toughs and keeping them from killing all the Jellies than we will subduing the Jellies in the first place."

"I hope we warned the three at the other end of the hall in time," said one of the others. "There hasn't been any word from them."

Placer flicked a switch on the intercom system.

"Touchstone, are you men safe?" he asked.

"Yes, sir," replied a voice on the other end. "We locked ourselves in, because there aren't any heatguns we can get to from here. The Jellies haven't gotten this far down yet. They seem to be cowed by the Toughs at the door to Miss Cara Nome's room, and the Toughs are strutting around getting themselves in the mood for an attack. We've been watching them through the window."

"Good," said Placer. "Between the Toughs at that end and our heatguns at this end, we ought to be able to force them back below without much trouble. Are we ready to move out?"

A different voice came in over the intercom, the voice of the tenth Master, who was on duty in the farm's control room.

"Placer, the screens show three groundcars moving up from the south," he said. "I've tried to contact them by radio, but they don't answer."

"We haven't been notified to expect any government visitors," said Placer. "It may be a convoy of travelers off-course in the desert, or it could be a wandering party of escaped rebels. Warn them away."

"Yes, sir."

Touchstone's voice came in from the other end of the hall.

"The Toughs are attacking, Placer. Space, it's awful! Those poor Jellies can't stand up to the Toughs."

Suddenly his voice changed, and became shrill with excitement.

"Placer! One of those Jellies has a heatgun! Two of the Toughs were just burned down, and the others are falling back down the hall. The Jellies are coming on, and I can see the gun in the hand of one of them."

"Great space!" muttered Placer. "All right, Touchstone. Hold tight and keep that door locked. We'll get to you."

He turned to the others.

"We've got to move out now," he said. "Use full intensity and shoot to kill. We'll have to burn our way through those Jellies and get to the other end of the hall."

Leaving one of the Masters at the intercom in the control room, the other six went out into the corridor, heatguns ready. The foremost Jellies had advanced almost to the door, and now that they had spread out along the corridor, they were not packed so closely together.

The six men advanced steadily, leveling their guns. They fired, intense, almost invisible beams stabbing into the group of Jellies.

Jellies shrieked in pain, several of them collapsing to the floor with smoking flesh. The others turned in panic and began to crowd back down the corridor, the beams stabbing at them and picking them off one by one.

Then, from amid the Jellies, a beam struck forth, and one of the Masters went down, his face burned away. Placer burned down the Jelly holding the heatgun, and the five survivors moved grimly on.

On the ramp ahead, Dark and Old Beard approached the open gate to the corridor, Happy and Shadow following them.

"I wish I had been able to find more heatguns at Ultra Vires," said Dark to Old Beard. "Only three, besides our four, are spreading them out pretty thin."

"At least the Jellies made the break into the corridor, and we've managed to discourage the Toughs below from following them up for a while," said Old Beard. The bodies of a dozen Toughs at the foot of the ramp behind them attested to the rear guard battle they had fought. That was what had held them up so long. "If we can hold the corridor and keep the Masters bottled up, your friends outside should be able to turn the tide."

"It will take them a while to break in," said Dark. "But I've already contacted Cheng telepathically and told him to move in."

They emerged into the corridor, into a scene of tremendous confusion. All they could see in both directions were Jellies, milling about and chattering. The mass seemed to be drifting gradually toward the left, while from the right came shrieks of agony.

"This way," said Dark, turning to the left. "We have to get Maya out of here before we can do anything else."

Forcing their way through the Jellies, they came to a door. Dark tried it. It was locked. He burned the lock off and pushed it open.

Maya was standing back against the wall on the other side of the room, alarmed at the noise in the corridor, frightened at the opening of the door. As Dark and Old Beard came in, and she recognized Dark, she ran across the room to meet them, joy transforming her face.

She threw herself into Dark's arms.

"Oh, Dark!" she cried. "I knew you'd come!"

He enfolded her in his arms and kissed her. Then he turned back to Old Beard, his arm around Maya's shoulders.

"Old Beard, this is Maya Cara Nome," said Dark. "Maya, this is my father, the real Dark Kensington."

"The older Dark Kensington," corrected Old Beard. "I am very happy to meet you, Maya. My son, you have chosen a beautiful woman."

Happy and Shadow had followed the other two into the room and were standing against the door, holding it closed.

"Maya, we're going to have to try to hold the corridor until the Phoenix gets here," said Dark. "I want you to go with Shadow and Happy down to the vats. You get into a marsuit, and they'll take you to one of the entrance buildings. I'll tell Cheng to pick you up in one of the groundcars, and then Happy and Shadow can come back here to help us."

"I'll do nothing of the sort," said Maya flatly. "You need them up here now, and I won't leave you. I'm going to stay here and help you. After all, I can handle a heatgun better than any of these Jellies."

"But, Maya, I want to know that you're safe."

"I don't want to be safe until you are. Please let me stay, Dark."

"All right," Dark surrendered. "Shadow, give her your heatgun."

The five of them left the room together.

They emerged into a scene of incredible carnage. The Jellies, with only three heatguns which they were inept at using, had been no match for the Masters. Almost all of the Jellies were lying dead on the floor of the corridor, and the remaining few were backed up at the end of the hall to their right.

Three of the men were advancing toward these last Jellies. The other two, returning to the conference room, already had passed Maya's door and were picking their way back among the scorched, twitching bodies of the Jellies. Dark and the others were between these two retreating forces of Masters.

"We'll have to try to save those Jellies," decided Dark at once. "Happy, you and Shadow move back up the corridor and hold the line in case those other two turn back to attack our rear. The rest of us will tackle the three to the right."

They split up and moved off. But they were too late. Dark, Maya and Old Beard had advanced hastily no more than ten feet when the last of the Jellies at the end of the corridor collapsed under the combined beams of three heatguns. Immediately, the door beyond the dead Jellies opened and three more Masters emerged. They joined the first three, and were given the heatguns taken from the vanquished Jellies.

Dark stopped and held up his hand, halting the advance of his little group.

"We're too badly outnumbered now," he said. "Let's collect Happy and Shadow and get back down to the vats, where we can hide until the Phoenix break in."

The Masters had seen them now, and started to move up the corridor toward them in a group, but were still ten or fifteen feet out of heatgun range. Dark was not surprised to see that one of the group was Nuwell.

Dark and Maya turned back toward the entrance toward the underground vats, but stopped as Old Beard emitted a growl of recognition.

One of the three men who had emerged from the room was skinny, goateed Goat Hennessey, and he was coming forward now in the forefront of the group, a heatgun in his hand.

"Dark, you and Maya go on without me," said Old Beard very quietly. "I have a score to settle."

Dark turned back, his mouth open to protest, but Old Beard had already started swiftly down the corridor toward the oncoming group.

"Wait!" cried Dark, and started to run after him. But, in his haste, Dark tripped over the corpse of a Jelly and fell sprawling. In the moments it took Dark to scramble to his feet and recover his dropped heatgun from the floor, the drama ahead of him flashed like lightning to its conclusion.

Old Beard ran down the corridor toward the group of Masters, leaping lightly over the bodies of Jellies in his path, his gray hair streaming out behind him.

"Goat Hennessey!" he thundered, his voice reverberating from the walls of the corridor. "You betrayed me and killed my wife! Now the time has come for you to pay for your crimes!"

The Masters stopped in their tracks, frozen at the sight of this figure of retribution charging down on them. In their forefront, Goat stood staring, open-mouthed, not comprehending until the full impact of Old Beard's words broke upon him. Then, recognition dawning, he squawled in amazement and fear:

"Dark Kensington!"

With that cry, Goat turned in terror to escape. But Dark was now within range, and the intense beam of his downward-chopping heatgun caught Goat at the base of the skull and swept all the way down his back. Goat Hennessey plunged forward to the floor, dead, his spine burned away.

Even as Goat fell, his companions emerged from their paralysis. The beams of five heatguns focused on Old Beard, and he died in a burst of flame that flared from wall to wall of the narrow corridor.

Appalled at his father's sudden death, Dark almost leaped after him, to attack the five survivors single-handed. But Maya grasped his arm.

"No, Dark!" she urged. "Please don't!"

Realizing on the instant that to die now would only leave Maya at the mercy of the Masters and Nuwell, Dark turned back. He and Maya ran for the door to the ramp leading underground, Dark calling to Happy and Shadow to join them.

But Happy, and presumably the invisible Shadow, were well up the corridor and they, too, were under attack now. The two Masters who had been heading for the conference room had turned back and were now in range of Happy, their heatguns blasting.

Happy had remained true to Dark's charge to hold the line against any attack from the rear. Frightened but staunch, he was standing his ground, waving his own heat beam at the approaching pair of Masters.

But Happy was too unfamiliar with the weapon and too nervous to hit either of his targets. The beams of both Masters found him at the same time, and, with a woeful shriek that was cut off in a choking gurgle, the unfortunate Jelly collapsed to a smoking heap on the floor, quivered once and lay still.

Apparently from out of nowhere, the unarmed Shadow descended like a thunderbolt on one of Happy's killers. The surprised Master went sprawling, his heatgun flying from his hand.

Shadow might have vanquished the other, too, except that this startled individual, waving his heat beam wildly in an attempt to catch the elusive, vanishing and reappearing figure, scored a lucky hit. There was a tremendous flare of flame, and the extraordinary form of Shadow appeared for the last time, a charred, flat body lying on the floor of the corridor like the shadow for which he had been named.

The whole tragedy ran its course in less than a minute. In that time, Dark and Maya reached the entrance to the ramp, ducked into it and ran down the incline to the sheltering dimness of the labyrinthine vats.

CHAPTER EIGHTEEN

Moments later, the two groups of Masters converged at the gate, two from one direction and five from the other.

"After them!" commanded Placer. "But stay together. We'll have to try to hunt them down in the vats, and maybe the Toughs can help us, but we don't want to get separated so they can pick us off one by one."

"Wait, Placer, there's something you ought to know," said one of the two Masters who had come from the direction of the conference room. "Greyde called out a few minutes ago to tell us he had word from Vidonati in the control room. Those groundcars that were hanging around had attacked one of the entrance buildings."

"Space!" growled Placer. "There must be a conspiracy involved here somewhere. We'd better stay up here, then."

He pulled the lever beside the gate to the ramp, and it rumbled down and crashed into place.

"At least, those two are trapped below," he said with satisfaction. "We can hunt them down at our leisure when we've repelled this attack from outside. If we can take them alive, I'm of a mind to make them pay well for their responsibility in our losing all our experimental Jellies."

The seven of them went on to the conference room, picking their way among the bodies of the Jellies. Placer took over the intercom from Greyde.

"Vidonati, this is Placer," he said. "What's the situation?"

"The groundcars attacked the south building," replied Vidonati. "They moved in and concentrated all three car beams on the airlock and burned it through. I counted nine men in marsuits who left the groundcars and went into the building. Of course, as soon as they started blasting the airlocks, I closed the emergency barrier to block off the downward ramp."

"Obviously, since we still have air in the place," commented Placer dryly. "You'd better call Mars City and get them to send help."

"I've already done that," said Vidonati. "A jet squadron's on its way."

"Good," said Placer. "They can be here in about five hours, and it will take those rebels, or whoever they are, two or three times that long to burn through one of the emergency barriers, even if they blast an opening and bring their groundcars into the building to bring the groundcars' big guns on it."

"Should I stick it out here, or seal all the barriers and come below?" asked Vidonati. The control room was in the north building.

"Stay up there so you can report on what they're doing, unless they start to move toward that building," instructed Placer. "If they do, seal the other emergency barriers at once and come below. We can switch to the emergency radio down here to keep in touch with the task force from Mars City, and just wait it out underground until they clean up these rebels."

"Good enough," agreed Vidonati. "I won't take any chances."

In the vats below, Dark and Maya made their way to Old Beard's hideout, their heatguns ready, keeping a sharp lookout for Toughs. They reached it without incident.

Dark looked sadly around the little recess beneath the tangled vegetation, where Old Beard had concealed himself successfully so long from both Toughs and Masters. He had hoped that this reunion with his father would mean many years of companionship between them, once they were free of the Canfell Hydroponic Farm and had found a haven in the Icaria Desert.

But he knew that Old Beard had died in an act that had great meaning to him, a savage revenge that had wiped out the bitter memory of the loss of his wife and had repaid him for twenty-five long years of exile. Old Beard had died nobly.

Dark picked up one of the smaller marsuits.

"We don't know what's going to happen above, and we can't help much by staying inside, now that we can't hold that corridor and bottle them up in a room until Cheng and the Phoenix break in," said Dark. "We'd best get up to one of the exit buildings, get out through the airlock and get picked up by one of the groundcars. I don't need a marsuit, but you can put that on as soon as we get above in the building."

"Have you been in telepathic touch with Cheng?" asked Maya.

"Yes. They've already broken into the south building. That's the one I came through when I left for Ultra Vires and when I came back. But the Masters let down a heavy emergency barrier on the ramp when they attacked the airlock, and we wouldn't be able to get through that. There's a ramp near here that Old Beard told me opens onto the north building. We'll go there, and I'll send a call to Cheng to move over and meet us there."

Dark sent out a call to Cheng and received an acknowledgement. He and Maya started for the ramp, unaware that the building which was their goal housed the farm's control room, and the watching Vidonati.

Above, a few moments later, Vidonati called Placer on the intercom.

"Placer, they've come back to the groundcars and turned them in this direction," said Vidonati. "I'm going to let down the barriers on the ramps from the east and west buildings, sabotage the controls so they can't raise them again, and come on down. I'll lower the barrier to this building from inside, as soon as I get past it on the ramp."

"All right," said Placer. "We'll start getting the emergency radio in operation down here. Do a good job, but do it fast, and don't get caught up there by the rebels blasting the airlock."

"I won't," promised Vidonati. "It'll only take me a few minutes, and I can be down the ramp before they can focus their beams on the airlock."

In the lead groundcar, as the three of them wheeled around and headed slowly for the north building, Cheng turned to one of his companions with a frown.

"I've been trying to get through telepathically to Dark, but I can't reach him," said Cheng. "He didn't give any instructions for getting into the building, but they seem to have locked these airlocks by remote control so they can't be operated. We'll have to blast this one as we did the other one, because I don't imagine Dark will be able to open it from inside. He seemed in rather a hurry to be picked up."

Dark and Maya hurried up the ramp toward the north building. Dark had been concentrating too heavily on finding his way through the vats to receive Cheng's telepathic call.

They passed the barred gate that opened into the corridors of the upper level, and a few moments later reached the top of the ramp and the gate to the north building. Dark had been prepared to open this by telekinesis but, to his surprise, it was already open.

They passed through it and emerged into the north building.

Dark had never seen one of the ground-level buildings in daylight, as both times he had passed through the south building it had been night. He looked around the place curiously as they entered.

It was about fifty feet square, bare except for the low, hard bunks on which the Toughs slept at night. On three sides of it were windows, now closed with heavy steel shutters. The airlock was across the room, opposite the ramp entrance. The fourth wall was blank, and apparently shut off a room at the end, because there was a closed door in the center of it.

They moved out into the room, and Dark said:

"Slip into your marsuit, and we'll go out the airlock. I told Cheng to bring the groundcars over this way, and they ought to be ready to pick us up by the time we get out."

"I don't see why we didn't stay down in the vats until the Phoenix break in," said Maya. "We were well hidden down there, and there might have been some way we could have helped the Phoenix from inside."

"Primarily because I'm not sure now that the Phoenix can break in," answered Dark. "I didn't know about that heavy emergency barrier the Masters let down on the south ramp, and I was surprised and relieved to find they hadn't dropped one on this ramp, too. If they had, we'd have been trapped below. If they have those barriers on all four ramps, the Phoenix can't stay around long enough to burn through them, because the Masters have probably already called for help from Mars City."

Maya had laid her marshelmet down on one of the bunks, and was pulling the marsuit on over her tunic and trousers.

The door at the other end of the room opened, and a man emerged, a heatgun in his hand.

Vidonati stopped in his tracks, startled, at the sight of Dark and Maya. Dark grunted in surprise, and reached for his heatgun.

Even as Dark freed his weapon, Vidonati fired. The beam missed them, melting away the top of Maya's marshelmet and setting the bunk aflame. Then, as the beam of Dark's gun swung toward him, Vidonati ducked precipitately back into the control room.

"He got your marshelmet!" exclaimed Dark. "We're going to have to go in and flush him out of there, and just hope there's another marsuit in there, before we can open the airlock."

Heatgun in hand, Dark started for the door of the control room, Maya at his heels.

It was then that the Phoenix, the three groundcars drawn up with their heavy guns focused, blasted the airlock of the north building. In seconds, the airlock was burned through.

There was no emergency barrier down on this ramp. The heavy, Earth-pressured air of the north building whistled out into the desert. As from a punctured balloon, the pressured atmosphere of the entire Canfell Hydroponic Farm rushed after it, roaring up the ramp, in a moment stripping the vats, the upper level and the north building.

Caught in the tornadic blast, Dark could only cling to a bolted-down cot with one hand, and hold onto Maya around the waist with the other. As the pressure dropped precipitately and oxygen no longer touched his lungs, he could actually feel his alternate metabolism shifting into gear, he could feel his breathing stop and the glow of solar energy begin to spread through his body.

As the wind faded and died, Dark released Maya and rose exultantly to his feet. Down below, he knew, Nuwell and the Masters were gasping out their lives in the thin air, like beached fish. Their recent attacker, Vidonati, lay half out of the door of the control room, his hands clutching convulsively at the floor.

"That's not the way I'd planned it, but it's just as good!" Dark exclaimed. "We've taken the farm!"

Then he remembered. Maya had no marshelmet!

Appalled, struck to the heart, he turned in his tracks.

Maya was standing behind him, calmly trying to rearrange her raven hair, tangled by the raging rush of wind.

"What's the matter?" she asked quietly, becoming aware of Dark's intent gaze.

"Maya! You don't have a helmet on! Are you breathing?"

She was silent for a moment, apparently examining herself.

"Why, no, I don't believe I am," she replied, just as calmly.

"How can you...? Wait a minute!"

Dark sent his mind into the invisible. His probing thoughts fled over desert and lowland, seeking. They found the Martian, Qril, and he recognized that Qril responded immediately.

Qril, how is it that Maya is able to live in the Martian atmosphere without breathing? asked Dark telepathically.

She is as you, replied Qril. *When she was a child, living among the Martians, we altered her physiological and genetic structure so that she, also, is able to utilize solar energy and exist without oxygen.*

Why didn't you tell me this before, at Ultra Vires? demanded Dark.

You did not ask, replied Qril, and the mental contact faded out.

Dark turned to Maya, his face alight.

"Darling," he said, "our children will need no embryonic alterations. They will be born as we are, able to live under Martian conditions. And never again will either of us ever have to wear a marsuit!"

He felt the questing touch of Cheng's mind.

Cheng: *Are you there, Dark?*

Dark: *Here.*

Cheng: *Are you all right?*

Dark: *We're both fine! We're coming out. Then we'll take off at once for the Icaria Desert, before the Mars City task force gets here.*

He and Maya walked hand in hand through the blasted airlock. The three groundcars were there, waiting.

The two of them stood for a moment, before getting aboard the groundcars, and looked out together across the red desert toward the sinking sun.

Death? Desolation? No, not for them. This was life, and free, bleak beauty, for them and for their children.

The future of Mars was theirs.

THE END

If you've enjoyed this book, you will not want to miss these terrific titles…

ARMCHAIR SCI-FI & HORROR DOUBLE NOVELS, $12.95 each

D-101   **THE CONQUEST OF THE PLANETS** by John W. Campbell
THE MAN WHO ANNEXED THE MOON by Bob Olsen

D-102   **WEAPON FROM THE STARS** by Rog Phillips
THE EARTH WAR by Mack Reynolds

D-103   **THE ALIEN INTELLIGENCE** by Jack Williamson
INTO THE FOURTH DIMENSION by Ray Cummings

D-104   **THE CRYSTAL PLANETOIDS** by Stanton A. Coblentz
SURVIVORS FROM 9,000 B. C. by Robert Moore Williams

D-105   **THE TIME PROJECTOR** by David H. Keller, M.D. and David Lasser
STRANGE COMPULSION by Philip Jose Farmer

D-106   **WHOM THE GODS WOULD SLAY** by Paul W. Fairman
MEN IN THE WALLS by William Tenn

D-107   **LOCKED WORLDS** by Edmond Hamilton
THE LAND THAT TIME FORGOT by Edgar Rice Burroughs

D-108   **STAY OUT OF SPACE** by Dwight V. Swain
REBELS OF THE RED PLANET by Charles L. Fontenay

D-109   **THE METAMORPHS** by S. J. Byrne
MICROCOSMIC BUCCANEERS by Harl Vincent

D-110   **YOU CAN'T ESCAPE FROM MARS** by E. K. Jarvis
THE MAN WITH FIVE LIVES by David V. Reed

ARMCHAIR SCIENCE FICTION CLASSICS, $12.95 each

C-34   **30 DAY WONDER**
by Richard Wilson

C-35   **G.O.G. 666**
by John Taine

C-36   **RALPH 124C 41+**
by Hugo Gernsback

ARMCHAIR SCI-FI & HORROR GEMS SERIES, $12.95 each

G-11   **SCIENCE FICTION GEMS, Vol. Six**
Edmond Hamilton and others

G-12   **HORROR GEMS, Vol. Six**
H. P. Lovecraft and others